RISE

AN ANTHOLOGY OF CHANGE

Edited by

NORTHERN COLORADO WRITERS

Copyright © 2019 by Northern Colorado Writers

Print ISBN: 978-0-578-57759-3

Ebook ISBN: 978-0-578-57931-3

Edited by Holly Collingwood, Laura Mahal, Bonnie McKnight, Dean K. Miller, Sarah Kohls Roberts, Ronda Simmons, and Lorrie Wolfe

Introduction by Amy Rivers

Cover Design by Carl Graves

For everyone who rises in the face of change.

CONTENTS

BIOGRAPHIES

INTRODUCTION

Change is a part of life.

From the moment we are born, change is our constant companion. The authors featured in this anthology have tackled the topic passionately, eloquently, and with empathy, humor, and, above all, with grace. Change inspires many emotions: happiness, anger, despair—but also hope.

From stories of loss and grief to tales of romantic love and lifelong friendship, you'll traverse the mountains and the valleys of change, the good and the bad—the nitty gritty—and everything in between. This is more than a book of poetry and prose. It's a carefully curated collection of memories and imaginings, each piece selected and placed with intention and deliberation, to take you, the reader, on a journey. We hope you enjoy it from cover to cover.

This has been a big year for Northern Colorado Writers (NCW). We've experienced a change in leadership and organizational goals but always with our mission in mind—to support writers in all genres and at all stages in their writing journeys.

One of the things I've always loved about NCW is the people. From my first conference, to the moment I made the decision to become its new director, my heart has been rooted firmly in this Fort Collins-based organization—so full of kindness, inclusivity, and generosity. This group has been integral to the direction and success of my writing career, and I am invested in giving back to this writing community by providing opportunities for learning, growth, and publication.

When I proposed that we create a mixed-genre anthology to be published in less than year, it didn't surprise me one bit to find that NCW members were enthusiastic about tackling this project. I wish I could share a fly-on-the-wall view of all the work sessions we've had over the past few months. The anthology committee gave so much of themselves, and the finished product is nothing short of stunning—a true testament to the talent of the writers and the love and fortitude of the committee.

Thank you to the anthology committee: Laura Mahal, Bonnie McKnight, Lorrie Wolfe, Sarah Roberts, Holly Collingwood, Ronda Simmons, and Dean Miller. This book wouldn't exist without you.

From the very first meeting where we discussed the theme, the timeline, and the guidelines, these amazing and wonderfully giving people showed up at the table with smiles on their faces and absolute dedication to making this anthology great. If everyone, everywhere, could work together so constructively and graciously, this world would be a better place.

In addition, I'd like to thank the following people: Matthew Starr and Sonja Cassella, who did a secondary reading and provided feedback for consideration during the selection process, and Tara Szkutnik, who volunteered her proofreading skills as we neared the finish line.

As we continue to change and grow as an organization, we hope to inspire and encourage the strength, hope, and resilience displayed in the stories and poems you'll find in the following pages. May we rise to the challenges in our lives and persevere!

Thank you for reading,
Amy Rivers
Director | Northern Colorado Writers

RISE!

AN ANTHOLOGY OF CHANGE

1

FOLLOW THE HULA GIRL

BY BECKY JENSEN

My stoic father never wanted to be a burden to anyone, in life or in death. Yet here I am, carrying this former Marine on my shoulders through the Rocky Mountains.

His ashes fill a snack-sized plastic baggie stowed in the top of my backpack—a zippered pouch called the brain. It's where I keep my valuables, including cash, driver's license, Colorado Search and Rescue card, and a one-hundred-calorie portion of my dad.

My father was a dead ringer for a young Charlton Heston, handsome in his dark blonde crew cut, with a strong jaw, broad shoulders, and powerful calloused hands the size of dinner plates. Dad worked hard to put food on the table, and when he walked into the house after a long day at the metal fabricating shop, we mobbed him at the door. He would stagger through the kitchen, laughing, with kids hanging off his neck, clinging to his back, and hugging his legs.

Although I grew up hiking with my dad, we never did much camping, so tackling a five-week solo backpacking trip through the Colorado Rockies is new for both of us. I know Dad would have loved roughing it like this, and, unlike me, he would have been fearless. At night I'm convinced every twig snap is a mountain lion padding through camp to break my neck as I sleep. And when my imagination runs wild, I unzip the brain and pull out Dad's ashes, a talisman to drive away my fears. Tonight is no different. His cremated remains are light-gray powdery ash, like the soft fluff at the bottom of a cold campfire ring, mixed with hard, skeletal bits of my dad that refused to burn. As I burrow into my sleeping bag, I rub a piece of Dad's bone between my thumb and forefinger through the double-bagged plastic, a child with a security blanket.

I think about my flesh-and-bone father and the tattoo on his left bicep: a topless hula dancer whose bare feet peeked out from under his short-sleeved work shirt. Dad got the tattoo in Honolulu before he shipped out to Midway Island at the end of World War II. The hula girl held one hand behind her long hair, the other arm outstretched in a graceful line, forever poised and ready.

"Make her dance, Daddy! Make her dance!" I'd squealed in delight as a little girl, and my dad always obliged by flexing his arm, making the hula girl's grass skirt bounce and sway over his muscles. My mom despised that hula girl like an old trashy girlfriend, the topless exotic dancer forever under Dad's skin, beckoning him back to the days before a wife and kids and bills had tied him down. Back to the bold days of his youth when he had slept on the deck of a troop ship at night, a breeze cooling his sun-kissed face, as he sailed across the Pacific. The hula girl was his constant companion, an indelible mark of independence and adventure, dancing with him beneath starry skies.

The tattoo artist, Dad told me, had used needles to draw the hula girl on his skin.

I furrowed my brow. "Did it hurt, Daddy?" I asked, tracing the outline of her bare legs with a finger as I sat on his lap.

"I suppose it did, Beck-a-boo, but it was so long ago I don't remember."

4

Come back to me, I imagine the hula girl whispering to my duty-bound father every time he moved a muscle, her blue-gray ink fading with each passing year. I like to think my dad heeded her call when he moved our family west from Iowa to Colorado the summer after he turned fifty. I was eight years old.

Dad's first job in Colorado was on an assembly line in a window-less manufacturing plant, and he quit after three days. "I felt like an animal trapped in a cage," he said as he threw the uniform's bow tie into the garbage. My dad joined a construction crew and worked as a trim carpenter until the market bottomed out and he was laid off. Eventually, he was hired at a cattle breeding facility north of town, where the barns were full of massive, valuable bulls for stud—beasts measuring over five feet at the shoulder and weighing close to 2,000 pounds. He looked after the huge animals during the night shift, and the bulls were so isolated and full of testosterone, they would often smash their steel pens in frustration. They could easily kill a man, and when my dad entered a pen, his only protection was a little blue heeler dog that nipped at a bull's back legs if it got out of line.

My mom brought my sisters and me to visit Dad at work one night. He took us on a tour, and then we did a little stargazing up into the cold, black sky. "See that up there, Beck-a-boo?" Dad pointed to Orion, one of the most conspicuous winter constellations. "That's 'OR-ee-uhn,' the Hunter."

I rolled my teenage eyes and sighed, "It's 'Or-EYE-uhn,' Daaad." A bull bellowed in its stall.

"Or-EYYYE-uhn," he said slowly, drawing out the second syllable as he smiled at me. "Good to know, smarty-pants." His gaze returned to the stars. "Can you see the knife on Orion's belt? He's raising his club and holding a shield," Dad continued unfazed, drawing his finger a short distance across the night sky. "Those stars below and to the left are Canis Major and Canis Minor, the big dog and little dog, and guess what animal the Hunter is facing?"

I shrugged.

"It's the constellation Taurus, the bull!" Dad burst out, hitching a thumb toward the barn. "Can you imagine facing one of these guys with just a club, a shield, and two dogs?"

"You're kidding, right?" I asked, dumbfounded. "You only have one little dog, Dad. Aren't you scared? Ever?"

He turned away from Orion and looked into my eyes. "When it's time to go, it's time to go, Beck," Dad answered. "But it's not my time to go just yet. I'll be fine. One little dog is all I need." On cue, the company cattle dog trotted over and sat at Dad's feet. "Well, come on, Canis Minor," he said to the heeler. "It's back to work for you and me."

The memory inspires me to pull on my down jacket and step out from the safety of my tent into the cold, black mountain night. Once my eyes adjust, I look up at the mass of stars. Layer upon layer of white pinpricks twinkle through clouds of hydrogen gas where Dad told me new stars are born. I search in vain for the fearless Hunter, but Orion is on the other side of the world, hidden from me. Frightened to be alone in the dark, I climb back into my tent, kiss Dad's baggie goodnight, tuck it in the brain, and crawl into my sleeping bag.

When I wake at dawn, the air is crisp in my alpine camp. It's the last Sunday in July, and I've already hiked more than 350 miles on the 500-mile Colorado Trail, a path that runs through six wilderness areas, eight mountain ranges, and six national forests between Denver and Durango. The CT is kind of like the Appalachian Trail only shorter, with more wide-open landscapes and much taller mountains. So tall, in fact, that in the five weeks it will take to hike the entire CT, I will gain the same elevation as climbing Mount Everest, sea level to summit, three times.

"You don't go on a journey like this without a reason," a fellow traveler told me. My reason was a matter of life and death.

· · ·

Six months before, I sat hugging my knees, naked and sobbing on the cold, wet floor of my shower, thinking of ways to kill myself. No single drama or trauma led me to that exact moment of desperation. It was years of steady social conditioning that nearly did me in. Cultural norms tell women from birth that appearance matters, perfection pleases, and we should be all things to all people, often at the expense of our own well-being. When I realized I would never measure up and there was nothing left of me to give, I sank into a groggy depression, my imperfect, exhausted body mired in a pit of joyless quicksand. There was nowhere to go but down.

My doctor suggested antidepressants after I sobbed my way through a routine wellness exam, but I declined and she never pushed back. And talking to a counselor was out of the question. I was raised to be tough. When we skinned our knees as kids, we were told to rub some dirt in it. I learned by example that you don't ask for help or accept a handout, that was for sissies and taboo in the family pride department. So I self-prescribed the Colorado Trail as a tough-love cure for what ailed me, a proving ground where I would learn if life was worth living. A gift of radical self-care. A chance to rub some dirt in it.

Temperatures at camp are close to freezing, and I'm slow to crawl out of my tent to relieve my bladder in the willows and to cook the oatmeal I'll need to fuel today's nineteen-mile hike. The long day ahead of me will be a roller coaster of climbs and descents, up and over the alpine spine of the mighty Continental Divide. Most of the hike will keep me above tree line, and the exposed tundra landscape is no place to get caught in an afternoon electrical storm. The weather is holding as I break camp and start hiking, but the clouds are already building.

The trail contours several mountains for miles before descending through tall stands of spruce trees. I fill my lungs with the clean, earthy smell of a living, breathing forest. Birds swoop and glide above purple delphinium flowers that tower over my head. All too quickly, the trees come to an abrupt end at a place described in my guide book as "the last forest-sheltered area before Spring Creek Pass." Translation: if a storm rolls in during the next eight miles of exposed hiking, I'm toast. Actual charred human toast.

A friend of mine was struck by lightning in the mountains a few years ago. He was lucky it only put him in the hospital instead of the grave, but it took him a long time to learn how to walk again, and he suffered permanent nerve damage. Electrical storms build fast in the Colorado Rockies, where mountain ranges make their own weather and people die by lightning strike every year, typically in the afternoon. I kick myself for getting a late start this morning.

"What should I do, Dad?" I ask the sky, but there's no response.

I pull a piece of dried mango from my hip belt and chew, wondering what my dad might have been doing on this same day when he was my age. He had probably changed out of his church clothes and was weeding the garden or pitching horseshoes on our farm in Iowa. It would be his last day of rest before Monday, when he would be up before dawn to feed the pigs. If I woke early enough, I could talk to him while he packed a sandwich into his metal lunch box, and wave as he drove his old battered pickup truck down the long dirt driveway to his second job as a steel cutter. I would have been too young to realize that my dad was starting to feel trapped and restless, like something was missing from his life and he needed to go find it.

I focus back on the task at hand: getting to Spring Creek Pass trailhead, and catching a ride into the remote mountain town of Lake City, before the weather hits. I do the math and realize I will reach Snow Mesa—a flat, featureless, four-mile plateau at 12,785 feet—by early afternoon.

My gut tells me to stay put. Late July is primetime summer monsoon season, I'll be hiking when thunderstorms are most frequent and severe, and I will be the tallest lightning rod for miles. From where I stand on the trail, it's impossible to see what I'm walking into, and I know better than to take one more step ahead. But it's been eight days since my last taste of civilization, and I'm seduced by the promise of a hot shower, a cold beer, and a warm bed in town.

"Let's do this, Beck-a-boo," I say and start walking again.

After a few miles, the fluffy clouds begin swelling into cauliflower thunderheads and a knot tightens in my belly. When Snow Mesa finally comes into view, the clouds are closing in at a rolling boil. I cling to blue patches of hope in the sky and cross my fingers that the worst of the weather will miss me like it has before. Even so, I pick up my pace. I'm at the point of no return where I'm closer to the trailhead than I am to that sheltered spot in the trees I left miles back, and nothing about either option feels right.

A memory of my father enters my mind. It's nearly a decade ago, and he's standing at the kitchen sink, a knife in his hand, making lunch. "Don't let anybody put me in a nursing home, Beck," Dad instructed as he sliced through fresh tomatoes from his garden. "And don't spend good money to keep me alive if I'm a vegetable."

Bladder cancer is a terrible illness for anyone to endure, let alone a former Marine hellbent on dying with dignity. Toward the end, Dad had worn a path in the carpet, slowly shuffling back and forth between the bathroom and the living room, using a metal walker. He became a shell of his former self, wrapped in a cardigan on the loveseat, swallowing a steady diet of oxycodone and morphine. It was not the journey he had planned.

Black thunderheads continue to build as fat raindrops hit the brim of my baseball cap. The temperature drops, and with it my morale. I stop to secure the waterproof cover over my pack and put on rain gear, including a rain skirt I made out of a drawstring Hefty bag. The electricity in the air makes my stomach sour and pulls at the hairs on the back of my neck. I hike faster across the flat mesa.

. . .

Several months after his diagnosis, Dad was determined to die on his own terms. And as soon as Mom left the house to run errands one day, he closed the garage door, taped a hose to the exhaust pipe of his car, and, taking the driver's seat, turned the key in the ignition. The exhaust fumes started to burn the back of his throat. And then his chest, filled with cardiac stents and atrophied arteries from a heart attack years earlier, grew tight and painful from lack of oxygen. "This wasn't supposed to hurt," he grumbled as he turned off the ignition. Disappointed and coughing, Dad opened the car door, looking for a better way to die.

A flash of lightning connects to the horizon, and my metal gear begins to hum. I scan my surroundings for any kind of depression in the terrain where I can hide, and I spy a small, dried-out gully. Forgetting about the weight of my pack, I jump into the shallow trench and land with a grunt. I fumble to unbuckle my hip belt, shove my metal-frame backpack under an overhang of tundra grasses, and run down the gully to hunker under another scoured grassy bank to ride out the storm. I look at the carbon fiber trekking poles in my hands and spring to my feet, chucking them javelin-style toward my backpack right before a simultaneous crack of thunder and lightning hit nearby. I shriek and scurry to my hiding place as the skies unleash hail and bone-chilling sheets of rain.

Under the embankment, I can see my poles and pack abandoned up the gully and worry that Dad's ashes might get wet. I imagine the hard-driving rain finding its way under the waterproof cover of my pack, seeping into Dad's plastic baggie, coating all the important things inside my brain with a thick, gray sludge.

"Oh, Dad," I mumble through numb lips, crouched inside a trash bag in the mud. "I don't want to die today, not like this."

. . .

He walked from the garage into the kitchen and spotted the knife block. Determined to see his plan through, Dad draped his hand over the sink and sliced one of his wrists open with the serrated blade of his tomato knife. As blood started to flow out of his veins and down the drain, his survival instinct kicked in and he drove himself to the emergency room.

By the time I reached the hospital, Dad was in a windowless room in the basement, imprisoned in the glass coffin of a pressurized hyperbaric chamber, wrist stitched and bandaged, breathing pure oxygen to counter the effects of the car's poisonous fumes.

"Well, if it isn't the Last of the Mohicans," he croaked, using the nickname he had given me as a little girl, the youngest of his ten children. As a white, thirty-seven-year-old, divorced mother of two, I knew the pet moniker was offensively appropriated and absurd, but I loved it. Dad's voice was weak and muffled from behind the walls of the chamber, raspy from his self-inflicted sore throat. I pressed a hand flat against the clear lid, and he reached up with his fingers to touch mine on the other side.

Eight years later, I'm huddled in a hailstorm on top of a lonely mesa, tempted to run the gauntlet over to my backpack, grab the baggie, and hold it close to me. I'm scared and I want my dad, but logic tells me to sit tight. I tuck into an upright fetal position, balancing on the balls of my feet, cold and miserable. Hugging my knees and squeezing my eyes shut, I rock back and forth, willing myself small as the storm rages overhead. Rain and hail pelt down, and another thunderclap splits my ears, as water flows in branching veins on the ground at my feet.

I left the hospital and drove over to my parents' house where I let myself in through the side door. My mother was staying overnight with Dad, and I had offered to lock up their house. It was a good excuse to escape the hospital basement filled with sick people, weak yet alive, trapped in doctor-prescribed caskets under artificial lights. As I stepped into my parents' quiet kitchen, I saw the knife in the sink and studied the room like a crime scene before reaching for the bloody handle. I washed and rinsed the blade, and slid it back into its block. Then I scrubbed the sink with bleach and wiped the counter with a clean washcloth, putting everything in order the way Dad liked it. I stared out the large picture window over the sink into blackness.

When I visited Dad in the hospital the following day, he motioned me over to his bedside. As I walked up to the side rail, he grabbed my wrist, startling me. "Didn't you think I was brave, Beck?" he asked, searching my face.

"Do I think you were brave? You never said goodbye," I choked out, making a fist and twisting my wrist free from his grip. "And you didn't give me a chance to say goodbye to you, Dad."

His eyes pleaded with me. "But didn't you think I was *brave?*"

The hula girl's bare feet and legs, limp and motionless, peeked out from under the sleeve of his hospital gown. Dad closed his eyes and I backed away.

The deluge on the mesa lets up after twenty minutes, and I emerge from the wet clay, muddy and shaken, but grateful to be in one piece. I retrieve pack and poles with trembling fingers and clamber back onto the trail, whimpering "thank you, thank you, thank you, thank you" in time with my footsteps as I hustle stiff-legged down the path. It rains steadily, and I keep hoping the next slight rise in the land-scape will be the last and I can get off this damn mesa. But then another rise pops up. And another.

My muscles and mental stamina, so tightly coiled and adrenalized for hours, finally release their tension. I am cold and exhausted. The shivers rumble through me in fits and starts, and then strike a steady percussion through my arms and legs and chattering teeth.

I've hiked fourteen miles, and have five more to go to the trailhead, but my legs are spent. I have nothing left to give and my body crumples to the ground, wet and vulnerable at the bottom of another cold shower. I need to pick myself up by my bootstraps and get the hell off this mesa. I need to stand and start walking. I need to . . . I need . . .

"I . . . need . . . hellllp!" I break down and wail, saying the forbidden words out loud, through ragged, gulping sobs, alone in the middle of this barren plateau.

As if in reply, a flutter of wings catches my attention, and a brownish bird lands on the trail in front of me as I smear my nose across the sleeve of my wet coat. The bird looks at me and takes a few hops along the path. I remain fixed to the ground, slouched and sinking into the mud, drained after the storm and my cry. The bird won't leave, and it bobs its tail and cocks its head as if to say, *Aren't you coming?*

When I was young, I followed other birds, clever killdeers that pretended to be injured, dragging a wing on the ground a short distance to lead me away from their clutch of eggs. I don't have time for games right now, and I want to tell the bird *I don't care about your fucking nest. Can't you see I'm trying to get my shit together?* But the bird isn't faking a broken wing. It looks me in the eye.

When it's time to go, it's time to go, Beck, I hear my dad say. "But it's not my time to go just yet," I whisper to the bird, and slowly stagger to my feet. It may seem too convenient an explanation, or a bunch of New Age horseshit, to think that this bird is my dead father in animal spirit form here to guide me off a mesa on the edge of the wilderness. But I know it's my dad. Step by step, I follow him down the trail, and when the rain finally tapers off and the first rays of sunshine break through the clouds, he flies away.

Dad lived for one year after his suicide attempt, and during that time I quit my job so we could spend more time together. We dug in the garden, played countless hands of gin rummy, weathered several of his cancer treatments, and had a proper goodbye.

"Make her dance, Daddy," I said to my eighty-one-year-old father as he lay dying in his hospice bed. He lifted his frail arm, flexed his muscle, and the hula girl danced.

Before I left home for the Colorado Trail, a study was published by University College London that explored the effects of suicide on friends and family. Research showed that people who experience the sudden death of a friend or family member are 65 percent more likely to attempt suicide themselves if their loved one died by suicide rather than natural causes. They call it suicide contagion.

Although Dad's suicide wasn't successful, his attempt normalized suicide as an acceptable exit strategy for me, as if committing suicide had Dad's stamp of approval as a legitimate way to end my pain.

I would have done it neatly and quietly with pills, none of that kitchen knife bullshit, and I had no preconceived notion that killing myself was noble or brave. I just couldn't see a way out of my depression and was exhausted by the daily struggle. I couldn't see an end to that lonely, stormy, dangerous plateau. For me, suicide was never about wanting to die; it was about not wanting to live the life I was living. So I hit the trail to figure out a better way to live.

Several days after Snow Mesa, I hike into another storm and flash flood advisory in the San Juan Mountains. But it doesn't frighten me as it did before. I respect the foul weather, listen to my gut, and find my stride.

After slogging through cold rain and fog all morning, there's a break in the weather, and rays of sunlight pierce through the clouds to illuminate a breathtaking landscape. The beauty of the place drops me to my knees, and I weep as the most intense sense of knowing sweeps through my body. *This is it.* As I descend the switchbacks, the sun dances across hanging lakes and down waterfalls as wisps of clouds linger and swirl around the cliff faces. Wildflowers are in peak bloom, red paintbrush splashed across a rolling carpet of emerald hillsides. I've been scouting every turn in the landscape for nearly 400 miles looking for the perfect place to scatter Dad's ashes.

"You'll know it when you see it," a hiker told me at mile twenty-seven, and she was right. I step off the trail at a rocky outcrop with panoramic views of the surrounding basin.

"How about here, Dad?" I rest my poles against a rock and unbuckle my pack, lowering it to the ground. Unzipping the brain, I carefully remove Dad's ashes. The waterproof cover did its job on Snow Mesa to protect my backpack's precious cargo, and the weight of the full baggie rests in my hands for the last time.

When my dad was in hospice care, I would collect my thoughts on a sofa located at the junction of two hallways in the hospital. The hall on the left led to the hospice ward where life was departing, and the hall on the right led over a sky bridge to the maternity ward where new life was arriving. Every time a baby was born, the nurses played Brahms's Lullaby over the speakers to announce the good news. The first time this happened, my gut plunged and I rushed from the sofa to my father's room, afraid the Universe had a "one in, one out" policy for the souls on this hospital floor. When I reached his doorway, Dad greeted me from his bed with a reassuring, "Hello, Last of the Mohicans," and I held his hand and fell asleep at his bedside, never wanting to let him go.

After spending several nights napping on chairs in the hospice ward, I drove home for a quick shower to feel human again. And when I stepped out of the shower, my phone revealed a missed call. I sprinted to my car, drove like a madwoman across town, and ran from the hospital parking lot to the elevator, repeatedly pressing the button until the doors opened and I scrambled inside. When the doors opened again on Dad's floor, I hesitated before crossing the threshold.

There was no need to rush. I walked over to the familiar sofa as the lullaby floated down the hallway. I sat in the heavy emptiness that lingered after the final note played, and I knew my dad was gone.

Back on the trail, I open the plastic bag, grab a handful of ash and bone, and draw the closed fist to my chest, hanging on to Dad for one minute longer. When I throw my hand into the air, the ashes catch a light breeze and float away from me, and the heavier, road-weary pieces of bone drop to rest on the soft bed of the grassy hillside.

"Yes, you were brave," I tell my father as I reach my hand into the bag for more ashes. "And I am my father's daughter," I say, scattering a second handful into the thin alpine air, smudging traces of Dad across my cheeks as I wipe my face.

I pour the last bit of ash into my open palm and imagine it contains the part of my dad that was the hula girl. And I blow it like a kiss into the beautiful wild.

Two years after completing the Colorado Trail, I sit in a dark tattoo parlor on the north end of town. At age forty-seven, this is my first time getting inked, and the artist asks me to hop up on the table so we can get this show on the road. I look at the design one last time before it becomes permanent: the brown alpine bird from Snow Mesa perched on a guide post, surrounded by fiery red paintbrush flowers. The tattoo artist hands me a pillow and reminds me to breathe. The machine buzzes and snaps, piercing my skin thousands of times per minute, and the artist only pauses to wipe the blood off my raw arm and dip his needles into a new color. I am inking a deal with myself to brave the elements, explore the world, and be true to me. I make a promise to live.

As I watch the alpine bird come to life on my arm, I fall in love with my constant companion, this bold, independent spirit, and I know my dad is with me.

One little bird is all I need. It holds its wing in a graceful line, poised and ready to soar across an endless sky. And when I rise to stand on my feet, I flex my muscles and the bird takes flight.

2

SUFFOCATION

BY MARILYN K. MOODY

I.
at the funeral, the bank manager softly said, come see me,
he gave her a teller job, he saved her, but she didn't know
that then, she had that job for thirty years, how else would
she possibly been able to survive, four little kids,
back then, when women didn't have jobs, stuck in that awful
little prairie town, she was Catholic, but why did she have so many?

her husband was a foolish man, he was obscenely happy,
he left it to her to figure out how they could live on his
farmhand wages, he was a hard worker, he wasn't a drinker,
but after they married, she realized he would always be like a kid,
another kid for her to take care of, she would have to make plans,
it made her become harsh and brittle and a nag and a worrier.

they guessed he lived about three minutes, as the thousands
of bushels of corn came down upon him, enough time to feel
the weight of grain pushing against his chest, to feel his heart
beating so so fast, to feel the dusty corn all around him, to feel

the unbearable pain of so so much grain against his twisted neck;
did he suffocate, did his heart explode, or did his neck break first?

II.
one of his daughters couldn't remember him much,
but she liked to tell
how her father would come home dusty and dirty,
with candy bars
he bought at the grain elevator
in his pockets
for the kids,
she liked to tell
how once, it was so so hot, the air
so so still you couldn't breathe,
she liked to tell
how her father couldn't bear for the kids to suffer,
she liked to tell
how he went to town,
she liked to tell
how he used the
very last of his money,
she liked to tell
to buy the kids an electric fan.

3

CHASING THE PHANTOM OF LOVE

BY MILLICENT PORTER HENRY

When I was sixteen I let an older man seduce me. I should have known better, but my head was atwitter with notions of true love and heart-stopping romantic men.

Ross Martin was his name, an actor famous for his role as Artemus Gordon in the TV series *The Wild Wild West*. But that momentous evening he stepped out onto an empty stage; the spotlight captured him inside a beam of white-hot heat, his hair slicked back like some dreamy Latin lover in a dark suit.

And the seduction began . . . when his silver tongue caressed the first lines of the poem "Little Word, Little White Bird."

> Love, is it a cat with claws and wild mate screams
> In the black night?
> Love, is it a bird—a goldfinch with a burnish
> On its wingtips, or a little gray sparrow
> Picking crumbs, hunting crumbs?

I sat—mesmerized—in front of our black-and-white television, praying the rabbit ears wrapped with tin foil would do their job. Ross

Martin spun out the words of Carl Sandburg in a cinematic reel of images. In one stanza, he conjured up love as a stupendous funny elephant tromping, traveling with big feet. In the next verse, love became a sneaky rattlesnake with poison fangs and then a red, red rose that turned to dust on the windowsill. His performance was riveting. I lost myself in that magical space where time and place disappeared.

When my world floated back into focus, I was thoroughly and forever seduced. Don't misunderstand. I did not fall in love with Ross Martin or Carl Sandburg. Oh no. I fell in love with love. Those two gentlemen started me on a lifelong quest—to find my own talisman for love. With the formidable arrogance of a teenager, I was positive they didn't quite have love figured out. Given a little time I'd finish the job for them. I started at once.

My romantic life in high school was a series of unrequited crushes. I was different from the other girls. While they flaunted speed bumps and curves, I was as flat as a paper bag. The stainless steel bands on my teeth were plentiful enough to set off a metal detector and rendered me almost unkissable. The only member of the opposite sex who paid any attention to me was my childhood friend, Steven.

Our friendship began in the fall of second grade when my family moved across the Nebraska state line to Iowa. Steven and I roamed the neighborhood like wild banshees, spent more time together than apart, told each other our dreams, our fears.

Right after I turned twelve, my father died shockingly young. His death was so sudden and absolute that I floundered in a sea of lostness. Gone was my anchor and protector. Steven stayed right beside me, a comforter, steady and true. During those bleak days, he even allowed me to play with his Lionel train. I assumed we'd be pals for life.

Not long after I began my love crusade, Steven trashed our friendship. He did the unforgivable when he asked, "Wanna go to the movies on Friday night?"

My best friend had just asked me out on a date. I was mad and refused to talk to him for a week. Didn't he understand his role was to be there to offer advice, to hold my hand while I discovered the mysteries of love on my own? He persisted for many months until we drifted apart with a slow but inevitable sureness. The closeness Steven and I once shared withered away forever.

With a young girl's naiveté, I wondered if love might be a teddy bear, a black-and-white oversized lovey won at a carnival, adoring, silent, and present.

The summer before I left for college, my girlfriend developed a crush on a college boy. She begged me to tag along while she chased him around town. We appeared like good little groupies at every one of his softball games, the art gallery where his pottery sold, and the Swarm-In Café on campus.

Two weeks went by. Then out of nowhere he called and asked me to the fair. What a shock. Out of loyalty to her, I turned him down. Only, he kept calling, and when my friend seemed to lose interest, I accepted. He was cute, older, and I figured good practice for college. That summer I decided love must be a hand-thrown pot shaped by long, tapered fingers and fired to luminescence. By the time freshmen orientation rolled around, though, his presence had diminished to a phone number in my little pink book. I was more than ready to depart for the small liberal arts college located two hours from home.

Mixers, rush, dances. Boys, boys, and more boys. Love was out there waiting. I could smell it, a strange concoction of burgers and fries, English Leather aftershave, and breath mints.

That first night on campus, my roommate, a street-smart gal from Chicago, took matters into her own hands and insisted we go to a dance. Terrified by my social ineptness, I begged to stay behind at the dorm. But she would have none of that. We flaunted mini skirts, high heels, and let our long, straight hair shimmer free. In the Student Union, strobe lights pulsed. The Beatles pounded out "All You Need is Love." Before long, a chiseled football player sauntered over.

"Would you like to dance?" he asked. A steamy flush crept over my face, chased by an avalanche of cold sweat. I turned him down. Then a slick fraternity man knelt before me with his hand out. The boys kept coming, only to have me send them on their way.

My roommate could take no more. She yelled over the music. "What's up with you?" Before the next guy came along, she dragged me outside to the patio.

"You are nuts," she said. "Those Big Men On Campus want to boogie. Don't you get it? They've picked you out of the lineup. Now, what in God's name is wrong?"

More than anything I wanted the concrete to open and swallow me whole before I died of embarrassment. I stalled, picked at my pink nail polish until it was ragged. "I don't . . . I don't know how to dance," I confessed.

"You what?"

I stuttered out my problem again.

"No way. If you breathe, you dance."

"Not if you grew up in a town where every family but yours belongs to a church that doesn't allow dancing."

Her lips settled into a thoughtful pucker; I soon learned this meant trouble. "You and I . . . have some serious work to do."

Until the wee hours of the morning, I struggled through the basics of the Pony, the Stroll, and the simple box step. I drifted off to sleep wondering if love could be a rock star, a longhaired hippie drummer who waltzes you away in the moonlight before your heart learns to beat in three-quarter time.

A wild and messy parade of young men populated my college years. One of them sang love songs beneath my dorm room in a baritone as mellow as the local beer. Another fancied himself a poet and stalked me with anonymous poetry. Then there was the rah-rah flyboy who wore his uniform with pride and championed God and country even during the Vietnam War. In those tumultuous years, I thought love might be a fly-by-night salesman who breezes into town and sells you a piece of blue sky.

Only one man kept coming back. His name was Greg, and he was nothing like the Romeo of my fantasies. He was tall, athletic, a sports-aholic, and dead set on a career as a math teacher and boys' basketball coach. I was short, an artsy type, determined to direct a show on Broadway. We dated off and on for several years in a stormy courtship. But even when the draft and the US Navy sent him across the country, the thread of attraction between us remained strong. When he returned to campus in the spring of 1971 with a diamond ring in his pocket, I decided that love had come for me.

Forty-eight years have passed since our wedding day. At least once a month, I've wondered what love is and where it is hidden. Shivering in the cold at one more hockey game, I've wondered. I wondered during the ten long years Greg spent in medical school after he changed careers. Sometimes I've wondered how love could hurt so much or stoop so low. Holding our newborn babies, I wondered how love could be so pure.

Unlike Mr. Sandburg—who decided by the end of his poem that love must be a plain white bird—I still searched for one elusive symbol that encapsulated the meaning of love for me. Maybe love was just a phantom: a kaleidoscope filled with ever-changing patterns of colored glass and beveled mirrors that simply taunted, "Catch me if you can." In utter frustration, I decided to abandon my quest.

After our youngest child left for college, I passed the days in a frenzy of cleaning. While de-nesting my office, I happened to run across Carl Sandburg's poem, "Little Word, Little White Bird." The yellowed pages drew me once more. I breathed in the lyrical beauty of his words.

Love, is it a tug at the heart that comes high and
Costs, always costs, as long as you have it?
Love, is it a free glad spender, ready to spend to
The limit, and then go head over heels in debt?

This time I read his poetic search for love with the maturity of middle age, not the impetuousness of a teenager. I was amazed to discover that Carl Sandburg was eighty-five when he penned this poem, irrefutable proof that time and age know no bounds when it comes to love. My surrender had been a trifle hasty.

Greg did not clean house to cope with our empty nest. Instead he obsessed over clearing out the emotional detritus we'd accumulated. He argued that we should try to heal the wounds left untended throughout our marriage, mend those many hurts that were swept under the rug and ignored. I agreed. As a beginning, we promised to help each other fulfill one of our own secret dreams.

My husband confessed a lifelong passion to own a motorcycle. With trepidation, I acquiesced to the purchase of a BMW cruiser. For several months, he donned the leathers and helmet, and practiced riding around the neighborhood at a sedate speed, gears grinding with every shift. An altercation with the pavement struck the fear of God into him. The beast now sits in our son's garage—nine states away. Dream over. Love was most definitely not a smoking-hot motorcycle.

Now it was my turn. I confided my lifelong desire. "I want to learn how to ballroom dance."

Greg blanched an unhealthy shade of white. His capitulation was slow and painful to witness. In the end, he honored our agreement. We signed up for line dancing on Mondays and West Coast Swing on Tuesdays.

Innocent and unprepared for what was to come, we arrived for our first lesson. About twenty men and women chatted as they changed into dance shoes. We had none. Jon Pardi's deep-throated rendition of "Head Over Boots" carried from the speakers. Several couples drifted onto that slick square of hardwood in an easy, rhythmic partner dance that we later learned was a Country Two-Step.

The evening was a revelation full of disasters. On our first attempt to move to the music, it became obvious my husband had no sense of rhythm. Absolutely none. Big problem. To make matters worse, his two left feet infuriated him. Bigger problem. We lumbered about the floor like two dancing bears lost in a swamp. I feared my dream was destined to flame out after just one lesson.

Tired and sore, intimidated and embarrassed, we returned the next night for West Coast Swing with grim determination. The dance instructors first demonstrated a proper dance frame. Greg vacillated between gripping me too tightly or letting me fly untethered around the dance floor. The basic six-count swing step morphed into thirteen steps when we tried it. Our promenade became a tug-of-war and the sugar push almost a shove. We lost our way somewhere during the instruction, decades behind the other couples, and still no rhythm. For some crazy reason we refused to quit.

As Greg and I tackled West Coast, then Foxtrot, simple swing, the waltz, and our favorite smooth and elegant Nightclub Two-step, we experienced a bewildering epiphany—ballroom dancing was very much a partnership like marriage. Dancing laid bare our shortcomings. Intolerance, battles for control, and thin-skinnedness leapt onto the dance floor with us for everyone to see. I wanted to shake him by the shoulders and scream in his face, "Left right, left right." He glowered at me. There was no going forward until we found middle ground and enough patience to resolve our problems.

So Greg learned how to make me feel safe in the turns. I grew to understand the panicked look on his face meant he'd lost the rhythm again. Amazingly, dancing fanned a passion between us, despite Greg's arthritic knee, my vertigo, and our senior citizen status.

Last Saturday night at an American Legion Hall in a minuscule town, Greg and I stepped onto the concrete dance floor. Heavy air swirled over our heads, laced with the scent of burnt popcorn. Veterans of several wars eyed us and whispered to the women beside them. A local band broke into the pulsing beat of Chris de Burgh's "Lady in Red."

We floated around the dance floor in perfect hold, twirled through the turns, and promenaded with style. Long after the music died away, we remained on the floor dazzled by the moment. A painful sob caught in my chest, and I knew.

You see Mr. Sandburg, with all due respect sir, I'm saying love is a dancer. A bruised and battered man who earned his dancing stripes the hard way, who strapped on those pointy-toed shoes every day and fought through the pain. A sexy guy with a slight limp, salt and pepper in his hair, and a soul big enough to eat humble pie. The ladies and gents around us smiled as if they heard him whisper, "Could I have this dance for the rest of my life . . . "

4

FLICKERING IMAGES

BY BELLE SCHMIDT

He sits beside her
gently patting her folded hands.
And she smiles, but only faintly
and a twinkle flashes
behind large, thick lenses.

There is a space
between the two recliners
where they sit.
But, it's not an empty space.
Across the gap
a sixty-year-old love
sparks like electricity
and warms the room.

She speaks, revealing a gap
where bridgework used to be.
But, the gap does not detract
from a face filled with love,

a face where youth is buried
just below the surface.

His mind, sharp and clear,
remembers travels in Europe,
tropical beaches, exciting
entertainment and high-fashion finery.
Her mind, not sharp and clear,
moves memories across
a checkerboard of gaps.

They sit, part of a somewhat
cozy semi-circle of dozing loungers
parked in front of a TV with its
endless flickering images.

He rises, then tenderly, teasingly,
grabs her slippered toes and gives
them a little shake. His visiting is done.

5

ASHES

BY GRETA TUCKER

You let the smile fall
You let her walk away
It all crumbles to dust
Blown away
Like it was never there

You let the pain grow
And sit
And fester

You let the embers form
And the fire spread

You let it burn you down
From your heart
To your head
From the inside out

You sit
Surrounded by ashes
Angry
Empty

Then you feel something
Lift you up
Put you back together
Piece by piece
Release
Recovery
Forgiveness
Freedom
Compassion
Love
And you welcome it
Like an old friend

You stand for yourself
Different now
You bring the smile back
Better now
A little more
Fireproof

6

PINECONE

BY DAVID SHARP

Thursday afternoon. I'm busy losing myself in the woods. Maybe it's Friday. Hard to keep track in summer. No school to pin me to a calendar. Whatever the case, I'm traipsing through the trees when I see them at the bottom of a hill.

Jenna Ludmeyer and a couple of her friends. They haven't noticed me. Jenna's back is turned. Without thinking, I snatch up a pinecone and rear back. I don't know why I default to these things. Maybe I like the way Jenna scrunches up her face when she's mad. Maybe I'm taking out deep-rooted aggression. Maybe I'm just a jerk.

I'm about to let 'er rip when I feel a tight grip on my wrist.

"Stop!"

Busted. I turn around to see a man I don't recognize. Still, he's kinda familiar. He wears a weird helmet. It's shiny, with a series of strange blinking lights. "Stop," he says again. "You don't know what you're doing, Mikey. You *can't* throw that pinecone."

"Mind your own business," I wrench my wrist from his grip.

He gives me a strange look. "This *is* my business."

"I don't see how. Are you some pinecone rights activist?"

He gives me a pained look. "You don't recognize me, Mikey?"

"I've never met you."

"You're wrong."

I squint my eyes and try to let recollection take hold. I snap my fingers. "You're that guy from the park who's always talking about how the president is a Russian weasel?"

"A mole, you mean?"

"Right. That's it."

He shakes his head. "I'm not the park guy. Mikey, you're going to find this hard to believe, but I'm actually—Wait, how could you think I'm the park guy? I don't look *anything* like him!"

I shrug. "Maybe a bit like him."

"Not even a little bit like him! He's lost half his teeth!"

"Oooh! Right. *That's* why I didn't recognize you at first. Dentures, right! Or implants? I can't even tell."

"I AM NOT THE PARK GUY YOU LITTLE SNOT! AND YOU KNOW IT!"

"If you say so. Who are you then?"

He grasps my shoulder and kneels to look me in the eye. "I'm you, Mikey. I'm you from ten years in the future."

"Of course you are," I say, "I should have guessed from your helmet with all the blinky lights."

"I don't really care if you believe me," he says, "So long as you *don't throw that pinecone.*"

I look at the pinecone still wrapped in my fingers. It's just right for throwing. Symmetrical. Weighted on one end. Full of little hooks on the ends that will snag in Jenna's hair. I can't imagine why such a little thing would be so important to this whacko, but I'm curious. So I ask. "What happens if I throw the pinecone?"

A grim expression takes hold of his face. "That pinecone will start a chain reaction of tit-for-tat pranks between you and Jenna Ludmeyer that will continue for years to come. Every prank will increase in intensity and elaboration until they've grown beyond anything either of you can handle. The Manicotti Incident. The Shoelace Conspiracy. The Orange Paint Affair."

I pull away. "Manicotti Incident? Which one of us is responsible for that?"

"She is."

"Give me the details."

"They're too horrible."

"The hell they are. Just tell me something."

"I had to wash my sheets ten times to get the smell out."

I have no response to that, but the muscles in my face betray my revulsion.

He tightens his grip on my shoulder. "Listen, Mikey. These pranks will continue for years. They will become legendary in your neighborhood. The sheer demented creativity you both display will echo in whispered conversations throughout the city. The consequences of this prank war in my time are . . ." He shakes his head and draws in a long breath. "Unimaginable."

"You can't expect me to take this seriously," I say.

The twisted glint in his eye grows more intense. "It *is* serious though, Mikey. More serious than a smartass like you could hope to understand."

I pull my face away from his hot breath. "What? Does somebody get hurt? We don't kill anybody, do we?"

"No, Mikey. It's worse than that. Listen. As the pranks get bigger, you and Jenna will develop a rivalry with one another. That rivalry will evolve into admiration. Admiration will grow into something else until . . . "

"Until what?"

He pauses to bite his knuckle before he says, " . . . I'm getting married."

"Wait, what?"

"Tomorrow."

"To . . . Jenna Ludmeyer?"

He shakes me by my shoulders with both hands. "I didn't know what I was doing, Mikey! I still don't! You gotta get me out of this, kid! I *can't* go down that aisle."

I examine the pinecone in my hand. "So, I don't throw this pinecone, you don't get married."

A wild, desperate expression takes hold of him. "That's it! You got it, kid! This is where it all starts. Just drop it now, and none of this will ever happen! It's so easy!"

I check over my shoulder. Jenna's still at the bottom of the hill with her back to me. She hasn't seen any of this. "Maybe I could just throw it not as hard?"

"Michael Jeremiah Flatbush!" Future me sounds like a scolding parent.

"Okay, okay. I mean, it didn't seem like such a big deal. But, I guess I don't *have* to throw—"

"Mikey!" says another voice.

We both turn our heads. Another me-ish guy stands a few feet away with another shiny helmet.

"Are you me too?" I ask.

He nods. This version sports a trim beard and mustache. I have to admit, it's a good look for me. "Hello previous Mikeys," he says, "I come from fifteen years in the future. Mikey the youngest, you have to throw that pinecone."

"What?" say me and the first other-Mikey in unison.

"You heard me," says the newcomer. "Throw that pinecone."

"Uh . . ."

"Don't do it," says the first other-Mikey, relinquishing his grip on me.

"Do it," says the new other-Mikey.

"He can't!" says the first.

"He must!" says the second.

"Do it!"

"Don't!"

"Yes!"

"No!"

"Stop!" I shout. They both turn their attention to me. "This is getting out of hand," I say. "First of all, it's confusing having three Mikeys. For now, you," I point to the newest version of me, "you are Beard Mikey. And you," I point to the first other-me, "you are Desperate Mikey."

Desperate Mikey recoils from his new nomenclature. "Why do you get to be in charge of names? That doesn't fit me at all!"

"Yeah, it does," I say.

Beard Mikey nods.

"Fine," says Desperate Mikey. "And you're Mikey the Snot."

"If it makes you feel better." I shift my attention to Beard Mikey. "Your turn. What's so important about this pinecone?"

He takes a breath and composes himself. "You have to hear me out, Mikey the Snot. If you don't throw that pinecone it will change things, but not everything. Jenna is still going to get married in ten years. But it won't be to you. It's going to be . . . " he stops and chokes back his emotions, "to Gabe Wilson."

"Gabe Wilson?" says Desperate Mikey. "Seriously?"

"Yes. Please understand, Mikeys. You can't let that happen. You don't know what it will do to you to see them together. Knowing what could have been! It's like dying a little bit every day."

"Whoa," I say to Desperate Mikey, "we get really melodramatic in the future."

Desperate Mikey nods. "Better Gabe Wilson than us," he says. "We didn't know what we were getting into. We were fools! Naive, impetuous fools, all of us! Avoid the horror of it all now. This is our only chance." He turns to Beard Mikey. "Think of the manicotti! The manicotti, man!"

Beard Mikey wipes a finger across his eye. "I would endure a hundred Manicotti Incidents to have Jenna Ludmeyer back. A thousand! A million!"

Desperate Mikey slaps him on the cheek. "Get ahold of your-

36

self! You're not thinking straight!" He turns to me. "Do you see? *This* is what she does to you. This is the power she wields. Gabe Wilson is throwing himself on a grenade right now. You can trust me on this!"

"Gabe Wilson is a putz!" shouts Beard Mikey. Sobs burst from him like floodwaters breaking through a dam. "What does she see in him? What does she *see* in him?"

I shift my focus back and forth between them. "Sooooo, what? Am I throwing the pinecone or not?"

"NO!" cries a new voice. The three of us groan. Well, two of us groan and Beard Mikey just kinda sobs with extra exasperation.

The newcomer looks like the rest of us, but with a little more wear in his eyes and hints of silver in his hair. I am not surprised to see he is wearing a shiny helmet with blinky lights on it. "I'm getting a headache," I say to the latest Mikey. "How many years in the future are you?"

"Twenty."

"And your problem is?"

"Your kids, Mikey! You have no idea what's coming. Do you understand? Your kids. They'll act just. Like. You."

"Is that a bad thing? I'm pretty cool, right?"

Parental Mikey shakes his head. "Remember the incident with the worms last month?"

"Nobody can prove that was me!"

All the other Mikeys roll their eyes.

"Oh, right. You were all there. Time travel is really complicated."

"How about the Sour Milk Scandal?" says Desperate Mikey.

"The House Plant Horror?" offers Beard Mikey.

"Okay, okay! I get it! We don't need to revisit my sordid past. So, my kids are a handful."

"They improve upon your methods, actually," says Parental Mikey. "They're the masterminds behind the Cricket Conundrum, the Basement Ballistics Debacle, the Chicken Casserole Catastrophe!"

"I've never heard of those," says Desperate Mikey. "Are they really worse than the stunts I pulled?"

Parental Mikey grunts. "It's biology, young Mikeys. Take two pranksters with sadistic imaginations, overlap their chromosomes three times over, and station them in a suburban pressure cooker. I leave it to you to visualize the results."

The other two other-Mikeys wince.

"So, what now?" I ask.

"Throw it!"

"No! Don't throw it!"

"Throw it! Do it now!"

The other-Mikeys argue. Arguing turns to shoving. Shoving to physical violence.

I squeeze the pinecone nestled in my palm, and glance once more down the hill. Jenna and her friends are laughing. They still haven't noticed us. Too absorbed in the freedom of a summer afternoon. Deaf to all but the droning music of the cicadas. A summer breeze wafts through her hair.

"Don't listen to *any* of them!" says a new voice, quiet, dusty, and withered. A wrinkled hand rests on my shoulder. The old man who speaks wears a rusted helmet. Several of the lights no longer blink. "Do it, Mikey. While they're distracted." He smiles with cracked lips and offers a wink.

I lob it.

"No!" shout two-out-of-three squabbling Mikeys.

The pinecone glides through the air with a spin that would inspire heart palpitations in the most seasoned NFL quarterback. It curves ever so slightly along the breeze in a perfect arc toward the back of Jenna Ludmeyer's head. I have a gift for trajectories. It hovers for just a moment at the apex before hurtling along its fateful path. It strikes Jenna dead center on the back of her head, snags in her hair for a fragmented moment, and then drops to the ground at her feet. She lets out a startled cry.

The old man chuckles and pats my shoulder. "You won't regret it."

Then they're gone. All four of them wink out of existence. I'm standing alone.

That's when I hear Jenna Ludmeyer's voice shouting. "I see you Michael Flatbush! I'll get you for this!"

7

PUPPETMASTER

BY GRETA TUCKER

She did it
Tore them apart like candy
Toyed with them like puppets
She pushed their knives
To the other's throat
Sharp as her wit
She did it

She let it happen
Watched the house burn down
Everyone in it
A smile playing at her lips
As the war began
Sweet as honey
She let it happen

She picked up the pieces
Put them back together

Held them close
Twisted words around
She picked up the pieces
And did it all again

8

THE POTATO SALAD WAR

BY CINDRA SPENCER

"Why don't you write it? Did you not take adequate notes?"

Officer Ahmadi closed his notepad and took a long breath. "Complainants must make their own statements, ma'am."

"Well, I've never . . . What do I include?"

"Everything you just told us," Detective Cox said.

I gasped. "The whole thing?"

Another officer burst in. "Hernandez called. They think they found our guy." Then he noticed me and his lips tightened.

I continued. "Even the part about the spoon?"

Detective Cox rubbed his forehead. "Ma'am, again, you don't have to file anything."

Officer Ahmadi slapped a pad of blank forms on the table. "Plus, the laptop's occupied. You'd hafta write it by hand." He tossed a cheap plastic pen my direction.

The pen rolled past me to an unintended destination. I looked up at him and blinked. The fluorescent lighting did his Mesopotamian nose no favors. "I actually prefer handwriting, thank you. Penmanship is a magnificent lost discipline." From my handbag, I retrieved the pearled Visconti Seamus gave me on our thirtieth. I hovered the fountain tip over a blank page. "Where do I start?"

"At the beginning, just like you told us," Cox said. "Take your time."

I entered today's date and began.

Like the other great wars our nation has suffered, it started with the union of two families. In fact, the first insult was fired not one hour after my sweet William was married. My memory of the wedding is stained now with the introduction to that horrible, tasteless woman.

"This is Natalie's mother, Irene. Irene, this is my mother, Agnes."

I made the expected embrace, taking in Irene's wrinkles and mottles of grey. I had my own grey, of course but she carried at least fifteen pounds more than the excess twelve I carried, so my nerves were put at ease.

"So pleased to finally meet you."

I could tell she was anxious, which calmed me a great deal. "Likewise."

The wedding was held in a garden, and Natalie glowed, a barefoot angel in the grass. I was glad to call her my daughter-in-law and believed she'd take good care of William. The sun lingered low in the sky, spreading golden luck over us as they exchanged vows. I wept, partly in joy and partly from the coronary taking my Seamus before he could see our son wed.

Fairy lights flickered in the tree canopies as the tables were set with food. A barbeque potluck seemed much too informal, given the occasion's significance, but it was too late to express further opinion. Besides, my heirloom potato salad brought a sliver of elegance to the affair.

Irene and her husband Ed moved down the buffet line opposite me. I noted the loose threads around the cuff of her jacket and scoffed that, as the mother of the bride, she did not purchase a new suit. I hoped Natalie was not merely one of William's charity campaigns. His bleeding heart had brought home more emaciated cats than I could recall.

"It's a lovely suit, Irene." I am not without my own philanthropy.

"Thank you. My mother wore it to my wedding and Natalie insisted I wear it today." She put a slice of brisket on Ed's plate and smiled. "Perhaps Natalie will do the same, someday, should we be so blessed." She winked at me.

"Perhaps." I busied myself with the greens.

"Gimme some of that, too." Ed pointed.

"This? I brought this." I passed Irene my Peruvian silver serving spoon.

She put a small dollop on Ed's dish, he gestured for more, and she added to it. We moved down the line, filling our plates with casseroles and nervous small talk. By the time we reached the bread I had decided I did not like Irene. It seemed her teeth were too small for her mouth. There was no relief, though, as we'd been seated together. I wished William would join us.

"Mmmm, this is good potato salad, Agnes." Ed wiped his mouth with a linen napkin.

Before I could thank him, Irene turned to me and asked, "Is it from the Kroger deli?"

I nearly choked on an olive. The sharp ring of her insult hung over the table, a startling but unmistakable challenge of battle, her saccharine innocence impossible to miss.

I touched the hollow in my throat. "That recipe, perfected by my great-nana, takes two days to make." I soon excused myself and made the rounds.

Over the following months I'd all but forgotten Irene's blunder. In fact, I had thought of it only once, when the other Red Hat Society ladies asked me about the wedding. I showed them photos and took in the compliments. The set of my hair. Natalie's figure. The fairy lights.

When Doris asked about the caterer I explained the potluck and Irene's affront; we all chuckled at her ignorance.

In July,

I looked up.

Detective Cox stood against the wall, sipping coffee. "All done?"

"No. I have a question. Must I reference exact dates? I'd need to go home and consult my calendar."

"Your best recollection is fine." He stepped closer and looked at my pages. "Oh, cripes."

"What?"

"You're writing it like a . . aw, hell." He scratched at his grey hair. "You don't need to write it like that."

"Is it not important to be thorough, Detective?"

"Ma'am . . "

We both knew he couldn't say no.

He nodded at me gently, by way of encouragement to keep going.

In July, William and Natalie dropped by to invite me to her family reunion. Natalie informed me they convened every summer: an entire day of cousins, second cousins, and cousins once removed running wild around the park.

"We have lots of laughs and get too much sun," she said. "Agnes, we'd love to have you join us."

I watched William's hand clench into a fist by his side, but he nodded in agreement.

"Well," I hesitated, "I don't . . "

Still smiling at me, Natalie reached down to pat his hand, as if to quell whatever irritant so often possessed him. I warmed to Natalie in that moment. We were allies combatting the silly notions that ran through my son's mind.

She continued, "You already know my mother, and Jen and Mike will be there." Jen is Natalie's sister. "You can meet Mike's parents if they can make it."

"It sounds lovely. Yes, of course I'll come."

She leaned in to hug me, then William followed suit.

I immediately thought to ask, "Shall I bring my potato salad?"

Natalie laughed. "No, no, my mother will bring some. A standing tradition. You don't need to bring anything."

"Surely it would be rude to come empty-handed?"

"Not at all. There's always too much food. Let others do the work for a change."

The day of the reunion I was reacquainted with Jen and her husband Mike, and Irene and Ed of course, along with numerous other relatives.

As William guided me to a seat in the shade, I remarked, "It's quite warm for a picnic, don't you think?"

"It's a beautiful day. Perfect reunion weather." He was so inclined to disagreement. I suppose it's what made him a fine tax attorney.

Under the pavilion, Mike and Jen said they'd make an announcement once everyone had their food. It took ages.

Irene made a gaudy fuss over making Ed's plate and I realized the whole production was simply to show my widowhood up. By the time she offered to refill his lemonade, I could tell she thought she really had one up on me. However, I knew from William that Ed was her second husband, and of course anyone could get one of those. Her real husband passed away when the girls were young, so in contrast, the many years I had with my Seamus were worth more than any second-rate contingency she had acquired.

The first time Mike tried to get everyone's attention, no one heard him. He attempted to clang a fork against a red plastic cup but obviously it didn't ring the way lead crystal would have. It made a faint rap which, for some reason, Jen found outrageously funny. Eventually,

Ed stuck his fingers in his mouth and made a shrill whistle, halting the chatter immediately.

Mike stood up on the picnic table. "Well," he paused, as if knowing he wouldn't get many words in, "Jen's pregnant."

The savages erupted into the requisite congratulations. The way they talked over each other was quite ill-mannered and overwhelming. Somewhere in the midst of all this, Natalie leaned in to ask me, "Have you tried Mom's potato salad?" She pointed to my plate. "It's amazing."

Out of politeness I took a bite. Despite its inadequacies, I chewed and smiled. I'm not a backward heathen. When Natalie's attention turned to gender predictions, I discreetly used the tine of my fork to excavate ingredients from the mound. Potato. Celery. Onion. "No egg?"

I had to ask again, louder, "No egg?"

William turned towards me. "What was that, Mother?"

"There's no egg in the potato salad?" I didn't want to seem confrontational, so I asked it of anyone, not pointedly at Irene.

His eyes took on that look he used to get when I rubbed dirt off his cheek. "Please don't," he whispered.

"I'm just surprised, is all."

Irene must've heard and shifted in her folding chair. "It's not meant to be egg salad, is it?"

William, always wont to take the corporate side, quickly added, "Of course not. It's very good."

I smiled, but did not take care to hide the debitage left behind as I dropped my plate in the trash barrel. Everything about Irene was utterly tasteless. Her blouse. Her whistling backup husband. Her snide remarks. And most certainly her potato salad.

The door clicked open and Officer Ahmadi returned. "Nearly finished?"

I sat up taller. "I'm up to the baby shower."

Detective Cox put his hand on Ahmadi's arm. "She's up to the baby shower."

Ahmadi shook his head. "The perp's Pro Bono is here. We don't have time for this shit."

I clutched my blouse. "Excuse me?"

"You take your time." Cox nodded to indicate Ahmadi should take his leave.

Once he was gone, I said, "My son's a highly reputed attorney, you know. He can see the river from his office."

Detective Cox snorted. "Does he represent meth dealers, too?"

"No, no." I laughed at the notion. "That sort of thing would bore him. William handles corporate taxes."

I leaned over the table and continued.

The invitation for Jen's shower arrived in January. Or perhaps February because the invitations were blue. They must've already known it would be a boy.

I looked at Cox. "Is it important to state exactly when the baby shower invitations arrived?"

"Ma'am, I can't say which details are important and which ones aren't." He said it with a rehearsed cadence; a reply given countless times. I concluded from the underlying tone it was not important at all. Why, I could have been a detective myself.

Jen's shower was on a Saturday. Mike's parents were unable to make it. I was informed that Frank, Mike's father, had been quite ill. Hospitalized with gout complications.

Naturally, there had been no central planning as to who-brought-what. "These things just aren't important to other people," William explained each time I asked him what to bring. As one might expect in the wake of this disorganization, Irene and I both brought our respective potato salads. I admit, I did smirk, knowing how well my dish would fare in a side-by-side competition.

They grazed like animals throughout the entire party, with no particular time marked to dine. The second time I checked for smudges on my silver serving spoon, it was missing. I searched everywhere—the floor, the empty space between the Jello and the green salad. When I realized it wasn't simply knocked off, I immediately knew it had been stolen. Irene must not have wanted me to have any advantage. She had motive and opportunity. Nana's legacy was then scooped with a squat, plastic spoon, cheap and small and mucked up with mayonnaise.

Despite the sabotage, my salad received plenty of compliments. And yet, an equal number of niceties were paid to Irene. It was impossible to tell which was actually preferred.

But, with each congratulatory remark on her grandparenthood, that smug tart grew more and more arrogant. 'Irene will make the best babysitter.' 'Irene's swaddling calms the fussiest infants.' 'Irene crochets the softest little booties.' She overtly relished the comments. As if Jen's fertility was her personal accomplishment.

"Agnes? Would you like a piece of cake?" Mike doled out disproportionate squares.

"No, thank you." I refolded my arms.

William joined me, licking a mass of blue frosting from his thumb. "Everything okay, Mother? You have your contemplative look."

"I've been trying to determine why they all pretend to like Irene's potato salad. I'm certain she uses russets, and everyone knows they're gluey when served cold."

My accomplished debater went silent, staring at me, and I gathered we were in agreement on this simple and rather obvious point. He stood and left without saying a word. I watched him have a quiet exchange with Natalie, and at one point she glanced at me. She was a smart woman and likely concurred russets were a lousy choice, too. A blend of reds and fingerlings made the nicest salad—but of course I needn't divulge all my great-nana's secrets.

As William drove me home, my crystal bowl and my silver spoon —recovered from the kitchen—sat in my lap, empty. The remnants had been packed for Frank, Mike's father, to enjoy when he got out of the hospital. It was too quiet in the car, and William failed to respond to the updates on my geraniums. I eventually asked, "Are you cross?"

His knuckles whitened on the steering wheel. "Mother, it frustrates me to no end when you're rude. Your disparaging comments about Irene's dish were out of line. And I don't think you offered any well-wishes to Jen and Mike."

"I gave them precisely two hundred well-wishes tucked inside a keepsake card."

He took a deep breath. "Has it occurred to you that some people make compliments just to be nice?"

I waved his nonsense away. "I didn't mean for Irene to hear me, if she did. The square footage in that home is rather deficient, isn't it?"

William tapped the steering wheel, staring straight ahead. "Okay. Okay, you know what? You know what, Mother? Maybe some people actually like her potato salad."

I scoffed at William and looked out at the traffic. He knows I won't respond to his ridiculous, fancy rebuttals. And to think of anyone enjoying that slop. I did not understand this breed of people, their warped preferences and values. For the first time, I doubted Natalie's abilities to look after my William. I wondered if she would attempt to impart this recipe onto my own grandchildren, when they came. This didn't sit well with me. Not at all.

"I'm going to check on a few things and grab another coffee. Can I bring you something?"

I looked up. The detective's manners indicated he, like William, had the clear benefit of a good mother.

"I could do with a chamomile tea, thank you."

"Cripes, I doubt we have that. Coffee?"

"At this hour! I should think not."

He left the door open and I continued to write.

I thought of Irene often over the next few months, the way she flaunted her growing bloodline in my face. And our Easter plans were spoiled. I had already pinned my wicker rose hat on when William called.

"Mother, we won't be getting together today after all. Jen went into labor and delivered baby Murray late last night. Or, well, technically early this morning. He's just over seven pounds, long fingers. Completely bald. Premature hair loss, just like Mike." William chuckled as if this little joke had already been told a dozen times.

"Oh? No one called me. You should have called me, William. I'd have come to the hospital."

"Yes, well, I didn't want to disrupt you, and besides, Jen wanted privacy."

"You should have called me."

"I'm calling now, and I just want you to know we'll plan to have brunch another time."

"You don't sound well. Are you ill?"

"No, we were up all night. We've only just got home."

"Was Irene there?"

William paused. "Yes, of course. She's Jen's mother."

I digested the notion that, like her sister, Natalie might permit that woman, but not me, to be present when my own grandchildren came. "Were Mike's parents there?"

William sighed. "No. Frank's gout still has the best of him."

"I see."

"So, everyone is tired and we've decided it best just to nap and skip brunch."

"What am I supposed to do with all this potato salad?"

"Take it to your church charity dinner? You told me a dozen times you'd have to leave early to make it to church in time."

"But it pairs well with deviled eggs. Natalie said she was making deviled eggs."

William's inhale and exhale grew longer. "Well, she won't be making them now. She's taking a shower and we're going to bed. Jen's doing fine, by the way. Murray is healthy, all is well. Happy Easter, Mother."

I paused. Low conversation in the hall disrupted my train of thought. I leaned closer to the door, eager to hear what the others might say about Irene and her atrocious behavior.

"I'll be there in a few minutes," Cox hollered over his shoulder as he entered the room. He saw I wasn't writing and he pointed to my papers. "Let's finish up your little *novella*."

Late October, William and Natalie called me over for a family dinner, along with Irene and Ed. I wore my pastel blue suit as I was certain what was coming and wanted to match the mood. Instead, however, William informed us he had been awarded a promotion after acquiring a big account in Juarez. "Next month, the firm is holding a Dia de la Revolucion party to celebrate, make the official announcement. I'd love it if you all came."

"I'll bring potato salad!" Irene and I blurted the words in unison. The dinner fell silent as we glared across the table, each daring the other to acquiesce.

Natalie, apparently still without child, finally offered, "It's a fiesta." When neither of us responded, she furthered, "So . . maybe bring guacamole? Or bean dip?"

William shook his head. "Not necessary. The firm will retain a caterer. All you need to do is come."

Ed shifted, looked at me, his wife, then back at me. He shifted again then raised his beer. "To William! Congratulations, bud. We're all so proud of you."

We then took turns toasting my son.

But that wasn't the end of it. In fact, that was the very night I real-
ized Irene was trying to kill Ed.

Detective Cox yawned.

I looked up to see him attempting to cover his mouth. I noticed
his wedding band sat loose around his finger. I wondered why his
wife didn't feed him well enough. "Do you like potato salad,
Detective?"

"Me? Uh, that's irrelev—"

"Because I'd be happy to make you some."

His lips parted but he remained speechless. Perhaps he wasn't
used to being flattered.

He gestured for me to keep going.

After the toasts and congratulations, the men moved to the sofa. Ed had
endless questions about William's new role, and I was pleased he took
such an interest in my son's accomplishments.

We ladies cleared the table, made a pot of coffee—decaffeinated of
course—and pulled lemon squares out of the refrigerator. Natalie
served them onto small plates. Irene took two, one for her and one
for Ed.

I watched Irene cross the kitchen, take the lid off a canister, and
spoon extra confectioner's sugar onto Ed's serving. Then she walked
into the living room and served it to him.

When William drove me home, I asked him if Ed still had
diabetes. William confirmed, and said unfortunately it seemed to be
growing worse. Ed's doctor had increased his insulin in recent weeks,
and his last podiatry exam wasn't promising. I was so proud of
William that I didn't realize what it all meant right away.

That night, it took some time to pinpoint what troubled me. Once I
realized Irene was deliberately destroying her husband, I couldn't bear

it. I had a kinship with Ed as he and I were both outsiders, both married into Irene's clan. I felt a duty to warn him, protect him.

The door clicked open and Officer Ahmadi poked his head in. "DA says he can't get that warrant signed until tomorrow."

I touched my throat. "A warrant!"

Ahmadi scowled at me. "It doesn't involve you." He looked at Detective Cox and gestured to the space behind him. "It's a shit show out there. We need you."

The detective sipped his coffee and nodded.

Ahmadi's lips twitched. He shook his head and clicked the door closed behind him.

"Detective Cox?"

He looked at me.

"But, there will be charges, against Irene? I wasn't certain . . ."

He raised one grey eyebrow. "Ah, I wouldn't count on—"

"But, that woman!"

"Listen, I'm not quite sure what you think—"

"Like I told you, she sprinkled arsenic all over her husband's, er, second husband's, dessert, and—"

The paper cup stopped halfway to his lips. "Arsenic? This is the first—"

"Well, confectioner's sugar. Ed's diabetic, so it's practically the same thing."

His shoulders relaxed. "I assure you, it's not."

I pursed my lips. "Well. You understand what I'm saying, nonetheless. You'll press charges?"

He closed his eyes. "That's not up to me."

I nodded and finished up.

Only a few days later I got the call that Frank, Mike's father, had passed away. His kidneys had failed. Though I'd never met Mike's parents, I offered my condolences to Norma and confirmed that of course I would attend services and help in any way possible.

Over the next few days I shared the names of the florist and funeral director that created such thoughtful arrangements for Seamus. I went shopping with Natalie. I bought her a smart grey dress for the service and we shared crab sandwiches at the club. It was a wonderful week.

I opted not to bring potato salad to the post-service reception. This decision seemed to impress William. I did not tell him I needed to watch Irene closely and determine if I could get to the bottom of her intentions with Ed. And I had a rebuttal of my own, a little payback for hiding Nana's spoon.

Being the designated helper, I slipped out of the service as soon as the last amen was uttered. It was my job to make sure the reception hall was ready before the masses filtered in. At the food table, I reached inside my handbag and discreetly opened a container. Confirming no one was watching, I retrieved hard dices of raw potato. Ugly, haphazard pieces battered with contusions of air exposure. I scattered them across Irene's salad and gave it a slight stir. We'd see how many compliments rolled in when they crunched into raw potato. Maybe she'd choke on her own hubris.

I engaged in polite conversation and listened to stories about Frank. He'd been in the Korean War. He enjoyed watching Ice Capades. He pruned his neighbor's plum trees.

As I listened, I watched Irene bypass the vegetable trays and fill Ed's plate with cookies, a bagel sandwich, and a slice of pie. Ed could be in a coma before the day was over at her rate. I needed to warn him.

When she returned to the food line to make her own selections, I approached him in the back corner of the room.

"Hiya Agnes! Pull up a chair."

I did.

"What did you think of the funeral? I thought it was a real nice turnout."

I looked at him straight on. This was serious. "Honestly Ed, I think you're up next if Irene has her way."

Ed gasped this news into the wrong pipe. He coughed with the hard force of surprise and rhubarb pie. He looked towards Irene but she, and many others, had her back to us. He continued to hack, which was a fair reaction to finding out your wife is trying to murder you.

I looked up too, trying to gauge how much time I might have to explain. But there was some commotion on the other side of the room. Irene and many others had formed a circle. I craned my neck but couldn't see what was going on.

As Ed quieted, it was evident a different obstruction had everyone's attention. Unlike Ed's coughing, it was stifled. Unproductive. I saw William vault over a table and snatch baby Murray, gone completely blue, out of Jen's arms. Jen was crying, screaming, "Help him, help him!"

Ed and I stood up, wide-eyed. The entire hall had gone silent, watching William turn Murray upside down, gripping his jaw. He whacked Murray on the back with his palm. Little legs flailed and a tiny shoe flew off. William whacked him again. Something flew out of Murray's mouth and he immediately howled an inhuman noise. William turned him right-side up and passed him back to Jen. She cradled him as they both sobbed.

Ed and I made our way over, my warning forgotten. William was shaking.

"What happened?"

Mike bent down and picked something up off the floor. He rubbed it between his fingers.

"What is it?" Ed asked.

"Potato," Mike said. "I think it's . . raw."

Irene and I both gasped. Jen gave a painful, beseeching look at her mother, but William and Natalie both looked at me.

"I, that's not, I don't . . " Irene struggled for words.

"I had raw bits in mine," a cousin's meek voice offered.

"Me too." The confirmation was but a whisper.

Irene went white. "I don't, I don't . . "

Natalie turned towards me and made a silent gesture, as if expecting me to explain. As if I would know. Which, of course, she couldn't know that I did.

She would not look away.

"What do you want?" I whispered.

"I want there to be a goddamned potato famine!" she screamed.

I blanched, nauseous at such an insensitive reference to William's heritage. Seamus was probably having another coronary right in his grave.

An uncomfortable silence followed Natalie's outburst. Despite the crowded room, Murray's muffled whimpers resounded, even cradled against Jen's chest. Those pitiful sounds went straight to my heart. The threat of tears filled my throat. Actual lives were at stake. The poor lad could've died. And Ed still might. The law needed to intervene. These were not matters I could handle on my own. I vowed then and there to rise above this nonsense. If I had to be the bigger person, so be it. I would not allow Irene's pettiness to take a life.

"Alright then, since everyone's listening . . ." Mike gave a strained smile, clearly about to make another one of his announcements and smooth over to nicer subjects. He put his arm around his mother. She looked extra slim, almost frail, but it may have just been the black dress. "So, Jen and I have talked with Mom." He patted Norma with reassurance. "Now that Dad's . . ." he paused, not yet accustomed to the right verbiage, "uh, passed on, Mom is moving in with us."

"That's wonderful!" Natalie clasped her hands together.

"I'll get to help with Murray." Norma reached her arms out and Jen passed the sniffling baby.

"It's true." Jen stood, and wiped mascara smudges from her eyes. "I'll be able to go back to work. We're going to buy a bigger house."

"More room for our little guy to run around," Mike added.

"We'll have a housewarming, of course, once Norma settles in."

Irene and I both moved to speak, but Natalie cut in above us. "No. No potato salad."

Uneasy chuckles from others went around.

"Not necessary." Mike beamed. "Mom makes the very best maca-roni salad you ever tasted." He poked Murray in the nose. "And that you ever tasted."

Norma beamed. "It's a true Southern classic, from my great-aunt in Georgia."

"Mmmm, I do love a cold pasta salad!" Ed rubbed his belly, as though he simply couldn't wait for it.

I glanced at Irene, and we held each other's gaze with mutual understanding. Like so many great wars before this one, our objective was now suspended. We had a more pressing matter to attend to. United by our new common enemy, we nodded in agreement, a silent pact to neutralize this new threat.

"Alright. I think that will do it." I capped the Visconti and put it back in my handbag. Detective Cox reached for my *novella*. His word might just stick, the clever man.

We both stood, and he stuck his hand out. "Good luck to you."

I gripped his hand. "And to you. So, you'll investigate Irene, then? Before Ed is murdered?"

He looked to choose his words carefully. "I won't *personally* handle it, but I'll process your complaint, as required." He paused, then added, "Mrs. Kelly, you'll move on from all this now, yeah? You'll take the higher road out there, set an example for others?"

I frowned. I hadn't likened him for a Democrat and didn't need to hear more. "Good evening, Detective."

"Good evening."

9

TABLES AND CHAIRS

BY KARI REDMOND

"These are sun setting chairs," I said. You raised your Toña beer to mine. We faced our plastic Adirondack chairs to the surf and watched the sun disappear into it. I met you in Granada where we discussed the merit of Tom Robbins, the unofficial, official rules of traveling, and the subtle difference between Victoria and Toña beers. We sat at the bar of the hostel, preferring it to the few tables scattered about with mismatched chairs. You said you were from Canada. I did my best not to hold it against you. I said goodbye to you that night; three beers in and a pack of cigarettes gone. Later, as I lay awake on the bottom bunk, I thought, I'd say goodbye to as many people as I'd say hello to in my life. It felt like I started with you. One week later, I spot you from the window of the bus that brought me to San Juan del Sur. You are walking, hands in your pockets. I think you are whistling. I rush off the bus, nearly forgetting my pack underneath it. Catch up to you. Casually say, "Fancy meeting you here." You show me around like I am an old friend, and you an old local. Take me to the bar you say you'll buy someday. I smile and nod, though I do not believe you. We spend our days on the beach and our nights at our bar in our sun setting chairs quietly sipping Toñas, each thinking of how we could possibly return. And you, the only Canadian I've ever liked, you bought the bar. Furnished it with plastic tables and chairs, red and white and green, the colors of the bottles of Toña we drank. And I've yet to return.

10

IN THE DARK OF EARLIEST MORNING

BY MEGAN E. FREEMAN

I wake in the dark of earliest morning knowing
that last night was the last night you will come home

into the quiet room where I am sleeping
and tuck yourself into my arms.

Letting me know you're safe.
Letting me know you love me too.

Like the first day of kindergarten, giving you up to the world,
never to have you fully back again.

Like the first day of your life, breathing air,
never again as safe as you were in my womb.

The next time I sleep in this bed, no one will wake me.
No one will interrupt my sleep to comfort me with confirmation.

Today I send you out of the known and into the other.
Tomorrow I come home alone.

11

THE OTHER DAY I FOUND A PENNY IN THE STREET

BY JACLYN FOWLER

Find a penny, pick it up
And all day long you'll have good luck.

I love the mornings in the United Arab Emirates when the weather's winter transformation begins and an almost cool breeze bathes our little community in hope. On these mornings, there is a promise of a long-desired liberation from the desert's oppressive heat; in the quiet of the pre-dawn light, there is a wish-fulfilling whisper; *better days ahead*, it says. As the moon glitters on the Gulf, its twinkling, twirling, almost amorphous light snakes its way from bank to bank and back again, indulging a little before its banishment with the coming of the sun's first rays. I wake early most mornings, mainly preparing for the long drive to Dubai, the UAE's most famous city, but also to contemplate a life without my father, to grieve on my own at a time when others still dream.

While work is no more than an hour away—in kilometers, that is —traffic can make the commute much, much longer: two hours, three hours, even four. The earlier I leave my home, the less time the drive to Dubai will take. Minutes matter in this quest. And so I sacrifice the extra sleep and breakfast and the morning light to lessen my time in the car. After waking, I have a small window of time that allows for a quick shower and a few spare minutes to do my hair and add the necessary eyeliner, mascara, and blush to the fifty-year-old face in the mirror that, these days, I hardly recognize. There is no time to wait for a sleeping husband to wish me good morning; instead, I kiss him goodbye in the almost light of a new day.

While my mornings are all about hurrying to avoid long waits, I have a duty I cannot ignore. Regardless of traffic, I must look after Doodles, my half Shih Tzu, half Brussels Griffon. The little guy fully depends on me. So before I pack up my computer, throw yesterday's dry cleaning in the back of the car, and begin the long commute, Doodles and I take a walk. Every morning. Without fail.

During the late fall, as the days shorten and winter approaches, it is quite dark at 4:30 a.m. The lamplights in my community are still calibrated to summer timing, so they flicker off just as Doodles and I emerge from our little villa. Outside, darkness envelops us in the night's last stand. Daylight does not begin its ascent for more than an hour when the fire-red sun sizzles its awake-ness, mirage-like, on the sweltering desert floor. Sunrises are brief here, the UAE being equatorial and all, but they are exceptionally stunning, animated and alive. Their brevity contrasts beautifully with the long, still darkness of night, especially in the winter months.

When I am not too wrapped up in my own head and I take whatever time is necessary to marvel at the daily sunrise, I find myself contemplating the almost spiritual role the sunrise might have in our lives—if only we noticed. I am convinced, you know, that the everyday-ness of the sunset is intentional, meant to be an all-too-obvious symbolic reference to the ups and downs of our lives. I don't mean symbolic in the ultimate sense: the life and death sort. No. That would be *too* too-obviously symbolic. It would be so overdone, in fact, that the symbolism would be trivialized. The daily sunrise is symbolic because, in regards to the way we focus our lives, we often miss the short bursts of light, too busy focusing too intensely on the extended stretches of darkness.

Yet, it is a fundamental truth that light always follows dark with the regularity and consistency of the sunrise. While the simple daily reminder of the sunrise should be enough to cue us in to this obvious point, we often overlook it, ignore it, just plain forget to take notice of it. A sunrise, after all, is extraordinary in its ordinariness. Even with its undisputed beauty, a sunrise happens every day. Every. Single. Day. Its regularity produces the ultimate irony in its symbolic power. Instead of the commonplace of a beautiful sunrise, then, we need a jolt to wake us up to the light, forcing us to acknowledge profound beauty in our lives, a profound beauty that always, always comes, even after times of lingering darkness. Every once in a while, that jolt comes. By God, it comes.

"Hey, buddy," I call, leash in hand. "Wanna go for a walk?"

There's really no reason to ask. Doodles is always ready for a walk; he'd go anywhere. Especially with me. But there's a comfortable symmetry in the routine of asking each morning, something that makes me happy, content. My asking this question might make us both happy, I suspect. So ask I do, preparing to head out into the shadows—into the darkness—of the too early morning. Darkness, I consider, is something I know a lot about these days, already forgetting my discussion of the symbolic nature of sunrises.

For a little more than two years, I have lived in the UAE in a little northern town called Ras al Khaimah. For a little more than two years, I have lived an altered life that was not altogether mine, but mine all the same. I had no choice, this move to the unknown, to an unfamiliar existence; I needed a job. I needed to care for my children, and I needed to prove to myself I was the strong, independent woman I had always been. For a little more than two years, I took what had become a Humpty-Dumpty-like broken life and put it back together again in a place where I no longer had to explain why. I simply worked on becoming whole. For a little more than two years, I have celebrated holidays and important family milestones without my family, most notably after the passing of my father, my best friend, my rock. So for a little less than two years, I have grieved for a father who died a little less than one year after I started my life anew in the UAE.

I am coping with my Middle East-sequestered grief, however, by recognizing the amazing coming together of so many disparate people, each contributing something unique to this new world of mine. I live in a little community of mostly expatriates, all nestled together in a sort of forced, yet agreeable, diversity on the edge of the Arabian Gulf. It is a pleasant place; the babble of our words adds to its charm, all of us searching for ways to understand and be understood. All of us polite to one other. None of us taking communication for granted as we might have done in our home countries. Our little community is picturesque, the sea and the sand marking its boundaries, so life *looks* idyllic too.

In the front of my house is the salt marsh, hazy in its humidity, the water view bursting with flocks of pink flamingos balancing on their stick-legs among herons and shrub brush. Past the salt marsh is a tiny strip of sand cut from the greater vastness of the Gulf Region desert. Here, waves of reddish-hued wind sculptures build into a still life, a portrait of rippling steps made from the dry and arid. An occasional camel lumbers into view, curiously out of place in this very small patch of wilderness; it and the great, lonely sands of the region are cleaved in two by the national highway.

To the rear of my home is the still, misty gulf and, just visible beyond it and to the right, is the open sea. On winter weekends, Doodles and I walk the sea on the spit of land between it and the edge of the salt marsh, paying our respects to the blinking reds of ships on the horizon, the tangle of coast-bound stingrays, the screech of native birds, and an occasional burkini-ed bather. But these walks occur on weekends, never in the early hours of working mornings.

"Let's go, buddy." I voice yet another of our morning rituals.

We take off down the street towards the community pool that sits within the lush greens of trees and bushes and tall, ornamental brown grasses with spikes of fluffy cotton; the pinks and mauves and yellows of the many planted flowers fill the spaces in between. So unnatural for the desert, such vegetation is the result of a UAE obsession with abundance, one that comes with the commitment of the country's most precious commodity—water. Throughout the length and depth of the desert greenery, workers install flexible, tubular water systems in and throughout the gardens, intestine-like in their right angle bendings back and forth. Workers converge on gardens to pick and prune, mow and nourish the colorful gifts, re-sculpting the desert from its more natural red-tan stereopticon image.

"Come on, Doodles; this way," I urge as he obstinately heads down the center of the street.

Only ten pounds, Doodles can put up a fierce battle when he sets his mind to something. And on this dark morning, he refuses to walk anywhere but in the middle of the street. There are no cars. There are no people. There is no reason *not* to walk down the middle of the street. In fact, most of the little villas are still dark, their occupants finishing their dreams. It is just me and Doodles. But I tug at his leash to move him towards the sidewalk where trees and grasses provide a better solution to his daily needs. He refuses, obstinate and deter-mined. After only a little, weakly fought fight, I relent. It is just too early for a battle. So we walk in the middle of the street.

There is stillness and silence in these morning walks. Even the birds' whistle-cries as they fly and the crabs' click click click on the stones by the salt marsh seem both more pronounced and more subdued, hidden in the blackness right before the dawn. The noise of daily life is all but absent. So it is a powerful few moments when *Adhan*—the call to prayer—emerges with its haunting, melodic chant. It comes out of nowhere, all at once, all around the city at the same time, from every minaret on every mosque in the skyline. You might expect Adhan to *break* the silence, but that would be wrong. It would be too simplistic a description. Instead, Adhan seems to enhance the silence. It heightens it. It fills the air with reverence, adding a sense of beginning to an almost-ended evening. A long, awesome *Allah* in all its rhythmic beauty begins each call, marking this end of darkness.

I close my eyes and breathe deep God's presence in the form of the invocation, even as Doodles continues to clip clop clip clop down the middle of the street.

"Doodles," I whisper, "what's up with you today?" I laugh at the sassy swing of his behind. "Who are you trying to impress?"

I am quite sure I don't speak out loud for the benefit of Doodles. Yet I do speak regularly; maybe it's just another of our routines. Or maybe I speak out to hear my own voice, mingling it with the emerging morning's song, a symphony of sorts in the sweetness of the almost-morning air. The loud silence of the approaching day beats out the symphony's percussion line. Adhan holds the melody. My voice adds yet another layer, a layer of ordinary sound in between the profound of the other two. My voice marks my presence within the greater world; it breaks through the lonely distance and connects me to my friends and family in other places. It calls out to my father somewhere far away, carried to him on the melody of the spiritual.

"Come on, Doodles. Come to the sidewalk."

I pull at his leash, and he glances back at me. He keeps on walking. I laugh at his doggie insolence.

October 18th, I think, beginning to lose the serenity of the pre-dawn hours, beginning to catalogue and schedule the rest of my day. *October 18th*, I think again and stop mid-step to recognize its importance to my life. Doodles notices and stops mid-street. He waits for me to unravel my thoughts.

"Happy birthday, Daddy," I whisper.

This is the third time I have celebrated my father's birthday since moving to the UAE. The first time I called home and heard his voice, laughed at his irreverent jokes, answered his questions about when I was coming home. The second time, a few months after his death, I sat at work and cried out my loneliness to no one but me. There was no reassuring voice on the other end of a phone call. No jokes. No father. Just a stinging, searing pain.

"I miss you, Daddy," I call into the night, my statement punctuated by the end of Adhan. "I wish you could hear me."

I make a move to push Doodles forward; I have lost the desire to walk. But he is immobile and inflexible, refusing to budge. "Stubborn," I hiss at him in play. I tug again at his leash. Again, he doesn't move.

My father's birthday weighs heavily on my mind, and this mental weight manifests itself in a physical way, making my limbs and heart heavy and unyielding. *Daddy*, I hear over and over again in my mind. Ache radiates outward from the word through my body and into my limbs.

"Come on, Doodles; I have work," I whine. The words carry the feelings of my father's absence.

Now Doodles sits. Right in the middle of the street, the dog's stubbornness and my sadness express themselves at a crossroads.

I stoop, trying to establish my own will in the matter, and I notice something on the ground glittering, shimmering, shifting my attention away from my dog. Abraham Lincoln's coppery face looks up at me; a penny, it twinkles in the absolute darkness of the early morning. The year of my father's death, 2015, is emblazoned on the bottom of it. For a few moments, I try to account for such a find, and the urgency to move collapses into bewilderment. Doodles, however, makes the decision that it's time to go. To the sidewalk. Off the street. To trees and grass and flowers.

I bring the penny close, trying to take in details. Doodles and I walk on through the garden, through the predawn darkness. *It defies logic*, I think to myself, turning the penny over and over again in my hand. I am the only American in this development. There are Jordanians and Palestinians like my husband, Egyptians, Emiratis, and Lebanese. There are British and Irish and the occasional Canadian. There are Indians and Pakistanis and a mishmash of others from so many other places. But there is only one American. Me. I have found a penny in the middle of a little development that sits on the southern side of Ras al Khaimah, a town that sits in the Northern part of the

United Arab Emirates which, itself, stands in the gulf region of the Middle East, far, far away from the United States. Nine time zones away actually. And far away from any place that accepts payment in American currency. *Daddy*, I think again, this time more in wonderment than in loneliness.

Doodles and I turn back towards home. His need to be sassy and stubborn is gone, and he is instead compliant, happy, satisfied with his role in our walk. Off in the far distance, the sun is beginning to show itself, darkness doggedly giving away to an inky bluish gray on the horizon. The first rays of daylight cast themselves out over the desert dunes that sit behind the salt marsh on the opposite side of the street from my home. Lights are beginning to blink on in the villas as we make our way, and enough time has elapsed since Adhan that prayer has begun, filling the air from the surrounding mosques with the name of God. *Allah*, I hear again and again. I walk home satisfied, aware of the gift that I have been given, the gift that moved me from darkness to light, from broken to whole, from far away to home again.

I have heard you, Dad. Happy birthday.

12

WITH FIONA NEAR REYKJAVIK

BY MEGAN E. FREEMAN

We whisper on the precipice
of the ancient parliaments
where thirty-six chieftains
gathered their clans
at midnight sun for
eight hundred sixty nine years.

Volcanoes rise around us
each named and sexed
and sleeping, though one
has six years overslept and
leaves the people watchful.

We squint at the gray sky
imagine eighteenth century
Icelandic ash blanketing France
in famine and revolution.

We place our toes at the edge

of minerals decorating the
circumference of geysers
like trim on a dinner plate.
Centuries of hot enthusiasm
belch and blow with
predictable ferocity.

Land of eruptions
and eruptive potential.
Tectonic dissection
shifting and agitating
measureable each year

like the temblors
of my human heart
and the seismic magnitude
of my daughter's
imminent departure.

She with the blue eyes and
black fur around her face
who laughs now into the glacial mist
but will soon leave me

will leave me as surely as
this glacier will continue to melt

as surely as
this ancient waterfall will cease
to thunder.

13

IT'S NOT THE RAIN I MISS

BY KARI REDMOND

I have a new relationship with rain.
Somewhere between Thailand and Laos,
we came to an understanding.
I told the rain she didn't bother me anymore
and she carried on . . like always.

I will say things are different now
and mean it,
but you won't understand.
I changed. You stayed.
There's that.

I remember you bought that guy's book
Ray, the bartender.
I didn't get it then.
I do now.

We are all aspiring.

I'll still wonder if you read it.
I will always wonder.

It will be different here—
the rain.
Our relationship (might be) strained
from the distance between us.

Her occasional appearance
too brief to matter anymore.

14

THE LAST DANCE

BY JENNIFER ROBINSON

"The National Weather Service in Denver has issued a Tornado Warning for South Central Weld County and Northwestern Morgan County until 6:35 p.m. mountain daylight time. At 5:15 p.m. mountain daylight time National Weather Service Doppler radar indicated a severe thunderstorm capable of producing a tornado—"

In front of me, visible through my grimy windshield, is a gigantic supercell thunderstorm making its way across the northeastern plains of Colorado. It's one of the most well-organized storms I have ever seen, according to both the radar looping on the screen of my phone and my personal experience. I've seen dozens of storms, and only a handful similar to this one. The main storm tower is well-defined against the cerulean sky. It's charging eastward as it spits lightning and drags wispy shadows of rain behind; the train of a bridal gown along the open range. It drifts peacefully through its journey, a mallard skirting across the surface of a lake.

I seem to only come out this time of year, when the low-hanging clouds, green and heavily pregnant with hail, hold me down to Earth like nothing else can. It feels as if clear blue skies will carry me away into nothingness; a balloon released by a child.

It hasn't always been this way.

"See, Chickadee? There's nothing to fear if you know what to watch for. When I'm not around to protect you, your mind will keep you safe."

I nod to the voice inside my head. It's an afternoon in early June and the light surrounding me is dim, as if the sun is already disappearing behind the western Colorado foothills for the evening.

I shift my truck into gear and make my approach. Dirt and gravel kick up a plume of dust in my wake. The mesocyclone is twisting in the air, slowly, as the strong updraft twists hot air from the earth and cold air from the sky together. Below rests the dark wall cloud.

"It's not too scary back here, is it, Chickadee?" Dad smiled at me that first time and reached over to ruffle my hair, pulling some of the finer strands free of my scrunchie.

No, it hadn't been intimidating when I saw it with my own eyes. In person, the beast that made all the town's sirens scream in terror was much different.

Back before I knew better, Dad would carry me down to the basement as I wailed in fear. The family cat followed us with her tail aloft in curiosity at this heightened level of excitement.

"Chickadee, look, Kitty isn't scared," he said as he flicked on the single light bulb before climbing back up the warping pine steps to shut the crawl space door behind us. I bawled while I watched the cat streak off into the darkness under the foundation of the house, happily looking for spiders in this hunting ground that was usually forbidden to her. I could hear the wind whistling in the foundation vents and the house creaking from the force of it all. Thunder shouted outside with no consideration for my childish nerves.

He lifted the hand crank radio. Big, work-worn hands spun the handle on the back, and soon grainy music attempted to drown out the sound of the ferocious storm bearing down around us. I was crying so hard I remember the pain in my stomach and how I gasped for air as my lungs refused to fill.

"Why are you crying?" My father chided gently, pulling me into his lap after settling to sit on the dusty floor. "We're safe down here, nothing is going to get us. We're all okay. Me, you ,and Kitty."

But what about the world above? What was happening up there away from my range of sight? I had only seen tornadoes of terrifying magnitude on television. Gigantic, unbelievable killers that destroyed everything in their unpredictable paths. They stole lives. They ruined the livelihoods of farmers like my dad and drove them into poverty and despair.

I attempted to voice my fear of not being able to see the monster outside ravishing our belongings, but the lightbulb above our heads began to flicker.

It was quiet for a heartbeat before the sound as fervent as a barreling freight train surrounded us. Our house groaned on its foundation, and a deafening boom sounded from the surface above. I caught a glimpse of Kitty bolting for cover under the tower of boxes stuffed with out-of-season decorations before Dad forced my head against his chest to protect me. I could smell dust falling from the rafters above. I screamed even though my heart was in my throat, nearly choking me.

I was certain I would never see the light of day again, that I would die there, at eight years old. The storm would take away all my dolls and stuffed animals and throw them into the fields. They would find my body with my ballet shoes still tied to my feet, fresh from dance practice. I can still remember which leotard I wore, and how my stomach tied in knots seeing the black clouds on the western horizon after Dad picked me up and took me home. I would never dance again, see Kitty again, or go to school again . .

And then, nothing.

The silence was intense, almost more terrifying than the noise that had just pelted the world above me. I couldn't see what happened, and I could barely breathe. Eventually Dad moved and I dared to open my eyes after pulling my head away from the protective warmth of his chest that smelled like alfalfa, summer, and a hard day's work. Everything looked the same in the crawlspace and Kitty was starting to get the courage to venture out from under the boxes.

My father told me to stay put while he went above to survey the aftermath. I gathered Kitty into my arms and kissed her warm, soft, dandelion-fur head for a little comfort. Soon, my father returned for us. He said it was safe; he was even smiling somehow after seeing what I had not.

The house looked the same as when we had left it for the underground a handful of minutes before. He then beckoned me outside. Pellets of hail blanketed the ground as if we had just awoken to a February snowstorm in June. Younger trees had been uprooted where they stood. However, the old apricot stayed untouched. She had only shed a few peridot leaves, and bruised fruit was scattered at her roots.

But would she always survive like that?

Instead of being thankful for what remained, I was filled with dread. There would be a next time—there was always a next time—and would our home and tree be okay then? And the next? What about the time after that?

Oh, what a fool I was . . .

And what a fool I still am.

I reach to crank my wipers on as dime-size hail begins to pound at my windshield. I reach over to hold the small cardboard box next to me securely in place. This storm is similar to the first one that I had experienced with Dad so long ago.

After that first storm, I had confided in him that I was scared of hiding. Scared of the unknown, of what made Kitty dash for cover and what had pulled our previously sturdy trees and fences out of the ground. My imagination ran wild with images of the tornado that had struck our home. What insane thing had the cataclysmic power to choose some things to destroy and spare others?

So the next time the looping doppler radar on The Weather Channel went red just northwest of us, Dad made sure Kitty had a safe place to hide and we loaded ourselves into the old Ford.

It was afternoon, and we drove into the sun, west into clouds that were black as night and eventually devoured the blinding daylight. Lightning shot around the storm. The thick white updraft was standing tall and strong suspended in the atmosphere.

A steady stream of trucks and cars passed us, heading east with headlights on and soaked in rain. We were the only ones heading away from civilization, driving toward the beast roaming the empty, untouched plains.

My heart pounded, but a small part of me was ready to confront my fears face-to-face. It looked as if we were driving into death itself with how dark the supercell ahead was, how violently thunder roared, warning us to turn back, how lightning shot out in every direction, unpredictable but beautiful in its fury.

Dad slowed and turned down an unpaved road to progress even closer to the storm. Since the sun had been completely swallowed by the overpowering clouds, the true power of the storm was revealed. In the distance, I could no longer see the horizon since wispy, dark tendrils of rain blurred it. Above, the clouds glowed a ghostly green.

Before I could process the power and beauty surrounding me, Dad stopped the truck, pebbles kicking up from beneath the tires at the sudden halting. My safety belt held me fast against the seat.

"Chickadee, there it is!" he gasped. I don't know why he whispered as he did at first, like a wild animal had just crept out of its cave, but then I saw it. Something stirred inside my soul like I had never felt before.

Like a ballerina's leg, pure and graceful, she descended to the world below and her pointed toe landed. She danced.

The cyclone kept her head above the clouds while her foot glided across the plains. She tugged at sand, cactuses, and grass as she pirouetted along the earth. Beneath the anvil of clouds, she turned grey with the debris she collected and playfully tossed. There were no trees, no barns or silos, no homes out here on the open range for her to take. She danced freely and recklessly, like no human ballerina I had ever seen. She moved with a grace and abandon that those not made of clouds and wind could only dream of. Lightning flashed around her, accentuating her curves as she bent and twisted over the fields.

She became more slender, a silver ribbon, and transparent as she dissipated into the breeze. As quickly as she came, she was gone.

Though she had gone so soon, she left with me a lifelong impression of how gorgeous tornadoes could be. Here, free and wild, away from where they could not cause harm or devastation is where I belonged with Dad.

The twisters never touched our home again. I believed that when we drove toward their thunderstorm homes and gave them an audience, we were unstoppable. I felt in my heart that we would watch them dance in the great plains of northeastern Colorado forever. I truly thought my life would always be the same and perfect like that.

We watched them for years. We watched them every summer while singing to the radio. We watched them as Dad's singing dissolved into coughing, and then it was the three of us: me, Dad, and the cough. We watched them as the cough got worse. We watched them after Dad's morning appointments, as we swapped roles and I started to drive the truck instead and he manned the radio and radar from the passenger's side. We watched a dancer on the late September day that he told me he no longer wanted to go to the doctor. I watched her through the tears that fell from my eyes like rain. Somehow, I knew that would be the last dance for us.

The dancers left, and the snow came with blizzards to replace them. And then my father took his leave too. His cough took him where I couldn't follow, and with him my courage left too.

I lost everything when I lost Dad. I lost my courage to go on with human normalcy. I lost my job, I lost the ability to leave the security of my father's house, and thus I lost the will to live. I spent that winter in front of the fireplace thinking of everything that was ever taken from me. My mother, my father, precious Kitty . . I was utterly alone.

The cardboard box I had brought him home in stayed where I had placed it immediately after the memorial service; on the dining room table we never used except when we had rare guests over for holidays. If I ignored it, maybe he would walk inside the back door and remove his work boots with two thunks again. Kitty would run to him, cooing to be scooped into his arms, and petted. And he would. He would toss the cat into his arms, hold her close and pet her. In an instant he would come in from the fields and bring all the love and light inside the lonely old house with him. I always knew it was fine that my mother had left, because I had him. I didn't need a mother who didn't love me because my father loved me enough for two parents, maybe even more.

I jump in my seat as a hailstone the size of a chicken egg collides with the windshield and a spiderweb of cracks shoot across my field of view. My hand clutches the box in the seat next to me tighter as I remember that this is the closest I have ever dared to venture into a storm. Dad always kept me far away where we would be secure enough to watch those gargantuan, powerful tornadoes waltz from a safe distance.

Now there is nothing he can do to keep me away. His arms and words aren't here to hold me safe and tight. They will never be here again.

The hail ceases with no warning, and the world turns deadly quiet except for the sound of the radio reciting its active tornado warning again and the screech of my tires sliding across sand and dry brush when I slam on the brakes and grind to a hard stop.

No hawks cry out and no wind rustles to send tumbleweeds skipping across the plains. I'm absolutely alone, and the radio drones on without Dad here to hum along to a country western song.

For the first time he's not beside me. He's not here to gasp as a pointed foot reaches down out of the clouds, descending, desiring to touch the ground. Under my breath I whisper, but I hear his voice in my soul.

"There she is, Chickadee."

She makes landfall, invisible save for the twisting debris she kicks up as she rotates. It's my turn to act as well, and I punch the gas to the floor. The tires on the old truck spin, kicking up brush and weeds, and I race toward her the moment I regain traction.

As she accumulates earthly debris, she reveals her true self. She's a slender rope cyclone, bowing beautifully and elaborately between the sky and the surface as she was born to do. Playfully, she collides with electrical lines to sway through bursts of electricity at her foot and lightning above her head.

She's the most beautiful thing I have ever seen, and I want her to be the last thing I ever witness. I want her to take me to my father. I clutch the box of his remains as I gain speed. The gauge on the dashboard climbs: sixty, seventy-five, ninety. Hailstones pop against the surface of the windshield. I see her as I have never seen a tornado before. She's spectacular, wrapped in eerie, bottle-green light from the hail-stuffed cumulonimbus clouds in the near distance. I'm so close I can see fragments of windmill and fence that she has pulled up in her journey across the great eastern plains. The wind is shaking the truck; she is starting to pull me off track with her unbridled power.

I want to be with her up close, something that I cannot accomplish in the shelter of the truck. Something tugs at my soul, wanting to say goodbye to the old Ford where Dad and I shared so many adventures, listened to the same John Denver cassette tapes over and over, but I don't want her to leave for the beyond without me. I don't want to say goodbye to Dad anymore. All I want to do now is to say hello.

I grasp the cardboard box and force the door open with all my weight against the strength of the wind. It feels as if the tornado is trying to keep me safe inside from her pressure and power, as if she knows that she is so much more than me. She is a goddess, capable of more than I could ever dream. I'm just a fragile human with a broken heart and an aching soul.

My hair whips around me, swirling and twisting, the same color and texture as my father's. He would be so upset at me now, running out into a dangerous situation because of emotions I refuse to control, not letting the knowledge of these storms that we learned together keep me from harm. Yet, I know nothing will ever hurt more than his death did, not even my own.

I don't know if I believe in heaven, but if there's even a small chance that I'll be able to be with him again, I'll take it. Sand begins to sting my face, and I am forced to close my eyes. She's right next to me and I can no longer see the force of her. I can only feel her wrath.

I feel my feet slip out from underneath me and only when I fall to the ground do I dare take a look. I will soon leave my body behind; this will be the last time I see with my eyes. I was always told they are the color of my mother's, but I always pretend for myself that they came from my dad too. He's the only one who mattered, who still matters.

I crane my neck upward and see the vortex above me. I am reminded of baths as a tiny girl, watching my toys swirl as the water disappeared down the drain and Dad scooped me up in a soft towel fresh from the dryer. I am filled with comfort and calm just like in those memories. I'm unafraid, but I no longer feel invincible.

In my arms the top of the box is tugged free from where it had been since my father's remains were placed there. The white powder I have refused to accept begins to lift out, and the twister takes them up into herself.

"Promise me something, Chickadee," I hear him inside my soul. In my mind's eye, I see him.

It was snowing that night. I could see the dusty flakes whip outside the hospital window, battered by bitter wind. The sky was orange.

The sterile hall outside the door was draped with garlands for Christmas.

"Yeah?" I moved closer to his bedside and took his hand. He was fragile, but I could still feel the rough calluses from all the years of hard work to give me the best possible life he could.

"That you'll take care of yourself like you've always taken care of me." His voice was rough, and it roused tears from my eyes. It was then I was certain I was going to lose him.

"You're crazy . . you're the one who's always taken care of me." I forced a chuckle despite the shattering of my heart. I had felt no greater pain up to that point in my life. I knew that would be the last time I would ever hear his voice or feel the slight warmth of his hand inside mine.

He simply shook his head and laid back against the pillows, falling back into sleep. That very night, while I slept curled in the chair by his bedside dreaming of wild antelope and ballerinas made of clouds, I lost him.

What would he feel knowing that I am unable to go on living because he is gone? Everything he worked for, everything he sacrificed for me during his life, gone just because I miss him so much. That isn't . . that's not what he would want. I haven't been respecting or paying mind to his last wish. He had never asked me for anything until that night and after everything he did for me . . I need to do this for him.

I need to go on living.

My heart stops in my chest as the empty container is tugged out of my hands and I feel my legs rise into the air, gravity losing its battle to wind. I'm losing control, the ground is leaving. The gale is dragging me up by my boots and, desperately, my hands search for anything to grab onto.

"No, please!" I hear myself scream over the deafening storm. My fingers find a tuft of dry brush and I hold it fast with all my strength.

My life, the life my father gave me and wants me to continue living, depends on it. "Please! Help!" I wail as my voice tears painfully at my throat.

"DAD!"

I cry for him, like when I fell off my bike on the driveway and skinned my elbow. When I broke my leg falling out of the apricot tree. The day Kitty and her aged body couldn't outrun a coyote any longer . .

The breath is knocked out of me as I fall back to the ground, my ribs and stomach hitting the dirt hard. I don't dare open my eyes, not until I feel hard, cold drops of rain hit my back and soak into my shirt.

My hands are shaking where they gripped the bramble bush and bright vermillion streams run between my fingers where I held on for my life. Rain trickles down my skin, diluting the blood where it soaks into the parched soil.

I'm alive.

She's spared me. As all those times her dancers performed in the plains for us, as the one that hit our home when I was a girl, my life has been in her hands. Once again she's given it back to me. I've been reckless, passionate, and foolish, and she's entrusted to me a second future. I know that with her kind, there is not often a third.

With this chance, I won't let Dad down.

15

WILLOW DANCING

BY SALLY JO

Silken moonlight on her face
Leaves a mark that can't be traced
Will-o-the-wisps caress her skin
Eager for the dance to begin
Slowly movement comes upon her
Bends her farther, farther, farther
Faster now she twists and flows
Spurred by wind that strongly blows
Her fingers rustle, her body creaks
Adrift in havoc the storm will wreak
Now gently descending comes down from her high
Settles into her roots as the storm passes by
Her hair slightly ruffled, her skin wet with rain
She'll wait to dance with the storm once again

16

THE LAST WHEAT FIELD

BY MARILYN K. MOODY

On my birthday, the 5th of July,
the wheat was always ripe and ready.

It was a different world then, a wilder world,
where the farmers still left the edges of the fields

in brush and weeds, and trees might still mark
the middle of fields, where ghostly houses flickered.

Now those fields are planted to the very edge,
every inch of prairie is worked and groomed.

My father was a hard-looking man, with leather skin,
big calloused hands, grey eyes, and oil-slicked hair.

My mother and I drove up with hot coffee in an
old glass jar, two meat sandwiches, and a bag of chips.

He left the red harvester running, while he
tore at the sandwiches and gulped the coffee down.

I was playing in the ditch by the side of the road,
humming happy birthday to myself and dreaming of cake.

I had only seen my father cry once before, but now
he cried loudly and angrily as my mother just stared.

He cursed the damn mother quails, who wouldn't leave
their goddamn nests as the wheels and knives of his combine

slaughtered the mothers and the baby quails alike, leaving
blood and guts and skin and feathers among the grains of wheat.

In a day's time, in only one field, he had killed dozens of them.
The next year my father planted tall hard stalks of inhospitable corn.

17

QUIET REFUSAL

BY SHELLEY WIDHALM

I absolutely refuse to move into that assisted living place. I've been around too long to have people tell me what to do with my life, especially my own children. I raised them to have manners, and here I am lying in this nursing home with my muscles not obeying my mind, my mouth swallowing my words, and my brain not letting them come together into sentences. I keep telling the nurses where I want to go— just the one word I can get out—pronouncing the "h" with a long, stuttering sound, so my house becomes h-ho-ome.

I've let the good Lord know I am ready anytime. I am ninety-three years old, for crying out loud. Don't tell me I have anything worth sticking around for when I'm stuck in this bed and my future outlook is an assisted living place. No one's listening. Not the nurses. Not the doctors. Not my children, who leave me out of their grown-up decisions as if I were the child.

The bed is narrow. It makes me feel like I'm in a crib. The sheets smell too much like bleach and not enough like a sweet spring breeze. I want my garden-level apartment, where I can look at heart-shaped pillows with embroidered patterns I'd stitched, ceramic wildlife I'd painted, and a quilted bedspread I'd made displayed over the couch's back end. I'd had hobbies to keep my hands busy, that let me make pretty things for my house I'd made into h-ho-ome. I imagine losing all of that for plain white walls in my square, beeping room.

A nurse swishes in to check my heartbeat. She takes my pulse.

"How are you doing today?" she asks, patting my shoulder.

Bright as sunshine. "Oh, ok-kay," I stutter.

"It'll get better." Another pat.

Right. As if.

She leaves me with the unstated promise she, or another nurse, will be back in an hour. It's too quiet, and my mind returns to the apartment I'd moved to after I left Richard, the children's father. An alcoholic who went on and off unemployment between his graveyard shifts as a janitor. He liked earning an extra dollar working nights, at least when he cared about the fact he had a wife and two children. He didn't care enough to stop our decline from a four-bedroom house to a three-bedroom apartment to a very crowded, dilapidated apartment with just one room. He wanted to engage in drinking binges lasting days, not listening to what we had to say, returning like a tornado blowing dishes off the countertops.

By the time Jack was fourteen and Lily twelve, I'd had enough and dragged them with me to yet another apartment. They screamed for their daddy when we left on a rainy night to get away from unpaid bills and, more importantly, from him. I'd traded my parents' house for Richard's college apartment as a pregnant sixteen-year-old and moved and moved until my head spun. My, the mistakes I made! But I've lived a long, a very long, life, and I know better now, like knowing I don't want someone taking care of me.

I try to hit my hand on the mattress for emphasis, as if someone was there listening, but my hand doesn't move. I used to want to be leisurely without having to worry about work and raising children. I wanted to read books all day and drink tea, and now I have all the time in the world. Ironic how I can't lift a book, or my thoughts.

As I've said, I'm ready to join the Lord. Oh, I am so ready. The reason is I've seen it, done it, read it, lived it. And I can't see, do, read, and live in this bed when my sentences—my very soul sometimes—cannot come out in self-expression. I do not have body language or the right side of my face to show my son and daughter how I can't just lie here and have my only activity be a search of my memory for comfort.

Sighing, I look out the window to see clouds shift in and out of the sunlight like white sheets bobbing on a clothesline. I see the brick building of the medical center next door and tree branches bounce shadows at high noon whenever it gets a little breezy.

I think of lifting my arms and spinning with the shadows. The physical therapist tells me when I can sit up in my wheelchair and regain partial movement of my limbs, I'll be able to sit underneath the oak tree making those shadows, as if they could become part of my own dance, our limbs in musical motion. Yes, a life, a full one and a long one. And, for the most part, a healthy one, until I had a stroke and broke my hip (don't we older ladies always do that?) and had another stroke to top it off.

I remember a wooden music box my mother gave me that came from her mother. It had a waterwheel in front of a one-story house, with the roof holding in my treasures. There was a little girl's ring with a bird's nest that came from a gumball machine, and a charm bracelet with a cat, a ballerina, and my initials—C.W. for Christina Walker, the ones I had before I got married and snagged back again. We had a cat, and I took ballet lessons until, well, the year I got pregnant. Before the baby made my belly into a balloon, I was graceful and thin and wore my hair, long and red, up in a bun. I'd given up that and my dreams, my children assuming I'd chosen to be a mother. Isn't that what women are supposed to want, especially back in my day?

I'm graceful now, at least in my mind, though my body is like a dreaming nap-taker halfway between here and there, the point where I could jump up if the telephone rings or slip into temporary blankness. I am in this place, my life on hold as my body takes me backward. I am spoon-fed, my bedding gets changed, as do I, and I am bathed, everyone's child now.

I cry after the light in my room shuts off, when it is just me and my narrow bed and its lousy, plastic-covered mattress. When I quit dancing, I also quit high school, returning to school in my mid-twenties to take night classes when I realized I'd need to work. After I left Richard, I clerked at a convenience store and kept taking classes. I wanted to finish my college degree. I had decided on nursing, but I needed to raise my children and work, and just didn't have time. I'd given up being a nurse to nurse my own family, only to get nursed later in life.

The decades disappeared, my son and daughter both got their degrees, and now they have families. They want to send me off to that place and not have to worry about me. They don't want to convert a part of their house into an in-law suite or even put me in the guest room. Or let me go back home.

I'd prefer to go home, because I don't want to be their burden.

They told me a couple of weeks ago it was time and that they were sorting through my things: dividing them into what I will need, what they want, and what can be salvaged for donations.

Did they ask me if I wanted to do the sorting or how or when? They just told me, like they were the parents and I was the child, when all I could do was say "n-n-o-o-o," that one word over and over. You don't know how many times I've used that word with them when they were children, and their reaction back then was just the same. *Why should we listen to you? You're not the boss of us.* Now, they are my bosses, the CEOs of C.W.

This has become my second reason for wanting to join the good Lord. My children refuse to take me seriously. I will be . . Oh, I can't even go there in my mind. I'll start crying, and then the nurses will come. They'll ask, "What's the matter, Mrs. Walker?" as if I'm still married to that rotten—I don't want to cuss, even if that man deserves every filthy word in and out of the dictionary.

Technically I was a Mrs. until Richard died of liver failure more than a decade ago, no surprise there. We didn't divorce, because I didn't have the money and didn't see the need to remarry. Plus, back then, times were different.

Oh no, I hear them coming down the hall. I know their footsteps. Lily's are like a short-legged girl in tap shoes trying to keep up with her mother, though she is quite tall, about five feet, eight inches. Jack's are heavy and slow, and I don't know how they keep pace with each other with the difference in their gaits.

I close my eyes, pretend I'm asleep.

"Mother, we let go of the apartment. And we have your stuff in storage, all ready for you when you move into the assisted living home." This Lily says after she greets me and gives me a kiss on the forehead. My eyes snap open at her touch, my concentration on pretending to sleep interrupted.

I yell "no," my word coming out in a whisper.

"We've been through this, Mother," Lily continues, acting as the sibling spokesperson.

"No-o," I say. My heart hurts. Is it a heart attack? Do I have a weak heart that's gone undiagnosed?

"Yes, we have," she says, drawing out each word as if I were five.

I shake my head, feel a little movement. Do they see? Do they hear my heart?

"You can't live by yourself. That's what your doctor has been saying. And we agree." Lily leans over the side of the bed to touch my hand. I try to pull it away. It moves a quarter inch. She doesn't notice.

"We want someone to be there for you, just in case. And we can't be. We have responsibilities with our children and grandchildren," she says.

"Mother," Jack says, taking my other hand in his. "We will visit. Often."

What does that mean? Often?

Jack lives across the country and Lily in another town sixty miles north of Denver. Denver is where I live, where I have always lived, apparently where I'm going to die because they will not let me have a say about my life. My life!

I close my eyes, pretend to fall asleep as if I were a child able to hide from the world with a drop of the eyelids. It works, and they, my children, get up after a few minutes and say hushed goodbyes. I open my eyes when I hear the door shut and hit the call button. My heart feels okay, the tissue part, not the insides where emotions and anger and the hurt get stored.

"Yes, Mrs. Walker?" a nurse says.

"Where go?"

She crinkles her brow.

I get out the word children. She looks over her shoulder. "They didn't tell me anything," she says.

"Come back," I say.

"You want me to call them?"

"I want, one go." I am trying to say I want to be the one to go, not them. She doesn't understand.

"Do your exercises and we will get you there," she says with a smile.

I look out at the branches against brick. I'm stuck here, and then I'll be stuck in that place.

"Mom." I hear Jack's voice a couple of weeks later on a day I can see the sky is a bright cerulean blue.

"Mmm," I mumble.

"I've been thinking. I haven't even told Lily yet, but you could stay with Nancy and me," he says, referring to his wife. "That is, when you are ready to leave here."

"Wha-at?" I stumble over my one word.

"Is that okay?"

"Tell Nancy?"

"Yes. We've talked. We realized we can't afford to send you to the assisted living home. And we want you with us, where we know you'll be happy."

My lovely boy, the one who hugged me after I left their father while Lily turned away, anger puffing up her eyes. She was Daddy's girl and blamed me for leaving him. She didn't understand about the drinking, didn't want to.

"No, no," I say.

It's a bargain I couldn't make. Same loss of freedom. Son in control. I turn to my window and let the tears come. My heart beats fine; physically it is fine.

"Mother, what's wrong?"

I try to wave my hand, make my son understand.

"There's the money. We, Lily and I . . . " He lets his sentences disappear into my understanding. Yes, after the money from my accounts run out, they'll have to pay my expenses. I realize this, of course.

"Mother, you can't be on your own, you know that."

I thought of my little boy taking out his toy tool set after we left his father, saying he could fix things. I thought at the time he couldn't fix my heart, and here he is lifting his hands toward me, a small hammering motion in his right fist when he sees I don't respond.

I take a breath and another, slow and raspy. "Okay," I say because what other choice do I have?

And that is that. Jack talks to Lily, and she says she will help out with financing a caretaker to come in when he and Nancy are away.

My refusal, I think as I look at the branch shadows, got me what I wanted, but not really, not at all. I am my son's mother after all, and he is telling me what to do, making decisions for me. I guess that's what happens when you have a stroke—not a stroke of good luck, mind you. A stroke cutting a line into the water of your routine. And my hand goes up to try the next stroke, as if I am swimming, when really, I feel like I am drowning.

"Beautiful day, isn't it?" a nurse says into my thoughts. I look at her. Her brows are wrinkled. "My son used to do that with his arms when he was trying to grasp things," she says.

Yes, I know. Babies do not have control of their limbs, are amazed when they see them in front of their faces, and when they are in the womb, look like they are still swimming.

I smile at her.

"Yes, it," I say, stumbling over the last word, sighing it out, "is-s."

I might as well try to be happy. I might as well do that. It might not be so bad living in L.A. where all the movie stars are and where the sun really shines, and year-round, too. Yes, I'll try this happy thing, I think, wondering if my face still shows my smile. I look out the window and blink up at the sky. Clear, blue, bright. A lovely day for change.

18

HENRIETTA'S REQUIEM

BY JOHN BLAIR

Because her son, Charlie, phones me from a new nursing home
and hesitates, *can you hear?*

Because Henrietta is moaning, *I want out of this place*
and more than words convey anguish

Because she lives in Laramie, I wonder if it's a zephyr
but hear a human quality to hopelessness

Because ground blizzards obscure roads
and uninhabited treeless prairies always hasten her despair

Because I can't touch her hand or lay a cool cloth on her forehead
and yet, she's not forsaken, not abandoned, not really, not reality

Because a week before we talked of her new bedroom
blue flowered wallpaper, white chair rail

Because with the bed in plain sight, she pointed to a door
and it goes to a lavatory and commode

Because she said, *that's where we sleep*
and the anachronous we, I let pass

Because *Ralph works a lot of overtime*
but he's been dead for thirty years

Because at least she's warm in a deserted world
and it matters so little the order of their going

19

STILLE NACHT, HEILIGE NACHT

BY LUANN ATKIN KOESTER

Joe stands tall and straight in front of slumping teens
despite his eighty years—
and more.

I understand you've been learning about World War Two.

Slouching teens in too small desks nod.
A deep breath and he begins.

I was only a little older than . .
That's when I felt the tip of a German bayonet poke my scalp
behind my left ear under my helmet.

And the less-slumped teens stop breathing.

Steh auf, schnell.
And we marched, and I was cold.

And the teens are breathing again, sitting straight in their too small
desks.

And we marched, and I was hungry.
He pauses, takes a sip of water, and asks the waiting teens to be
patient.
Some of this is hard for me to talk about.

On Christmas Eve they gave us soup, hot water with a little potato.
It was a holiday feast. Outside, on an asphalt slab,
in our European theater under a German sky,
we drank our soup out of our combat helmets.

His voice snags
and the teens try to swallow the lump for him.

Someone started to sing *Silent Night*. For a bunch of tired, hungry
soldiers, we sounded good.

He blinks away a mist.

Stille Nacht, heilige Nacht
Alles schläft; einsam wacht
Nur das traute hochheilige Paar . .

And we all sang together. There was harmony in the German
Theater.

There's no swallowing the lump in their throats.

Until a British bomber flew over.
Asphalt chunks showered down.
A hundred and sixty men died.

Steh auf, schnell

And we marched, and I was hungry.

*Steh auf, schnell—get up, quickly
*Stille Nacht, heilige Nacht—Silent night, holy night

20

RINSE, REINCARNATE, REPEAT

BY SARAH REICHERT

"Oh, my God." Gabriel stared, horrified, at the scene.

"You don't have to call, I'm standing right here," She said, exasperated. "I saw it too." God crossed Her arms in front of Her chest and stared at the mirror where the two young corpses lay in a pile of sprawled hopelessness. The girl's strawberry birthmark lay exposed on her neck like a gem. The boy's gray eyes, forever gazing skyward.

"That's what I get for trusting teenagers with reincarnated souls. It's like giving a sixteen-year-old keys to a Maserati. Ugh . . . hormones. I really need to rethink that design." God paced to the large drawing table where Her diagrams and disheveled paperwork lay.

"Well, sure but, the passion was nice!"

"Nice?" She scowled. "Chemistry is volatile!"

"But fun?" Gabriel winced.

"Sure . . . fun, I guess. I mean, humans wouldn't have lasted this long without it but—the side effects!" God blew a curl off of Her forehead. "And why is it so hard to listen to your parents? It's in the top ten list!"

"Their parents didn't want them to be together!"

"Yeah, at fourteen, what normal parents would? If they could have waited a few years they wouldn't be all . . . expired! I'm telling you, the teenage brain has no room for rational thought or foresight!"

Gabriel sighed and watched the image fade.

"So now what? We go older? Have them find each other when they're less . . . saturated? Two humans, well-versed in adulting?"

God snapped Her fingers. "Good, I like it! I've got just the era. Let's jump ahead to a better time for making humans more responsible."

The battlefield was dark with blood and mortar residue. He had to find her. His last transmission hadn't gone through, and the news passed down through his unit that the medical tents had taken fire. It took him a day and a half to scramble down and out of the abandoned trenches, over the springs of curved barbed wire, and through the smell of death from bodies not yet claimed.

The sodden green cloth was faded gray and lay in a crumpled pile. The support beams stuck out at odd angles like broken bones beneath skin.

"Ruth!" he shouted. Silence shouted back. "Ruth!" He scrambled over the tent, lifting its edges and diving beneath.

"John?"

"Ruth!" Renewed hope filled his heart and he clambered towards the sound of her voice.

There, beside a leaning beam, he found her covered in a dirty, wet blanket. Her face was pale but her lips still pink. Too pink. Blood-red.

"Ruth." He dropped to his knees at her side.

"You found me." She smiled, teeth stained. "You found me in time."

"Darling," he whispered, and knelt to kiss her forehead. The gray of her eyes forever burned in his memory. Her cold hand touched the strawberry mark below his ear.

"Angel kiss or stork bite?" She smiled. "I think I prefer angel." Her

104

voice receded. John pulled back the cover and she shivered as her insides were exposed to the cold air.

"You can't go," he whispered. "You saved me, now I'll save you." Love and fear make such stupid declarations.

"You already have, John," she reassured as her hand went limp against his neck.

Gabriel cleared his throat and winced.

"Uh . . . boss that—"

"Don't throw up on my rug." God handed him a bucket. Gabriel held it to his chest and stared at the unfading scene.

"That was—" he swallowed.

"War. Surely you remember."

"I don't—I don't want to . . . I'm more of a lover than a fighter these days. I mean . . . who knew humans had so much . . . wet stuff on the inside—" He curled around the bucket.

God scratched at Her nose and turned back to the mirror.

"Well, shit. That might have been too much adulting."

Gabriel coughed. "Maybe."

"What about a more . . . lighthearted era? Huh? Something bright and colorful? 1960s? 70s? California? Still with a challenge but not so . . ."

"Squishy?"

"Yeah, not so squishy."

He glanced over his shoulder again. The dark shape was still behind him, dodging in and out of the shadows. Just a few more blocks until his apartment. Jimmy took in a deep breath and blew it out in a puff of steam. He listened for the other man's footsteps and wondered if the other man had been following him since the club.

Jimmy glanced back again; was he getting closer? With heart pounding, his feet quickened. Just a little farther. The stoop of his apartment came into view and the orange streetlamp glow felt like a welcoming set of arms thrown around him.

He reached for the apartment keys just as the man's hand closed around his elbow and pulled him back. He started to yell but the man covered his mouth.

"Easy, easy," the voice said beneath his ear. "'s just me. It's just Dan."

Jimmy relaxed and melted into Dan's arms. Dan kissed the strawberry mark on his neck and sighed beneath his ear.

"Sorry to catch you like that, but . . . you know how it is." Dan's gray eyes lowered to Jimmy's lips. They stood beneath the streetlamp, embracing the moment of safety and the love and passion that couldn't be denied from the moment they'd met.

That's how the car full of hate found them, bathed in orange glow and wrapped in each other's arms. With bats in hand and their own brand of righteousness justifying the bloodlust, the dark figures sprung from the sedan.

"Hey, ladies," a man in a ski mask called. "Did we catch you at a good time?"

The four joined them on the street and left the dark world two souls lighter.

"Goddamn it!"

"Hey!" Gabriel swung his head to look at Her.

"It's not technically in vain if it's my own name." She waved Gabriel off. He looked down at the scene and shook his head.

"Well, you did write that whole Sodom and Gomorrah thing . . ."

God scowled at him.

"You know that's *not* what that story is about! And when did my words become so literal? Men wrote that book! Men, Gabriel! Fallible, stupid men. How can a man even begin to understand a goddess . . . I mean, look at how they draw me! Some kind of love child of Zeus and Santa Claus? Ugh! Morons, the lot of them!"

"Well, I'm sure they did the best they—"

God's hair turned bright red. Gabriel shrank back.

"The best they could?" She yelled and threw Her hands into the air. Fire bolts shot down, sparking a wildfire somewhere in Nevada. "Why is this so hard?"

"Well—"

"What?" Her hair was singed in the aftermath and the smell of burning caused Gabriel to cough behind his hand.

"It's just—you keep throwing these soul-pieces into really . . . well, horrible circumstances."

"It's a test, Gabriel! It's not supposed to be easy! Otherwise everyone would find their soul mate and well, they might . . ." God stopped.

"Find enlightenment? Happiness maybe?"

He flinched as She raised Her hand to lick Her fingers and put out a burning lock of hair. Sensing the danger passing, he continued.

"I mean, maybe *we* could even take a goddamn day off?"

"Hey! Watch it." She scowled.

"Sorry." Gabriel rocked on his heels as the image of the bodies lying in the blood-painted street faded. "Maybe—"

"What?"

"Maybe life is hard enough, you know?"

"What do you mean by that?"

"Life, war, the human capacity to hate, the normal trials of survival . . . maybe we could just ease up a bit?"

God growled. "That's not the point."

"I know, I know! They have to suffer for it. But I think they're already suffering enough—"

"The sweetest fruit is the hardest to reach," She countered.

"Anytime we start talkin' fruit, things go downhill. I'm sure I don't have to remind you about the apple—"

"You're pushin' it, kid," She said and pointed a finger into his feathered chest.

"Okay, okay . . . but how about you just make it a normal amount, you know? Ease up on the severity of circumstance and see what happens on their own?"

"They're selfish."

"Yes."

"Self-centered and narcissistic. They've become spoiled and hate-filled!" She paced, talking under Her breath.

"Yes. They are all those things."

"They're losing their compassion, their empathy. It'll never work, not now. By the time we try again it'll be, well, twenty years and . . ." She stopped and looked at the darkened mirror. "I just don't know if I can take another failure. Maybe it's time I wipe the whole slate clean."

"Wait, you mean . . . ?"

"Yeah, seven plagues, end of days, real dark shit, Gabby. I've had it."

Gabriel held out his hands. "Whoa, whoa! Hang on, chief. At least let me plead their case. I've seen good, too."

"Oh? Have you? Today? You mean here? Today? Poison, family feuds, wars, famine, disease, greed, hatred. I honestly think it's time we start over and let the dogs rule. We all know they're the better species."

Gabriel nodded. "You are right about that."

"Good!" God rolled up the sleeves of Her flannel shirt, spit on Her hands, and rubbed them together. "Let's mayhem."

"Wait!" Gabriel stepped between Her and the mirror. "Just . . . please try one more time."

"Why?"

"Because . . . yes, they're dark, and twisted, and greedy. They're broken and awful. But sometimes—God, sometimes they rise up, and they give, and they love, and . . ." His throat closed with emotion.

"Are you crying?" She scowled.

"Sometimes, they are all you had hoped they could be. And if you can find one set, just one, that can love each other against the odds, find each other after hundreds of thousands of years of their stardust being separated . . that would be a good day's work, don't you think?"

She looked into his eyes, swimming with silvery angel tears.

"Damn it. Who made you so pretty?"

"You did."

"I'm an idiot."

"You're an artist, you can do anything."

"Flattery is not going to get you anywhere, Feathers."

"But you'll do it?" he asked hopefully.

God sighed.

"Fine. Once more."

"But it's my Bobo and I can't live without it!" the child screamed through the bathroom door. Her father's calming undertones followed.

Chelsea was paying for her coffee, late as usual, with an unforgiving boss waiting for her next mistake. She looked down beside her clunky boot where a loved-to-gray stuffed basset had fallen between the stools.

She didn't have time to help today. The dad would find it. Isn't that what parents were good at, she thought, finding things? The screaming turned to sobbing and the door burst open. A flustered man, carrying his red-faced child, staggered out.

"I'm sorry, Daphne, I can't stop to look. Daddy's got an interview and we'll never get across town if—"

Chelsea's heart stilled at the site of Daphne's fallen face; the tragedy of her eyes squeezed shut against the loss. Chelsea had known that loss. It seemed like her whole life was that loss. She could turn away; let the girl learn, as she had, that life was not fair.

Everyone loses what they love.

Daphne's brokenhearted whimper was muffled in her dad's shoulder. Chelsea watched as he tried to comfort her on the way out, worry in his gray eyes for all the ways he was failing that morning.

. . .

God held Her breath.

Gabriel's eyes bored into the mirror.

"You're not going to hit him with a bus, are you—"

"Shhh!" She waved Her hand without looking away. "This was your idea, Genius. Let's see if a human heart is really worth anything."

Chelsea's toe touched the toy. She'd had a basset growing up . . . Bailey. Her chest filled with warmth at the memory of the kind brown eyes and velvet-soft ears; the comfort a loyal soul could provide.

Did we all have to suffer?

She bent low, balancing her coffee cup in the other hand, and picked up the stuffed dog. Her finger traced its faded brown ears.

"I think I'm going to pee my pants," Gabriel said. His fists clenched in anticipation.

"You don't have pants . . . or pee," God scoffed.

"What's she going to do?"

"Well, I don't know! Free will, remember? Maybe my biggest mistake."

"Look!" Gabriel pointed to the mirror.

"Excuse me?" Chelsea's hardened voice carried down the sidewalk to reach them. The man turned, crying child in arms, haggard and broken. All recognizable defeats that Chelsea understood. "Does this belong to you, young lady?" she asked and wiggled the floppy dog.

The instant relief that flooded the man's face was like the sun breaking through. His kind gray eyes welled up.

"Yes," he breathed.

"Yes." God and Gabriel clenched their hands, still not sure if a bus would come barreling around the corner.

Daphne scrambled to face forward and squealed. She bounced out of her father's arms and ran to Chelsea.

"Bobo!" She flung herself into Chelsea's arms. The carefully balanced coffee cup tumbled into the gutter and the warmth of the tiny body took its place. Daphne snatched the dog away.

"Daphne! Honey, you can't—I'm sorry, I'm so sorry!" The man ran to them, the case sliding off his shoulder and tie askew. He peeled Daphne from Chelsea's arms, Bobo now securely fastened to her chest.

"No, no, it's totally fine," Chelsea laughed, a sound she'd not made in months, as he scooped up his daughter and Bobo.

"I'm Chelsea," she said and extended a hand.

"Peter," he returned in kind.

Daphne took in a breath and squealed. "Daddy! Look! She's been angel kissed!" Daphne pointed to Chelsea's neck. Chelsea covered the mark with her hand self-consciously. Birthmark, blemish, "ugly thing" was what her mother had always called it. Never angel kiss.

"Uh . . . yeah," Peter's eyes were suddenly focused on Chelsea. "Your coffee!" he burst out. "I'm so sorry about your coffee!"

"No it . . . it's fine, I should probably cut back anyway," Chelsea said, equally intrigued. "Aren't you running late?"

"I was . . ." he said, eyes dropping to her full lips. "I—interview . . . I have an interview . . . But can I make it up to you? I mean—you, you really saved my life there . . ."

"I would love a new cup of coffee sometime . . after you nail your interview." Chelsea and Daphne's eyes met, the same gray as Peter's.

"It's scary to lose something we love," Chelsea said to the girl. The warm smell of Daphne's strawberry shampoo still lingered on her neck. They felt—she fought the urge but it stuck in her throat—like home.

"It is," Peter said. "But it sure is sweet to find it again."

The world stood still for half a rotation.

"Ha! See! I told—"

"Shut up, Feathers." God smiled.

"Humans *can* do it, they *can* love."

"Don't give them too much credit. The dog really saved the whole mess," God said.

"Well yeah, but still. That was a nice touch. Real artistry."

God cleared Her throat. "Well."

"Well?" Gabriel asked.

"I'd say that constitutes a good day's work, don't you?"

"I think we did pretty well."

"So—?"

"Taco Tuesday?"

"Yes! But you're on a two margarita limit this time."

"Oh, come on, it was just that once . . ." He blushed into his wing.

"You're way too friendly a bird. I still have feathers stuck in my favorite jacket."

"I'm only almost human." He chuckled.

"Maybe that's not such a bad thing," God admitted.

21

FOR THERAPISTS BELIEVING IN ANGELS

BY ELLEN KRAMER

The day I told
my therapist about my writing,
she photocopied the page of notes I'd written
on the word *liminal*.
Then she asked me if I believed in angels.
It being therapy,
I believed maybe she was telling me
that *I* was an angel, it being therapy
and I being the center of
that universe.

The day I read aloud
to my therapist the story I'd written
about the man I loved,
but wasn't allowed to love,
she told me maybe he was
a messenger of God
in my life.

I tried not to believe her,
because I wanted him to be
just the man that he was, the one for me.
I wanted his message to be just for me,
not for everyone.

The day the man I wasn't allowed to love
told me of a good book to read,
I laughed.
It was a book I believed I was too intelligent
to read.

But then
I stopped laughing and read it,
because I loved him.
I read it and I imagined it was about him
and I hoped it could be about me, too:
about both of us—maybe together.

The day I told a man of God
about the man I'd loved and hadn't been allowed to love,
and who I'd just moved across the country from—
he listened.
I believed he listened
because he saw in me the face of God
because he *always* saw God,
in everyone.

And then I saw *him;*
I wrote him a letter and he wrote me a letter.
He told me he saw the face of God in everyone--
but that in me
he also saw the face of *me.*

So maybe I'm writing my story about me,
and my therapist,
and the man I wasn't allowed to love,
and my man of God.

But it could be
that the poem is still about all of us:
the therapists who are angels
and believe in them,
the messengers of God,
the men of God who arrive at the last minute
and save our faith—
and the ones writing about all of them,
about all of us—
each and every one of us the center of the universe for
our one-and-only
God.

22

THE EVIDENCE OF CREATION: A DIARY

BY KATE HANSEN

August 19, 2017

I've been a mother now for two weeks and five days. Or, depending on how you count it, 290 days. Mary's motherhood journey began when Gabriel showed up in her backyard, but did that begin a General Motherhood Counting Rule? Either way, I find myself in possession of a tiny baby girl.

Today I fed this tiny baby girl, and she fell asleep on my chest. I looked down at her curled on my front and marveled that she ever fit inside me. I was filled with wonder that my body created her.

How did it know to align her eyelashes in an almost invisible fringe along her fluttering eyelids? How did it know how to make her ten pink fingernails, each the size of a baby ladybug? This baby—my body—are literal miracles.

I kissed the top of her sweet-smelling head and silently praised the Lord that baby-making does not require skill. There are no expert mothers who create higher quality babies than the apprentice mothers. Look at Mary—a teen girl made the only perfect Being on her first try.

Every mother takes credit for making her baby, but really, we can only take credit for swallowing prenatal vitamins, eating well, and exercising. Ultimately, we all just marvel as our bodies do the single most impressive thing in the world.

August 21, 2017

Last night I took a bath before bed and stared at my belly that once created a miracle. I sat in the hot water, listened to Mozart's violin concerto no. 2 in D Major, and relished the luxury of a few minutes to myself. Taking my belly in my hands, I squished it together to see hundreds of wrinkles and creases appear. It looked hilariously like Jabba the Hutt. I giggled even as I felt slightly disgusted by the sight.

Staring at my naked body in the mirror after my bath, I felt the slight disgust rise again. Even after experiencing the creative miracle of my pregnancy and birth, my body still feels like a stranger's. Parts and pieces shift, and I constantly leak blood, milk, sweat, or tears. A sneeze or cough can rattle any number of things.

Moving slowly, partly from exhaustion and partly because of the aforementioned shifting pieces, I pulled a clean pair of hospital mesh panties and my gray sweatpants up under Jabba's chin. Oh, the underappreciated luxury of fresh clothes after a hot bath! I wonder what Mary's sweatpant equivalent was—although her New Testament style was probably conveniently airy. Did she ever get a hot bath? Or even a cold one? I doubt even she felt immaculate after giving birth.

Creating a baby comes with expected changes: the not-sleeping, the diapers, the altered social life. However, the evidence in my postpartum body surprises me every day, and it has forced me into an unexpected mental adjustment. This particular adjustment snuck in like the processing fee for online ticket sales. I got pregnant like I accept Terms and Conditions—say yes and hope for the best. For the most part, the terms were what I assumed. But this clause snuck in: *"By creating the miracle of life, you also agree to pay the price, includ-*

ing, but not limited to, a dramatically changed relationship with your body."

August 25, 2017

Sometimes in the middle of the night I turn on the lamp to change a diaper, and the sight of my baby surprises me as I fall in love with her nose and fingernails and elbows all over again. When she sleeps in her bassinet, I miss her warmth against me. But when I set her down and she stays asleep, I sigh and thank God. When my husband comes home from work, I eagerly hand her over and enjoy doing anything besides nursing, even putting away the laundry. But when she inevitably wails with hunger, I just as eagerly take her back and offer milk from my tired nipples. Every night I take a bath with the door closed and music on, and I bask in being alone. I feel incomplete without her close, yet I long to be alone.

The push and pull along my journey has surprised me. I am drawn to my baby, bask in her miraculous presence, celebrate her creation. And yet, the very real demands of motherhood physically and emotionally drain me. I resist them; I long for relief, a break, time off. I've created a baby, but my journey toward motherhood takes longer than I anticipated. Stumbling down the path, I often trip as I turn to look back while being pulled forward. Creating babies is easier than creating mothers. I'm drawn into my new life and identity, but change comes slowly.

September 2, 2017

It's been a month now, and I've tentatively ventured out into the world again. Again my body and my feelings surprise me. Over the past week, four women have told me how cute my body is. While relaxing by the pool in the warm sun, I listened to a woman exclaim over my tiny baby. "This can't be *your* baby! You're so cute and skinny! There's no way you just had a baby!" she said as she looked me up and down over the top of her sunglasses. I was suddenly newly aware of my appearance: the milk-factory boobs and deflated belly I'd crammed into last year's swimsuit. *Actually, she is my baby, thank you. I made her with this body. Stop looking at it.* [Smile] "Thank you."

I'm not flattered by these comments for two reasons. First, my size is evidence of the months I spent vomiting saltine crackers. The pounds I managed to gain vanished when my baby nursed every two hours around the clock for a month. I'm annoyed that my thinness is praised instead of being evidence that I desperately need an enormous roast beef sandwich and a three-hour nap.

Second, I'm puzzled that these women think my body's size is important. Would they compliment an Olympic athlete on her appearance? I hope not, because that would be ridiculously misplaced praise. I just completed a nine-month marathon with a beautiful baby as my medal, and still I get comments on my jean size.

In theory these compliments should make me feel good, but I'm surprised that *I do not care how they think I look.* I used to care, but birth has separated my appearance from my identity. Now I find the social weight of my thin body strange and irrelevant. Because of motherhood, my body is not the same, and I am not the same. I have little desire to return to my former self. Not on the inside, not on the outside.

People talk about "getting your body back" as if it were stolen instead of willingly given. If they knew my journey, our conversation would be different. But they don't, and I don't correct them. Instead I smile and say thank you and face my miracle being cheapened. It's comforting that most people missed Mary's miracle too. To them, Jesus was just another honeymoon baby, just another crazy out-of-town delivery story, just another runaway twelve-year-old, just another carpenter. So I take a lesson from Mary. She kept her mothering journey safe in her heart, away from unthinking opinions. Mary didn't let them cheapen her miracle.

· · ·

July 13, 2018

After almost a year, I am reflecting again. My baby no longer fits curled up on my chest. She's a tiny person who crawls and laughs and explores. We've both learned a lot this year. My awe that came with new motherhood is fading, but I've learned a deeper respect for my body's experience and the triumph that belongs to it. I've worked hard to ignore the alluring messages that I can get my smooth, firm body back.

Most postpartum marketing features photos of bared abdomens with varying degrees of tautness. These campaigns assume I am not happy without a perfect belly button and that having one will make me so. The irony is that belly buttons are universal evidence of the mother-baby relationship. Evidence of my mother's miracle is surrounded by stretch marks I gained from mine. My greatest joys—life received and given—stemmed from that little circle on my belly. My body's imperfections are the evidence of creation; they are inextricably connected to my miraculous experience.

No mother would ever forget crossing the bridge of birth into motherhood. So why do we obsess over erasing the evidence manifested in our bodies—the keystone of this bridge? We rejoice over the physical bodies of children, but shame the physical evidence of their creation. Creating a child requires the journey from maiden to mother, and our changed bodies are evidence of it.

The journey to motherhood is not a downward or an upward course; it is simply a movement forward, like the change of seasons. We remember Mary as both the Virgin and the Mother of God. We recognize and remember both her roles, but do not elevate one above the other. Likewise, we discredit ourselves and our experiences if we try to move backwards in our journey.

Before I was pregnant, and even during my pregnancy, the bodily changes scared me. I worried about getting fat, about getting stretch marks, about postpartum hair loss. I clung to my maidenhood. I wanted to keep a foot on each side of the bridge. Even so, it takes work to accept my mother-body and all that comes with it. It takes work to recapture some of the awe I felt in the beginning.

But when I do the work, I want to keep the marks on my body. In my mortal way, I have performed an act of creation and suffering. The marks on my body are reminders of the sacrifice and triumph of motherhood. It's a tiny taste of divinity—unglamorous, tired, often-frustrated divinity. I have to consciously seek divinity in the sleep regressions and teething, in the oatmeal on the floor. Although much of my day-to-day as a mother feels trivial, my journey is not. It's not something I want to forget or want my daughter to forget. I chose to give my body to my baby, and if the Lord Himself chose to keep the bodily evidence of His sacrifice for creation, why should I try to erase mine?

23

BIRTHING

BY MEGAN E. FREEMAN

In the university bookstore,
she stands helpless in front of the pens.
    I've never done this before.
    I don't know what I'm doing.

After midnight,
she climbs into my bed
and my arms. Burrowing
like she's trying to get back
into my body.

Back to the origins
of our very first night together
as two separate beings
breathing separate oxygen
no longer nested one inside the other.
Separate but still clinging.

I hold her and she weeps a little.

In this small, twin bed high
on the thirteenth floor of this small hotel
in this small city-state where
she is about to launch her new big life,
she sleeps in the fetal position.

It took me forty hours to birth you,
I whisper. And when we stand
on opposite sides of this small planet
and stretch out our arms
they   almost   touch.

24

THE MOST BEAUTIFUL PARTS OF MY BODY

BY MEGAN E. FREEMAN

the most beautiful parts
of my body
are the broken puzzle pieces
jumbled
in the column of my core
the ones that squeezed
the equilibrium from my step
caused pain to rival labor
though
this labor was unceasing
and pushed from bed
to toilet to shower
on all fours
crawling like the lowliest
Roman beggar
all shame eclipsed
by primal incomprehension
prehistoric need
but now the puzzle's edges

are assembled once again
the missing pieces snapped
back into balance
collateral damage
mitigated by vigilance
and gratitude
and daily salutations
of the sun

25

SYNTH

BY KATIE LEWIS

The choice wasn't a hard one. My original body wasn't going to last long, and I wasn't about to let that stop me. At twenty-three, I simply wasn't done yet.

The replacement of a limb or a vital organ had been routine since well before I was born. Most people were walking around with at least some piece of SynthCorp in them. An entire body transplant, though, what they called a "full transfer," that was still relatively new. Not unheard of, and certainly the next logical step by all accounts, but still new.

There was mandated therapy, of course. Months of it before I could even be approved for the transplant. But the truth was, by that point my body had become nothing more than a prison. By the end of my illness, it was barely recognizable, even to me. The chance to escape from it felt like nothing short of a miracle. No more pain, no more fatigue: like dying but without an actual end.

Waking up in my shiny new Synth body was, without a doubt, the strangest experience of my life. I had been warned of so many things. That my senses of sight, hearing, and smell would be sharper. That taste would be a bit lacking and touch would be extremely dulled, at first. All part of the process as my brain relearned its new artificial nerve pathways. Paralysis was also not uncommon, especially in the first twenty-four hours, and I had been given strict instructions not to panic. Nor did I, to my credit. Instead, I lay quietly in my bed, counting the minuscule imperfections on the ceiling visible to my new Synth eyes until a nurse finally noticed I was conscious.

It was another day before I could speak. And several more before I could move around very much. The whole first week blurred together, both out of boredom and the simple fact that my poor, inefficient organic brain was too busy with its remapping job to encode many long-term memories. I had also been warned about that. The main thing I remembered from those first days was the absence of all the tubes and machines I had grown so used to. There was no heart monitor. No IV. A SynthCorp body could sustain itself for weeks on a single electrical charge, and all of my vitals could be tracked wirelessly. Of course, eating and drinking were still possible and highly encouraged, albeit from a purely psychological standpoint, but it wasn't necessary. Still, it was important to keep that grey matter happy in its new shell, after all.

Visitors came and went, but eventually there came a day when I awoke alone in the room. Moving my limbs at will had grown slowly easier as the days went on, though I had yet to really dig into my physical therapy. Like most hospital rooms, mine was equipped with a bathroom which had seemed to be more for the comfort of my steady stream of visiting relatives and friends than anything else. Today, however, I shifted my legs one by one off the side of my mattress and managed to stand by holding onto the metal railing along the side of my bed frame.

I didn't so much walk as shuffle, clinging to the wall as I went. My knees seemed to have forgotten how to pick up my feet, and I dragged them across the ground, hearing the slight squeak they made now and then as my bare Synth skin slid across the linoleum tiled floor. I stopped once when I heard voices approach my door, sure I was about to be caught, but they passed by and I continued my painfully slow progress to the bathroom. Once I got close enough, the wall offered a helpful railing to lean on and I made good use of it as I forced my uncooperative body the final few inches into the room. I knew that my muscles couldn't actually be burning, that it was simply a phantom sensation my brain was producing based on the level of stress, but even so I clung to the sink with trembling legs as I panted for air. Another unnecessary autonomic response.

For several moments I simply stood there, catching my breath and refusing to raise my eyes. I stared into the sink, trying not to focus on the buildup of grime around the drain that was only visible because of my newly enhanced sight. *Really, a hospital should be more clean,* I thought.

Finally, I closed my eyes and forced myself to raise my head. When I opened them, the face that stared back at me in the mirror wasn't mine, but I had been expecting that. It had been a large part of my therapy, proving I could accept that my appearance would change. The transplant was barely covered by insurance as it was, and even then only in extreme last-case scenarios like mine, where the "birth body" was totally unsalvageable. Facial matching was considered an elective enhancement. But I figured why not? A new body might as well have a new face.

What I hadn't expected, what I had failed to appreciate, however, was how uncanny it would be. The skin was flawless, not a mark or blemish to be seen. No acne scars or beauty marks. My new eyebrows were perfectly shaped in a way that I never would have had the patience for in my old body. My eyes seemed to be permanently rimmed with eyeliner and my lips were an unnatural shade of pink that gave the illusion of lipstick. Even my heightened cheekbones were slightly rosy and perfectly contoured.

With clumsy fingers, I managed to turn on the taps and splash water on my face. It was cold enough to make a normal human cry out in shock, but my nerves weren't registering temperature just yet. I scrubbed my face with the palms of my hands before blinking the water away and raising my eyes to the mirror once more.

There was no change in my appearance. But of course there wasn't, because I wasn't actually wearing any makeup.

The sound of the running water filled up the tiny room, but I ignored it as my numb fingers fiddled with the ties of the hospital gown next. I didn't have the dexterity I'd once had, though, and within seconds frustration got the better of me. The thin fabric tore with the satisfying noise of ripping cloth, and I let the garment slip off my shoulders to pool at my feet.

The story was the same as with my face. No moles or freckles dotted my Synth flesh. Perky, perfectly balanced silicon breasts stood up without any need for support, moving slightly with every breath. My titanium rib cage was just barely visible before my waist tapered just so towards the bottom of the mirror. I looked down at myself and confirmed the same was true all the way to my toes. Every inch of my skin was unmarked and hairless. Every part of my body was beautifully sculpted. I looked . . . unreal.

"Miss Smith!"

I turned towards the source of the voice, heedless of my own nudity. It wasn't my body, after all. What did I have to be ashamed of? My doctor, Dr. Jones, and a nurse were watching me from my empty bedside. The nurse wore a look somewhere between embarrassed and horrified. She had been the one to call out. Dr. Jones was harder to read, his face betraying only a stern narrowing of his eyes.

"It's wrong," I said. I was still getting used to the sound of my own voice. It was too high and too soft. It hadn't bothered me before, but now it was grating.

"Miss Smith," Dr. Jones began, laying the tablet with my chart aside to take a step towards me.

"Let's get you covered up," the nurse said at the same time, stepping in front of her male counterpart.

"It's wrong," I said again, louder this time.

"There is an adjustment period. You know this, Miss Smith," Dr. Jones said calmly. He had stopped advancing and was merely watching me, the way someone watches a dangerous animal. And that was right, that was smart, because a Synth body was several times stronger than a normal human one and I hadn't yet gotten control of all my motor functions. The nurse, however, didn't stop her advance. Suddenly, I didn't want her to touch me.

"You're not listening to me!" I shouted, slamming my fist down on the edge of the still-running sink beside me. I heard the ceramic basin crack. The nurse stopped in her tracks.

"I am listening," Dr. Jones said calmly. "Tell me what is wrong, Alexis." I blinked, turning my full attention back to the doctor. His hands were at his sides and he had widened his eyes again. He was trying to make himself look inviting, trustworthy. I couldn't say if I noticed it because of my newly heightened senses or simply thanks to months of watching my therapist do the same thing.

"I'm perfect," I whispered. For a moment I worried I'd been too quiet and would have to repeat myself, but then Dr. Jones nodded.

"You are," he agreed quietly. "As I said, there's an adjustment period." I just stared at him, the sound of the running water filling my ears.

"I'm perfect!" I shouted back, resisting the urge to strike the sink again. I might break it. "Don't you understand? People aren't perfect! People have marks and scars and fat! I'm . . . I'm not a person anymore . . ." By the end of my tirade, my voice had begun to wane, losing both strength and volume until I was nearly whimpering. Could my new body cry? I wasn't sure. I couldn't remember. Dr. Jones sighed and turned back to pick up my chart and begin making notes. He seemed annoyed. Or disappointed. Or both.

"This type of body dysmorphia isn't uncommon with full transfers," he muttered as he tapped away at the screen. Now that he said it, I did remember my therapist saying that it was a possibility. By that point, however, I had been so desperate to get out of my dying body I would have agreed to just about anything, no matter what the risk. "We can begin tracking it now. And if it persists we can see about making adjustments."

I blinked again.

"Adjustments? I thought that was elective," I said blankly. The nurse had begun to inch closer again, I noticed, but had wisely chosen not to touch me until she was sure my anger had evaporated.

"Facial mapping is elective, in most all cases," Dr. Jones corrected, finishing whatever note he was making to glance up at me again. "Body dysmorphia, on the other hand, is a recognized psychological disorder that SynthCorp takes very seriously. They want all of their customers to be happy with their products. Well, as happy as possible," he finished with a shrug.

"What can you do?" I asked, my mind whirling with the possibilities. Would I want to try and recreate the marks from my old body, or make something from scratch? And just how far could these adjustments go?

"They can adjust just about anything you want. Create scars, add fatty tissue if you prefer, even some adjustment to facial features—so long as your therapist agrees that you are suffering from body dysmorphia, anyway."

I glanced back at myself in the mirror, now getting a side view of my impossibly airbrushed body. There wasn't an inch of body fat to be seen, and the wrongness of it all struck me afresh. My hand rose on its own in my reflection to cup one of my too-perfect breasts.

"What about these? Can they get rid of these?" I asked, turning back to Dr. Jones. Now he was frowning again, taking a moment to scroll through my chart before answering.

"You didn't present with any signs of gender dysphoria before the procedure," he pointed out as he flicked his finger across the electronic screen that held all of my medical information.

My lips turned up into the hint of a smile.

"I wasn't aware that I had a choice in the matter, before," I replied simply.

I sat on a barstool, sipping my fruity drink through a cold metal straw. Over the past months my new taste buds had begun to grow stronger, bit by bit. The process came with waves of cravings for certain foods, sweet or salty or savory. This week I was on a strawberry kick: all strawberry, all the time.

The music pumping from the speakers droned in the background, though even with my enhanced hearing all I could make out was the steady thump of the bass beating against my eardrums. A gaggle of girls erupted into giggles behind me. Their voices were shrill with alcohol and the excitement of a night out. At least one of them was wearing perfume, a sharp scent that clashed terribly with my strawberry drink. I wished they would leave.

"Hey," someone said to my left. I turned and found a man suddenly leaning against the bar beside me, holding out his wrist so the bartender could scan his credit chip for a beer. He had the sort of face that made it impossible to tell where he fell in the twenty-five to forty range, though the cut of his sandy hair and the light in his bright blue eyes suggested youth.

"Hello," I replied simply. My voice still wasn't the way I remembered it but it was lower now, lower than it had ever been, actually. And that felt right, even if most of my family still couldn't recognize it over the phone. He accepted his beer and took a swig from the bottle before turning his blue eyes on me again.

"So, human or Synth?" he asked bluntly. I barked out a laugh, mostly out of surprise. Most people weren't brazen enough to ask such a question in public. In fact, most people couldn't even tell. Which raised the question, how could he?

"That's not the question that people usually start with," I said, twisting in my chair a bit to show off more of my entirely even torso. He only grinned, displaying a row of perfectly too-white teeth.

"I'm not your usual kind of guy," he said simply. It was a laughably bad line, but I didn't laugh again. Instead I took another sip of my booze drowned in strawberry syrup and considered him. He was well built and his face had a pleasing symmetry, which was how my Synth eyes measured attractiveness these days. Or maybe my brain had always functioned that way and I had simply never noticed. More importantly, there was something in those sparkling blue eyes of his, some kind of boyish excitement that seemed to draw me in and excite me too.

"Does it matter?" I asked. He had tipped his head back for another drink of his beer, but he stopped short as soon as I spoke.

"Does what matter?" he asked, dragging the sleeve of his shirt over his lips. I could smell the mix of sweet corn and skunk from the cheap beer he was drinking and took another sip of my own drink to chase it away.

"Human or Synth. Does it matter?" I asked, tilting my head with the metal straw still caught in the corner of my mouth. I expected his eyes to move over me. I expected them to go to my flat chest or even the unhelpful waistband of my jeans, but instead they stayed fixed on my own eyes, staring into the particular shade of hazelnut brown I had picked out of a book only a few short months ago.

"Not from my experience," he said, lips quirking in a coy grin. I sucked the last of my Strawberry Fizz through my straw and hopped off the bar stool.

"Alex," I said, holding out my hand.

"Charlie," he replied, trading his beer to his other hand to give my slightly smaller one a firm shake. Touch was another sense that was slowly evolving, but I could feel that his palm was chilled and slightly damp from holding the bottle.

I had never been the type to go to bars like this on a Saturday night, even when I was healthy. Even on the few occasions when I had, I had never gone alone and *never* talked to strangers. But as

Charlie wiped his hand on his jeans after the fact and offered me a goofy grin, I looked past him to the mass of bodies moving on the dance floor and considered all the things I never would have done before. And all the things I could do now.

"Come on, Charlie. Let's dance."

26

UNREQUITED

BY JOHN BLAIR

You never met my father. He could do anything, tinker on the Model T or build a house from ground up, framing, plumbing, everything. An educated man, he taught at Colorado A & M in the Industrial Arts Department. He built furniture including the oak breakfront for the house where my mother birthed me, where I lived eighty-two and three-quarter years. Mother insisted on lessons. She brought her family's piano from Missouri, and "It's not just for decoration," she said. Later, a Baptist organist taught me to play at church on a hydraulic instrument, compressed air via a manual pump. My legs ached for two days after each class. Mother died, and Father followed mere weeks later. Too lonely I guess. Quiet permeated the house. Can you hear silence? I filled it with music from piano students. You attracted me, a young man from church, your blue eyes and curly auburn hair. But it was your gentle manner and unending curiosity that kept me fascinated, reminded me of Daddy. You took me for shared hot fudge sundaes at City Drug Saturday afternoons. We sat on stools and ate with extra-long teaspoons until our teeth throbbed from cold. I thought our relationship progressed to a point where you might propose. I would have said yes. Do you know loneliness?

That's when you told me of your partiality for men. I could tell no one without revealing your secret or shaming you . . . and me. I lost weight, closeted myself except for long walks to City Park. I accepted my spinsterhood, but never forgot you. When I saw your obituary in the Coloradoan, unexpected tears recalled my fondness, my longing for your embrace.

27

WRITE, CRY, BREATHE: SURVIVING THE PROCESS OF TRANSFORMATION

BY WREN WRIGHT

When the universe pushes you to join an online dating service, insists you accept an invitation to tea from a pleasant-sounding British gentleman, then instructs you to *kiss him when you see him,* it's wise to comply. Alan and I met (for tea, of course) on a hot sunny afternoon in August 2005. The next day, he asked me to marry him. I wondered what took him so long.

The wedding was a few months later. It was the second marriage for both of us, and our bond was lovingly fierce and uncompromising. Our souls were on fire, and they burned hot, quick, and bright. But before the end of our sixth year, he was gone.

Nine months after we were married, my new husband was diagnosed with dementia. Love can be a trickster. It can be innocent and affectionate or cruel and gruesome, all the while disguised as transformation.

We understood that this dementia, this thief, would take its time fracturing our union. No one and nothing but this wretched disorder would pull us apart. There would be a significant, progressive decline in Alan's cognitive functions, his balance and motor skills. His thought processes, reasoning, memory, attention, language, and problem-solving capabilities would come and go. Mostly go. Finally, his body would forget how to carry out normal functions—like swallowing and breathing. And then he'd make his transition to the Great Love in the Sky.

Four years after the diagnosis, Alan fell at home. He was standing at the bathroom sink when his legs simply gave out. Within hours, he went from having moderate dementia to severe dementia. Before the fall, he required minimal help. He'd ask me to tie his shoes or button his shirt. After the fall, he couldn't pick up a spoon to eat breakfast. When I put it in his hand, he didn't know what to do with it. Silently, I railed at the universe while gently taking the spoon and feeding him as if he were my infant son.

Two days later and still unable to feed himself, Alan was admitted to the hospital where he was given an anti-anxiety drug. He had a bad reaction to the medicine, which caused his symptoms to worsen. The irony in that was not lost on me. We endured ten agonizing hours of trauma while the drug worked its way through his system. The experience unraveled my already frayed nerves.

At home by myself late that evening, while Alan finally slept peacefully in the hospital, my inner compass steered me to the computer and demanded I document the day's events. Still reeling from the violence of Alan's ordeal, I did just that. I wrote:

He fusses with his blankets, tears off his hospital gown, picks at his clothes. He hallucinates. He grasps the air, peels bananas that aren't there, asks me to pull the needles out of his legs. I go along with it all, especially making sure he understands I removed all the needles. He's satisfied and falls asleep smiling. At last he's at peace, and I can take a break from being with him in his dementia. But that lasts only a minute.

He wakes up, flails about like a fussy baby, arms and hands and head moving in short, jerky, out-of-control motions, his hands pulling my hair and necklace, holding on as he falls deeper into the nightmare only he experiences. He squeezes my fingers so hard that I remove my wedding ring to prevent injury. He reaches for me, misses, unintentionally grabs and bumps and punches me. He's fighting something. Part of me wants to cry, but my crying would not make this double helix of hell easier for him, so I search my mental landscape for the thing that will make it easier. And there it is—my presence, my strength of presence. More of that, then. I'll give him my attention and his dignity and ask that I'm gifted the power to sustain them.

Here, then, I thought, is how I can be present for Alan, myself, and this dementia. I'll look that dastardly dementia thief in the eye and write about it throughout this journey. I'll write everything— every sorrow, failure, disintegration, descent, every emotion of despair as well as the joy—there has to be joy hidden in there somewhere. I realized I needed to give voice to our love and suffering, our grief and loss, to light a flare for those in similar situations, to put my perceptions and knowledge into a format others could relate to as they navigate the uncharted terrain of dementia. My soul was on fire, my passion lit.

Writing was one thing, but there could be little writing without crying. And there was a lot of crying, a lot of release. This new life with Alan would take superhuman strength, and crying was my second ticket to the other side.

During my caregiving and grief process, and throughout the writing and crying, I discovered the third secret: breathing. Taking a pause, a step back, observing from a distance, as if it weren't happening to you and your loved one, as if it were a movie. Watching space open up where there was none before, and deciding how to fill it. This was my way of breathing.

But for now, our tale was just revving up. I had the mistaken idea that I needed to write our story in novel form, but I didn't know how to do that without having lived it through. Anxious days followed anxious thoughts before my inner compass suggested there was only one way: to write one memory at a time, exactly in the manner I wrote that first journal entry. I would commit everything I remembered to the page. I'd call it up later and copy and paste it into a semblance of an order. I'd add to it, subtract from it, and edit it into cohesiveness, something that made sense. This, I believed, would complete my personal cycle of the experience, and it might even help heal me. I had no clue at the time how much more would unfold, how much more I'd learn about myself, how much more broken I could get, or how my wounds would heal.

This drive and passion to write our memories rooted and quickened within me. It carried me through Alan's hospital stay and the subsequent fourteen months in a nursing home. It magically flittered about in the background, like a ghost note hovering above the sacred mother drum as it beats the rhythm of our lives. Sometimes that drive shook my foundation, sometimes it soothed me. I don't know if one can cultivate such obsession, but if I hadn't been guided to write, I'd like to think that I would have had the sense to invite such passion to stay beside me all of my remaining days with Alan.

After finishing my first journal entry, and with the day's trauma still rattling my core, my brain was a mush of bottled-up emotion that wanted out. I let go of all we had been through since Alan's fall. I wept for having traveled through the dark night of the soul without a map or chart to guide us. I shed tears for having to battle monsters, demons, horrors of the heart. I howled, wailed, whimpered, sobbed. And when I finally came out the other side in the wee hours of the morning, I fell into a deep, sound slumber.

I wrote, I cried, I breathed. It was the repetition of this pattern time and again that rescued me. It protected me, liberated me, and created the space for me to grieve, the strength to thrash about with the dragons and demons, to keep on writing.

Write, cry, breathe. Repeat as often as necessary.

Because my intention was to capture my unedited memories for no one's eyes but my own, I was free to spill them out like so much raw sewage. I vented and vomited words on the screen. I praised love and condemned it. I wrote my confusion, my bliss, my grief and gratefulness. I wrote thoughts and reflections about each day's events and ensnared the memories from our earlier days.

What I wrote was unprocessed, so coarse that I usually cried as I wrote. It was my first therapy, my first attempt at healthy self-soothing. Writing the events of my caregiving life validated the path I had chosen—to be present for Alan. Writing the events and my feelings each day helped me maintain a strength of presence for him, to be a grounded witness, to take on and deflect as much of the pain and suffering he needed to offload, to honor and uphold our love for each other.

For example, there was the night Alan forgot I'd be late for our visit because of an earlier appointment. When I arrived, he uncharacteristically and vehemently chewed me out. Astonished, I let his verbal abuse run its course. I listened and recognized it was dementia running the show, not him. At home afterward, I wrote:

Daggers shoot from his eyes, heading toward me, hundreds of tiny daggers. I take the hit. I take all of them. They pierce my skin, my heart, stomach, lungs, and throat. I'm in great pain, but Alan's pain is much greater. He thinks I abandoned him, that I'm gone for good, never to return. Fear, anger, and loneliness simmered in him all day. By the time I appear, he's a pressure cooker of ugly notions soup, and when I walk into his room, the pot explodes and the fuming contents spatter all over me, burning me to a crisp. I couldn't prevent it, but I could clean up the mess. So, Alan and I take our pain and fear out for tea. We make friends with it, and we become a big happy family of pain and fear. We hold hands, the two of us mewing like abandoned kittens, each forgiving the other, ourselves, this atrocious dementia, the universe. Finally, finally—we laugh.

I documented my bouts of frustration, jotted down recipes for healthy food meant to comfort me and how they turned out after I tried them. I transcribed dreams and nightmares from the night before. I imagined our lives as Romeo and Juliet, living in Dementiaville instead of Padua, and modeled a poem in the style of Shakespeare's prologue to the play:

One loving household, torn apart by dementia,
In the fair Rocky Mountains, where we lay our scene,
From ancient karma break to new chaotic placenta,
Where primal love causes new love to teem.
From forth the celestial loins of opposing forces
Our two star-crossed lovers live their lives
Together but apart, alone on separate courses,
As their devotion to each other moves forward, ever strives.
The fearful path of this frightening disease,
And the continuance of its terrifying rage,
Which, but all cries and hearts nought could please,
Is now passing across this, our stage;
The which if you with patient ears attend,
What here shall miss, our toil shall strive to mend.

Each writing session tidied up my psyche and guided my search for meaning. I documented the horrors that popped up, like when Alan forgot who I was for three days. I recorded my happiness, like when Alan remembered me on the fourth day, not recalling he'd forgotten me. Writing begat more writing, more emotion, more release. In this way, I slowly built an invisible but sturdy scaffold reaching from my heart to his, my silent offering to him in his dementia.

Write, cry, breathe. Repeat as often as necessary.

As my husband's illness progressed and for several months after his death, I'd take my laptop to a coffee shop to write. I found comfort in the change of scenery and the warm drink. I limited those sessions to an hour. That was as long as I could write before risking crying into my chai in front of strangers. When I could hold in the tears no longer, I'd pack up, drive home, and only then would I weep. Sometimes I'd cry for ten minutes, sometimes for several hours. I wept, sobbed, bawled, and blubbered until there was nothing left to release. I didn't force it. I simply let it happen. I gave my grief and sadness sovereignty over its expression.

In the privacy and cocoon of home, I sniveled and whimpered over nothing and everything, usually each day. Once, I started to cry after I put on a CD of African and Celtic fusion music and noticed that my mood matched the music—a sad cacophony of perky pipes and flighty flutes, dastardly drones, demonic drums, galloping guitars, and wailing whistles that somehow formed the perfect background for my lament. Often, I'd sit cross-legged on the floor in front of the living room fireplace or on the loveseat overlooking the veranda and our expansive lawn, crying myself dry.

During a snowstorm late one winter night, situated at my desk in the study, comforted and protected by the overflowing bookshelves surrounding me, I struggled through the drudgery of paying bills and sorting through incessant stacks of paperwork. In frustration, I scattered the documents on the floor, lay down on them, and moved my arms and legs as if I were a child making a snow angel, crying while I did so.

And then there was the time five days before our fifth wedding anniversary when Alan told me he didn't love me anymore and never wanted to see me again. I drove home and took to the bedroom. With the fireplace blazing, I curled up under the covers and wept like the tormented soul I was. We were apart for eighteen days, until he called to tell me an angel revealed to him the absolute *wrongness* in his decision and that this angel advised him to bring me back into his life. I cried tears of joy to see him again.

There were occasions I'd shed tears unexpectedly, with nothing to set me off. My bawling was cathartic, but behind my weeping was a support system that had been with me from the beginning of Alan's illness. This network of friends, professional therapists, counselors, and support groups validated the voice and urgings of my inner compass to continue crying it out.

Crying is the body's way of releasing toxins and stress hormones, of cleansing us mentally and physically. To move forward in this wild excursion we call life, all our emotions must be experienced and expressed safely and fully. That doesn't mean forcing the expression or experience, but it does mean surrendering to it, consenting to let it safely take us where we need to go.

Write, cry, breathe. My tears propped me up and made it possible to carry on, to keep on writing, loving, and living.

Each of my writing and crying sessions rendered my psyche empty. With teardrops spent, my heart contained only space and air. My grief had left temporarily, and my inner compass offered therapeutic activities to fill the void. It guided me to take breathers from the physical and emotional demands of writing and crying, to take respite, and to recharge.

For me, breathing was anything I enjoyed doing at any given time. Sometimes crying would exhaust me and I'd take a nap, letting the rapid eye movements of sleep sort out the day's events. Sometimes crying awakened contemplation, so I'd meditate, work on a painting, read, listen to music, or have a long soak in my jetted bathtub. Other times it would energize me, so I'd play my djembe drum, walk, or go for a drive. Or it would nudge me to get out in the world, so I'd visit bookstores and coffee shops, go to a movie, or hang out with friends or family.

To live my own life while Alan was in the nursing home, I inhaled deeply, and I exhaled just as intensely to live my life without him after he died. Breathing is the sacred space between release and feeling, between ending and beginning again. It's the first ghost note of life, and of living in the joy and misery and light of our own presence.

Write, cry, breathe. If we don't breathe, we don't live. And life is in each breath.

Five months after Alan died, just before what would have been our sixth wedding anniversary, I finished writing a draft of the memories of our life together. The last words I wrote:

There's nothing more to do but wait. I hold Alan's hand, wanting to be with him forever, to walk with him, to fly away with him. Outside, it's growing dark, quiet, calm. I'm at his side, still holding his hand, when the sun sets gracefully, exquisitely, with his last exhaled breath. At last he's free, and I'm empty, eerily at peace.

A year after that, I finished another draft. The write-cry-breathe routine continued to work. I was on a roll. But for as much passion as I had to polish my notes further, there existed an opposing force just as determined to foil my efforts.

As I began writing again, I stalled, stuck in crying mode. I'd weep, breathe, then try to write; weep, breathe, try to write—over and over again, always with the same unproductive result. I took a stab at rewriting different journal entries, thinking I needed only a gentle push to pop the clutch and start up again, but I stalled.

My work came to a standstill as I coasted deeper into despair and depression, lost the spark of what little energy I had, and finally shut down. I landed in a darker place of grief than I'd ever been. I was broken, and I was done trying to write. I needed to breathe. I needed to play more ghost notes.

Two years passed, but even then I was unable to write. My inner compass—the same intuitive voice that led me to Alan—lured me from our home in Colorado to the Pacific Ocean and the redwood trees of California's North Coast. It accompanied me daily as I walked along the shore, sensed the rhythm and power of the ocean, and presented myself for renewal, begging for help. This crying was too much. I took deep breaths of air, full of sea spray and healthy negative hydrogen ions that balanced my serotonin levels and lightened my psychological load with each visit.

After a few months of wandering up and down the beaches of the North Coast, my inner compass escorted me to my laptop, sat me down, and announced I was ready to write again. And I did. This time, however, there was no need for the write-cry-breathe routine that had served me in the past. This time I wrote without weeping, mostly. I still couldn't keep it together as I rewrote the initial scene at the hospital where Alan had a bad reaction to the anti-anxiety drug.

Still, I wrote, and I kept on writing. By then, I'd learned more about how to write our story, and I was finding my groove as a writer.

I finished my notes and published related essays in literary journals and local papers. Finally in the zone, I found the neighborhood to be lovely.

Write, cry, breathe. Repeat as often as necessary. I continue to write. The crying is done. And I still breathe.

28

THE ABUNDANCE OF ONE

BY SHERRY SKYE STUART

I've never been just one.
My life was entwined;
children, husbands, church,
their demands and delights
blurring the oneness of me.
Now I am alone.
Celebrating the abundance of one.

I savor the tranquility
of my home:
sunlit windows, worn rugs,
overflowing bookshelves,
beloved quilts, glowing candles.
My sanctuary.
Celebrating the abundance of one.

I gather the bounty
of my garden;
calming lavender, tangy chard,

crunchy lettuce, rainbow carrots,
fragrant mint, juicy melons.
My serenity.
Celebrating the abundance of one.

I bask in the satisfaction
of my writing;
journaling yesterdays,
imagining tomorrows,
long-ago women's stories.
My inspiration.
Celebrating the abundance of one.

I savor the blessings
of my life;
fulfilling desires,
meditating at my altar,
gratitude for all that I am.
My healing.
Celebrating the abundance of one.

29

BIRD FOR BIRD

BY JIM BURRELL

Chatterbox of house finches,
a sunny outburst
of backyard glee,
soprano festivities
ring behind birch leaves—
a riot of high summer
singing.

Talons plunge, and with wings
spread wide—grey angel
ignoring the graceful leaves—
a hungry Cooper's hawk
reaches into the shrieks.
Turning back overhead,
it stares down clear-eyed
and carries off
a tiny silence.

30

THE LAKE HOUSE

BY MICHAEL KANNER

The lake no longer held any secrets. A long drought had stripped its ability to conceal them. Calling it a lake was an overstatement. It was never more than a large pond stuck in the foothills. At best, it was never more than one spring melt and one rainstorm from being the mud flat it is now.

I could write a history of my family in the exposed debris. Over to the right, a pile of bottles from where Granddad threw his empties. Off to the left, the tail fins of my uncle's car from when he got drunk and drove it into the lake. Local legend was that there was a body or two from the "Moonshine Wars" in the sludge from when the local bootleggers, including some distant cousins, decided that the easiest way to deal with competition and tax officials was to shoot them and throw their bodies in the water. When I was a little kid, my brother Tom and I would lay out on the dock talking of the treasure we were convinced was at the bottom.

But in reality, it was just muck; a mix of dirt, plant life, and waste that had stewed in standing rainwater for generations. It had taken an act of nature, or God, to expose it all.

"So, Jim Bo, what are you going to do?" my sister Jane called from the shore side of the dock.

Standing up, I brushed my hands on my jeans. "Not much good having a lake house when there's no water."

"It might recover." Jane always saw the possibility of something better.

I walked on to the shore to where she was standing. Shorter than me by a head, her blonde hair tied back in a ponytail, she was dressed in jeans and a t-shirt with an old afghan around her shoulders. She was as slender and endearing as when she was a little kid. It was hard to think she was in her mid-twenties. The years had not been decent to me as the wrinkles had piled up and my hair had departed. I was no longer in fighting trim like I'd been in the Army.

"If Tom was here, he would know what to do." For Jane, 'if Tom was here' was the solution to every problem.

"Doubt it. Even he couldn't bring on the rain."

"I wish Tom hadn't gone away." She still looked up to our older brother, even though he had been gone for a decade.

"Well, he had to." Looking down at her feet, I noticed she was barefoot. "Jane, where are your shoes?"

"On the porch. I like the feeling of the grass and mud when I walk around."

"Well, there's no mud. It's time for lunch. Let's head back up to the cabin."

"Race you!" And off she sped with her arms outstretched so the afghan fluttered behind her like wings. That was Jane, all spur of the moment.

Like the lake, the cabin wasn't much. Originally built right after World War II when separation pay let some cousins buy the property, it was timber frame construction with a tar paper roof and a collection of mismatched windows. I suspected the materials had been "liberated" from construction sites during the post-war building boom. There was just a single large room that served as everything— kitchen, dining room, living room—and two bedrooms for the adults.

The three of us and our cousins usually slept in hammocks and sleeping bags out on the porch, or mattresses thrown on the floor. You had to go outside to use the "necessaries." Electricity had been provided by a series of generators, each one replaced rather than repaired whenever they broke down. Most of the furniture was second or third hand, each piece dragged up by branches of the family when newer furniture was bought.

When I got to the cabin, I was greeted by Jane dancing around. "I win! That means you make lunch." Between my limited cooking skills and what we had brought up for the weekend, lunch was canned tomato soup and grilled cheese sandwiches. Fortunately, the combination was Jane's favorite and I was rewarded with a big hug. She wouldn't let go until I returned her hug and kissed the top of her head. She called it her "release button."

Lunch didn't take long. As soon as we finished, I started to wash the dishes. Jane grabbed a towel to dry, but I told her we would let them air dry. I hadn't decided if we were leaving them with the rest of the trash. No reason to chance her getting upset about dropping one.

"Why don't we come up here anymore?" Sitting on the floor next to me, Jane was eating one of the apples we had brought with us.

"No one really wanted to."

"I wonder why? We always had fun up here." She was the only one that still had good memories of the place. "Say, let's play a game. You know, like we used to."

"Sure, see if you can find one while I grab a smoke."

Jane scrunched up her nose, "I don't like you smoking. It's not good for you and it makes you stink."

"I know. I'll quit one of these days. I promise."

Standing up, she wagged her finger at me like Mom, "Okay, but just one."

"Just one. Promise."

Stepping out on the porch, I tore open the bottom of a fresh pack. That was a GI thing. Opening the bottom kept the filter part clean, so you wouldn't be sticking dirt, grease, or worse in your mouth. I took a long inhale to calm my nerves. Coming up here had been necessary, but also meant dealing with a lot that I would rather have forgotten. If I thought I could do it without starting a forest fire, I would have torched the place. That's what it deserved.

I thought about the years since we last came up here. I'd supposedly joined the service because I could learn a skill and have some benefits. But I think it was a way to run away. In high school, having a sister who was "different" was an obstacle to any social life and made staying home an effort. "Serving my country" seemed like a good escape. Anyway, I came out of the service with three things—the GI Bill, a fifty percent disability rating from a back injury, and a cigarette habit. Between the GI Bill, my disability, and money saved during deployments to Afghanistan, I had enough for college and a teaching certificate. This landed me a job as a high school history teacher near where we lived.

Finishing my cigarette, I went back inside. Jane was already sitting next to the coffee table. "Look what I found: *Sorry!* Remember, we used to play it when it rained. I'm green." Jane was busy laying the game out on the table.

"Okay." I sat down opposite Jane. I reached across to brush her hair back and was greeted with, "Busy!" She was so absorbed, like putting out the cards was the most important thing in the world.

We started the game with Jane making me promise not to let her win. As it went on, she took great joy in being able to declare "Sorry" and send me back to home even though she got angry and pouted if I did it to her. No matter how old we got, she still acted like she did when we were little kids. Jane finally won (after I palmed a card or two), which let her cry "Loser!" I put off another game by telling her I needed to pack some stuff to take back with us.

"Jim Bo, you know who would love this place? Kathy. You should bring her up here sometime."

"I told you, I'm not dating Kathy anymore."

"Why not? I liked her. She still says hi and stops to talk when she sees me. I made her some really nice flowers last week. She said she liked my arrangements."

"She liked you, too. We just quit dating." I'd liked Kathy also, enough to consider marriage. She was pretty, smart, and easy to talk to. But she just wasn't up for what I needed to do.

At first, Kathy thought it was sweet that I was taking care of Jane. Jane's smile and personality were great for winning her over. Kathy treated her like a little sister, despite the two being about the same age. But, after a few months of dating with Jane as a constant third wheel, Kathy said we needed to talk. I had just sent Jane to bed so Kathy and I could have some time alone.

"Is she ever going to get better?"

"No."

"Are you ever going to leave her?"

"No, she's my sister."

"You know there are some good—"

"What? Group homes? She's not an inconvenient puppy to put in a shelter."

"But we—"

"Could visit every weekend, and then it would become once a month, then holidays and birthdays, then maybe once a year. No! I'm not abandoning her."

Kathy left after that and we decided we should just be friends. Or she decided, and I was forced to agree. I still see her. Hard not to since we are both teaching at the same school. I heard she was getting serious with one of the science teachers. Most women didn't understand why Jane had to join us or I needed to get someone to stay with her. If I dated anyone, it didn't survive the first time they spent the night to be woken by Jane bursting in my room asking for breakfast and chatting them up while they tried to cover themselves or get dressed.

Changing the subject, Jane asked, "Why did Tom have to leave?" This was an old conversation that always started like this. I knew exactly how the script would go.

"Because he did."

"But, why?" When her mind was set on a subject, she could be as stubborn as a two-year-old.

"Because he hurt you."

"That's what you always say, but I don't remember it."

"That's okay." It was probably better Jane didn't remember. For her, Tom was the fun brother who played with her and made her laugh. I was the mean brother always telling her what she could and couldn't do.

"Is that why Dad left?"

"I guess. Who knows?"

Actually, I did know. Mom said she came back one day to Dad's empty closet and a note on the dining table saying that he had left. He said he couldn't deal with it anymore. Every time he looked at Jane, he was reminded of what happened to her and to Tom. Personally, I think he was following the family tradition of being a drunken loser. I don't know if they ever got divorced, but we never heard from him and Mom never talked about him after he left. She never dated from then until she died.

Another game of *Sorry!*, dinner, and a movie on my computer kept Jane busy and her mind off why Tom and Dad left, at least for the rest of the night. While she was occupied, I packed my truck with fragments of summers spent up here. Not that there was much worth anything. It was mostly old paperbacks, linen, and the odd collection of pots and pans that, like the furniture, had gotten dragged up as families got replacements for home. Deciding to leave most of it, all I loaded was a couple of family albums (which I would go through later to take out pictures of Tom), some quilts and blankets, and a portable record player and records that I knew I could sell to a fellow teacher. I hadn't told Jane, but I was selling the cabin and property. Deaths within the family had resulted in me being the only owner. The realtor said she had a buyer that was interested in doing a scrape-off and building a proper second home. A scrape-off was appropriate. While the cabin and lake may have been part of my family's history, it wasn't a history worth preserving.

"Jane, time for bed. It's a long drive back and I still need to get ready for next week when we get home."

"Okay. Will you play the tickle game with me?"

"NO!"

"Tom and I used to play it when we were up here."

"I know. He shouldn't have. It was wrong!" I was trying hard not to raise my voice. Shouting got Jane upset, which was the last thing I needed.

"Is that why he had to go away?"

"Partly." Speaking more calmly, I hoped to defuse things.

"He had to go away because he played the tickle game?"

"No, I told you. It was because he hurt you."

"You always say that, but I don't remember it. I think you're lying." In the weird world that Jane and I lived in, her thinking I was a liar was the best option.

"Fine. I'm lying. Now go to bed."

After Mom died, I became Jane's guardian and saw the police report and her medical file. Both were very graphic. Even what I had seen in Afghanistan had not prepared me for the description and pictures of the crime scene or the injuries Jane suffered. During the investigation, it came out that Tom had been molesting Jane for a while. But it went beyond that one summer afternoon. Way beyond.

My folks and I were in town. Tom had challenged me to climb one of the taller trees. I fell out and broke my arm. The trip to the hospital in town was long and they didn't know how busy the emergency room would be, so they decided to leave Tom and Jane at the cabin. Having updated the family tradition of addiction from alcohol to drugs, Tom got high on something as soon as we left. The police couldn't determine whether he had lost control or Jane had decided that she didn't want to play his games anymore. When we got back, Tom was gone. Jane was unconscious on the bed, looking like a broken doll. The human body wasn't supposed to bend that way, not the body of a 12-year-old girl. Mom and Dad weren't even sure if she was still alive. After the ambulance took Jane away, I saw that the sheets and mattress were covered in blood. The walls looked like someone had been finger painting with red paint. Mom and Dad found out that Jane had also been raped. Repeatedly. And in every way possible. Tom was picked up by the police the next day while he was hitchhiking. The trial was fast as there was no question what Tom had done to Jane. A few years later, we were informed he had been killed in prison. My parents let the state bury him.

Jane never fully recovered. Physically, most of the broken bones and injuries healed, although her nose had a bend to it and some internal injuries were permanent. I don't like to think about them or how she got them. The part that didn't heal was her mind. It was still stuck in that last innocent summer. The doctors said it was a combination of extreme trauma and physical damage. The police think the blood on the walls was from Tom repeatedly bouncing her head off them with enough force to break her cheek and her nose. She had limited long-term memory and almost no emotional control. What she felt always showed. We got used to her outbursts and that she had to be repeatedly told things. Regular school didn't work, so Mom homeschooled her. Dad left. Mom tried to keep it together and take care of Jane, but she got cancer. That plus my disability got me a quick and early discharge. Mom died soon after I got back. Jane and me were all that was left of the family.

The next morning, we had breakfast and I loaded the generator into the truck. It wasn't much, but I could probably sell it for a few bucks. I explained to Jane we couldn't take baths because there wasn't any water. She insisted she had to take a shower, so I rigged an Afghani field shower with the last jerry can of water I had brought up. Once she was done, we got in the truck and drove away.

"Do I go to work tomorrow?" Jane had a hard time keeping track of what day it was.

"Yeah." Some friends from church owned a flower shop and had hired Jane to help clean the shop and make arrangements. The customers loved her big smile and friendly attitude. Since she didn't have an idea of what arrangements were supposed to be like, she had a flair for original designs that helped the shop's business.

"Good. I like it. Everyone is so friendly, and they let me play with all of the flowers."

"They like you, too." With Jane, it was hard not to.

"When can we come back up here?"

"We can't. I'm selling it."

"Why are you selling the cabin?" Her tone was not good. Any change upset her, and this was a big one.

"Because no one goes there, and we can use the money."

"Tom wouldn't have sold it." And there it was.

"Probably not."

"I like Tom better." There was the little girl anger.

"I know."

Jane went into a pout, playing with the radio until she found a station that was playing a song she liked. After singing along to a string of pop songs, her mood improved.

"Can we stop for ice cream?"

"Sure."

"I love you, Jim Bo, you're the best."

"I know. I love you too, Jane."

31

CONSIDER THE GIRL SINGING

BY FRANK COONS

Spring, and she sings
in the children's choir under
a 40-foot cross and a 30-foot savior,
along with 50 other fifth graders.
And her mouth is the softest O
I've ever seen or heard.

On this evening, I believe
I can hear her individual notes
rising above the rest and directed
at me, the long-ago familiar words:
hallelujah, risen lord, and all
the ancient glories in a rush
of gratitude and guilt.

The young man in me, dressed
in the altar boy's cassock and surplice,
presents himself in almost innocence.
I gather him to me and wonder

at the composite of us. There is nothing
I would trade.

And still she sings of joy and new
beginnings. No, all is not right
with the world, but some things
are right—like this young girl
singing to me in spring. Not only
right, but (say it!), holy.

32

VACANCIES

BY JONATHAN ARENA

A man floats into pure white clouds and comes out the other side to a brilliant blue sky. He lands on his feet, standing on the same clouds he passed through. He looks at his hands, legs, chest, his entire body, and seems confused, like he expected something different.

Theo sits on a hovering chair behind a hovering desk looking upon the man. He adjusts his eyeglasses and surveys the large screen in front of him. He's had a long day and his shift ends after this evaluation. Then he can go home. Home, sweet home.

"Is this—" the man begins to ask.

"Yes," Theo interrupts. He hates that question. Not because it is a bad one, it's the most logical, but because he's just been asked it too many times. Everyone asks it. Sometimes more than once.

Columns and columns of information spread across the screen. It begins with the man's birth and sorts through his entire life history. All the data, absolutely everything. Certain events are highlighted. Theo speeds through them.

The screen calculates the verdict. It does not take long. Gatekeepers can override it but only in special cases. And nowadays, overriding is highly frowned upon. New policies prohibit most of it. Tons of paperwork if you do. Tons of scrutiny from management too. Some have even been fired over it.

"Dwayne Richardson," Theo reads from the screen. "Age forty-three. Cause of death: stabbed—by an eleven-year-old girl." He looks to the man standing before him. An unusual death to say the least. "Twenty-nine times in the neck and chest?"

"That bitch—" the man mumbles under his breath.

"Excuse me?"

"I didn't deserve that. I was a decent man. I provided."

"Well, let's see," Theo reads more. "Your childhood looks normal. Father was an alcoholic, but whose wasn't back then? So naturally, you became an alcoholic by age seventeen. Able to keep your nose relatively clean with the law, that's good. Married, divorced, married again. The second one was for the last three years. She was previously married too and had a young daughter. Eleven years old."

Theo looks from the screen and finds the man's eyes. They lock and never let go. The discontent he had for the man quickly turns to anger and disgust. Theo can see the guilt from where he sits. The man reeks of it.

"That's where it gets bad, Dwayne. Very bad."

The man hangs his head in shame. He knows he's guilty. He knows he doesn't deserve to go to Heaven. Theo slams a gavel onto the desk and the man drops through the clouds and falls below. He is sentenced to Hell.

Theo looks to his watch. The end of his shift. He goes to sign off from the screen but another death is loaded and appears before he can cancel. A young girl floats through the clouds and stands in front of his desk. Dwayne Richardson was supposed to be the last in his queue. His shift is supposed to be over. He was not *supposed* to get any more deaths.

What the Hell?

The girl bounces up and down on the soft cloud and giggles. It's nearly contagious, but Theo frowns harder to fight it off. He hates when children end up in his queue. He always seems to get all the young ones. He had wanted a daughter so much when he was alive. Most men wanted boys, but he wanted a daughter. He and his wife failed to bring either into the world.

"Hello, mister," she says.

"Hello." He watches her life information take over the screen. It's short, only eleven years. Killed by shotgun.

Mary Rose is her name. To say her life was turbulent is an understatement. Drug-addicted mother, new school every year, a revolving door of men in her mother's life.

Theo looks at the young girl and fixes his glasses. She murdered a man right at the end of her short life. She stabbed her stepfather with a knife twenty-nine times. He cannot believe it.

It's her.

The screen tells him murder is always a Hell sentence unless in warfare or self-defense. You shall not murder. It's one of the commandments. Dishonoring a commandment will always send you to Hell, except for those two special occasions. But is her case included in self-defense? Dwayne was asleep on the couch when she killed him. That's the kicker. He was doing nothing to her in the moment, and the policies are clear about that.

The screen delivers the verdict that this deserves a Hell sentence. Age is no factor.

Theo shakes his head. Murder is never the answer, but he cannot blame her for what she did. He would want his hypothetical daughter to do the same in her shoes. Ridding the world of a man like that should not be a hard decision.

And her own death came one minute and forty-two seconds after her stepfather took his last breath. Twelve-gauge buckshot spread across her face and killed her instantly.

Her mother pulled the trigger.

"Hi." She scares the shit out of him. He hadn't heard her approach his desk. She stands right next to him, eyes wide and staring, as children do.

"Hi." Theo forces a smile. He's a little scared in her presence. She did just stab a man twenty-nine times. And now look at her. She seems like any other happy eleven-year-old girl.

"Is this Heaven?" she asks.

Theo nods. That question again.

"I knew it! I knew God would understand. He deserved it."

"Your stepfather?"

"He will *never* be my stepfather," she says with furrowed brows, then relaxes her face and smiles out of nowhere. "I bet he's in Hell now. He is going to burn for eternity. Right? Isn't that what happens?"

"Hell is a cold, dark place, so no burning. Eternity though, yes."

"And you're the Gatekeeper of Heaven?" she asks, smile growing by the word.

"Well, sort of. There are a lot of gatekeepers, and we all work different gates, like an airport. Over a hundred of us across all shifts now. Lots of folk dying these days. But it's just a job, you know. Pays the bills."

"Just a job? You get to welcome people to Heaven for a *job!* That's amazing!"

"Well, the hours are long. Break room is small. And there's not exactly a retirement age."

"May I welcome the next person with you?"

"No, my shift is over." He looks back over to the screen. "No more welcoming today. And to be honest, there isn't much welcoming these days."

"What do you mean?"

"The new policies are very strict. Heaven has never been so hard to get into, and to be honest, humanity isn't looking great right now either."

Theo decides the case of Mary Rose *was* self-defense. Therefore, it follows the new policies, and there are no exceptions to the policies. They must be followed. He slams the gavel and Mary Rose does not fall through the clouds. She is sentenced to Heaven. She wraps her arms around Theo with all her strength. Her warmth spreads through his body and he smiles and hugs her back.

A woman floats from the clouds and stands before the desk.

"Oh, come on!" Theo says. Another death snuck in before he could sign off. His shift is supposed to be over. To top it off, he doesn't even get overtime pay this week since he called out sick on Tuesday.

The woman is crying and falls to her knees. She buries her face in her hands as tears flow between her fingers.

Mary Rose peers around the desk at the woman.

Their eyes meet.

"Oh baby!" The woman rushes over to her and lays kiss after kiss on her forehead, cheek, nose. "I'm so sorry, baby! Forgive me! Please forgive me!"

The woman's information falls down the screen like a curtain. Rachel McNeil. Thirty-seven years old. Married, divorced, married again. Mother of an eleven-year-old daughter.

Theo reads further. He needs to know.

Rachel heard the commotion from the other room and thought the worst. She grabbed Dwayne's shotgun that rested on the wall. It was loaded. She rushed into the living room to see her bloodied daughter standing over a stabbed-up corpse—her husband.

Her finger reacted. One shot fired. She screamed.

Theo breathes again. The gunshot was accidental.

Rachel stared at the two bodies in the living room for quite some time before moving again. Her Mary Rose did this. Why would she do this? She was always so sweet.

Then it hit her, and it hit her hard. The little details suddenly pieced themselves together to make a whole. Her spine shivered as the idea flooded her mind, her every sense. It was difficult to breathe. She couldn't live on.

Theo glances at the mother and daughter beside him. They embrace and cry on each other's shoulders.

"I'm so sorry," her mother weeps. "I had no idea."

Mary Rose cries harder. The way the two bodies form around

each other seems surreal to Theo. Love binds them and appears to relieve some of the pain.

But there's a lot more to Rachel's story. Five misdemeanors, one felony. She spent a total of thirteen months in prison on three different occasions. But all of that was before she gave birth to Mary Rose. She cleaned up her act after having a baby, only two relapses. She became a better person, but still struggled to attract a decent man. She started to settle.

The screen highlights particular life events from Rachel. She has many offenses to her name. She helped a friend overdose. She did everything for him. Figured the dosage, set it all up, then did it with him. He overdosed. She did not.

Theo looks away from the screen. Rachel and Mary Rose remain tightly bound together. Tears spill from eyes and snot runs from noses.

"I love you so much, baby," Rachel says.

"I love you too, Mommy."

Theo keeps reading.

Rachel was directly involved in another death. Drunk driving in high school. Her best friend in the passenger seat died instantly. That was the primer to the rest of her life, but the end was the worst of all.

Kills daughter with shotgun. Kills self with shotgun.

The screen suggests a Hell sentence for Rachel McNeil. Demands it. The new policies are crystal clear about who is allowed and who is not allowed into Heaven. The policies allow no room for exceptions and must be followed. Suicide is especially clear.

Theo remembered his wife and her many problems on Earth. He loved her despite all of it. They were married for forty-seven years, but he died first. He applied to this job in hopes of welcoming her. He dreamed about it. Fantasized about it.

But it's been sixty-four years.

He must accept it.

She will not be joining him in the clouds.

Theo reviews Rachel's good qualities once again. Loving mother, no drugs for six years, faithful wife. She grew and developed as the years went on. She always strove to be a better person. She *was* a better person.

Mary Rose breaks from her mother's embrace and looks at Theo. She wipes her eyes and nose and her cute smile returns.

"This is my new friend," she says, pointing at him. "But I never got your name, mister."

"It's Theo," he says and shakes Rachel's trembling hand. "Nice to meet you."

"You as well," Rachel says. "Thank you so much. Thank you, thank you, thank you."

"For what?"

"Bringing us together. Welcoming us to Heaven."

He smiles faintly and glances at the screen. It flashes with the verdict. Rachel needs to be sentenced to Hell. No exceptions.

"Are you an angel?" Rachel asks. The glimmer of a smile emerges on her face.

Theo chuckles. "No, no, I'm just a regular guy. Who died. And this is just a job."

"Just a job?" she asks with blanketing confusion. "You get to welcome people to Heaven! How amazing is that?"

Theo laughs for real this time. Like mother, like daughter. He gazes upon the two of them with a genuine smile. Love radiates from their souls and he can feel it. How can he possibly separate them? How can he sentence her to Hell?

Mary Rose glances at the screen and the smile vanishes from her face. She gestures to her mother. Rachel gasps in horror.

All eyes on Theo. Silence lingers in the air like a dark cloud.

He slams the gavel down with authority. His authority.

Rachel remains above the clouds just like Mary Rose. She is sentenced to Heaven. Another smile and kiss between the mother and daughter.

Another beautiful moment.

Theo finally signs off from the screen. *Thank God!* His shift is over. He takes a deep breath and gathers his belongings for the last time. All of this will surely get him fired but he is okay with that. Relieved, actually.

"Well," Mary Rose slips her hand into Theo's and flashes a smile impossible to say no to, "aren't you going to show us around?"

33

EVERY WOUND IS A PORTAL

BY FRANK COONS

I
On nights when you
   are the loon's call
ululating over unusually
   calm water,
and I am the sturm und drang
   of the magpie
on a branch of hawthorn,
   I wonder how we were able
to shape space to fit into
   our one dimension.

II
Every wound is a portal
   where demons escape
& angels enter with lanterns.
   By now we must be
nearly sanctified & bright
   as the dog star.

When I think of the om in us,
   something resembling peace
descends, though it stings
   beautifully, & sizzling,
leaves a little cicatrix.

III
I remember only increments of time
   before you, small vignettes,
like moths fluttering against the pane.
   They can't get in because they
can't get in because they have
   been replaced by the you of you
in me, the near
   and now of you.

34

RISING FROM DISASTER

BY BILLIE HOLLADAY SKELLEY

At 5:41 p.m. on May 22, 2011, the city of Joplin, Missouri was hit by an EF-5 tornado.

When I first saw the aftermath of the tornado, I was struck by how quickly one's world can be turned upside down. Everything I had grown accustomed to and taken for granted had changed. Initially, I was at a loss to understand what had happened. My mind searched for reasons, but there was no logic to be found. I had to compartmentalize my encounters just to function. I was so overwhelmed by anxiety, confusion, and fear that events become fragmented, and many of these fragments have become indelible memories.

FIRST FRAGMENT:

I am relieved to discover that the walls of our house are still standing. Our roof is damaged. Shingles are everywhere, but no serious leaks seem to have occurred. Television and internet are gone, but by some miracle we still have electricity. A huge Bradford pear, a tree planted with my own hands twenty-five years ago, has fallen against the dining room window.

Second Fragment:

Through the rain and cloudy skies, I realize the damage to our yard is considerable. Huge trees are crumpled and split like tooth-picks. Pieces of jagged wood cover the ground. Gigantic limbs and split branches lay across the road and driveway, prohibiting move-ment by vehicles. Bushes are tossed about like tumbleweeds, and leaves are scattered everywhere. Pink insulation hangs from the trees that still stand. It resembles the Spanish moss that drapes live oaks in the South, but the color looks strange and unnatural. We do not have Spanish moss in Joplin, and my mind rails against the idea.

In the backyard, a forty-foot section of wooden fence is woven between a stand of trees. I have never seen it before and have no idea in what yard it was previously located. A portion of a child's plastic castle, various toys, and a silver helmet—perhaps from a motorcyclist —are also present. None of it is ours.

The most astonishing thing I witness is in the front yard. On a slope rising toward the street, perhaps a hundred wooden stakes are equidistantly jammed into the earth. Each is approximately the size of a yardstick, and they look as if a meticulous giant forcibly stabbed them in a pattern across the front yard. An engineer could not have arranged them any better, for they are all at the same angle and equal distances apart. Like the pink hanging moss, however, it seems so unnatural. There is a sinister nature to it. I want to remove them, but there is no time. I have to check on my elderly mother and stepfather.

Third Fragment:

Since the roads are blocked, I walk. At Schifferdecker and Twenty-Sixth Street, I encounter the National Guard, and a U. S. marshal gives me a ride on an ATV to my parents' house. I've never ridden on an ATV, and this ride adds to the surreal nature of every-thing that is happening. The images along the way are disconcerting. Anxiety and fear begin to overwhelm me.

The damage is unbelievable and catastrophic. The sheer scope of the devastation is hard to process. As far as I can see, houses are crumpled and leveled. Some appear to have been moved, and others are not there at all. Whole neighborhoods have been obliterated. Much of the landscape is flattened. Electrical poles and wires cover the ground. Splintered wood, nails, and glass lay in scattered piles. It looks like a war zone. It is all so wrong.

Huge pieces of metal siding are wrapped around denuded trees. A washing machine, with its lid open, sits high above the ground in what is left of a large oak. A mattress hangs from a flagpole. One car is standing on its headlights, and several others are crumpled together in a pile like a child's discarded toys. The top portion of a huge stuffed bear, severed at the waist, lies in a ditch. It looks back at me as we pass.

None of this can be real. It has to be a nightmare that I will wake from soon.

The few people I see in the neighborhood appear okay, but dazed. They all have a vacant look in their eyes. The ATV can only get so close to my destination. As it drops me off, I hear a middle-aged woman call out, "God, I don't know what we've done wrong. Just tell us what we've done wrong, and we'll stop." I don't know what to say to her. I'm tempted to put my hands over my ears so I don't have to listen. Instead, I reach out and give her a hug.

FOURTH FRAGMENT:

I hurry toward my parents' house. At least, I think it's their house. I hardly recognize it. I want to close my eyes and run away, but I cannot.

Their home is disfigured and distorted. The front is covered by a heavy, white, tarp-like material from the roof of a nearby elementary school. Circling the house, I see their crushed deck, shattered fencing, and broken and split trees. Windows are cracked or blown out. Glass and wood litter the ground. The garage door is twisted and mangled, but it is partially open. Squeezing through this opening and praying my parents have survived uninjured, I enter the house.

I find my 88-year-old mother sitting in a chair, surrounded by towels, in what is left of the family room. She is covered in blankets.

My stepfather quickly recounts what they have been through. They were unable to reach an interior bathroom and its protective tub because they had so little time before the tornado hit. Consequently, my stepfather had covered my mother in the hallway with his own body. Looking around, it's clear he saved her life.

I feel a sudden rush of rain, and for the first time I realize two-thirds of their roof is missing. Almost all of their belongings that I can see are soaked. My stepfather has pulled my mother's chair to the only section of the house where the roof is still intact.

The bedrooms of the house are pretty well demolished. In the bathroom, the sliding glass doors on the tub are twisted off their tracks and have been forced through the back of the unit. Had my mother and stepfather made it to their desired destination, they surely would have been killed.

My parents have no electricity, no running water, and nothing else that I can classify as "functioning." I know they cannot remain in their home. Fortunately, my brother is able to take them to his house. In my dazed state, I have no idea how he got there or how he got them out.

I begin trying to save some of my parents' clothes, papers, and other belongings by pushing them into the remaining dry area where the segment of roofing remains. I am able to get some important items covered, but the rain continues. As I stare up into the sky from this roofless room and feel the rain on my face, I am once again overwhelmed by the feeling that this is all so wrong.

· · ·

The police stop by to tell me I need to secure the house, especially the garage, so looters are not tempted to take things. I go outside to evaluate how to "secure the house."

As I am standing in the rain, staring at the front of the house, a man appears at my side. His arrival is like magic. I could swear he just materialized out of the soaked earth. This man is short, wiry, and middle-aged. His red shirt and jeans are wet. I am so startled I cannot speak.

"Do you want me to cover the roof with that tarp?" he asks.

I realize a tarp would help keep out the rain, so I nod.

I watch as he cuts a piece of the massive white tarp that covers the front of the house and carries it up to the roof. He moves with ease, like a squirrel climbing a tree. I watch in amazement until I realize I am chilled from the rain. I go back into the house and keep moving books and clothes under the intact section of the roof. When I fill up that area, I go back outside to check on the "magic" man.

He has cut a piece of the tarp to cover the garage door. Staples hold it in place at the top and on one side, but the other side is open so I can come and go. The garage is secure, and its contents are hidden from the outside world. I slip through the open side of the tarp to thank this clever, talented man, but he is gone. I never even got his name. He has covered most of the roof, and I am so relieved and grateful.

Though it seems like minutes, hours have passed. It is getting late, and I need to get home. Without an ATV to spur me through the chaos this time, I have to walk. Up close, it's harder to compartmentalize all that is happening. Scenes come rushing in, not waiting to be stratified and labeled.

The neighborhoods I walk through are alive with sawing sounds and yelling voices. Everywhere, people are struggling to find some normalcy. I realize that, like me, they are looking for something familiar to hold on to in the chaos. A man walking by says it is much worse toward Range Line Road. Worse is hard to believe as I survey the damage all around me.

What should have been a thirty-minute walk home instead takes about an hour and a half because of the debris and destruction. I talk with people along the way and each story seems more horrific and impossible than the last.

There are reports of airborne cars, babies torn from their mothers' arms by the devilish wind, and severed limbs being found in strange locations. One hospital is closed because of the damage it suffered. Patients are being moved to other towns for care.

The power unleashed by the storm is more and more apparent. No longer will I imagine Mother Nature as a gentle lady, dressed in a long white gown, softly caressing a flower petal. She is a raging bull wildly knocking down houses, trees, or anything else in her path—not for any reason, but just because she can.

Finally, I reach my driveway, but I do not recognize what I see as home. The yard is not the same. The house is not right. It is standing, however, with a somewhat intact roof, and I say a prayer of thanks. Now that no one is around, I let myself cry.

Sixth Fragment:

A week goes by. The struggle for a return to normalcy continues. Phone service is intermittent. Still no television or internet, but I have found a radio. A radio announcer confirms that an outside world still exists and gives daily updates. I come to regard him as a friend because he gives order and structure to my days. I want to hear his voice and learn the news so I can fill in the gaps about what is happening.

From radio broadcasts and neighbors, I learn that the winds during the tornado are believed to have exceeded two hundred miles per hour. Pieces of wood have been found rammed straight through concrete curbs. Every school my children attended, from grade school to high school, is either badly damaged or completely destroyed. I hear about a dental office that has been totally blown away. There is no evidence that the office was ever there. Dental chairs, x-ray machines, and file cabinets are all gone. Medical records from the damaged hospital are being found on lawns an hour's drive away. People are also still looking for loved ones.

With help, I've discarded the scattered tree limbs obstructing our driveway and the Bradford pear covering the dining room window. I pick up most of the shingles, and I remove the sinister, invading stakes in the front yard.

SEVENTH FRAGMENT:

One of the most harrowing events occurs when I find two empty infant car seats in a stand of trees behind our house. I notify the police because we know children are still missing. The police come, and we form a line of people to walk the area and look for the seats' occupants. I do not want to find a baby. With each step, I look, but I do not want to see anything. I cannot imagine a mother waiting for news about her child. The police finally conclude no infant can be located. Either the children were blown further away, or the seats were empty. One of the policemen takes the seats in the hope that parents may recognize them. It is hard to imagine trying to identify an empty car seat. My mind refuses to go there.

EIGHTH FRAGMENT:

I make daily trips to my parents' home to continue trying to salvage some of their belongings, but there is less and less to save. I now put damaged items and rubbish near the curb for the city to haul away. What started as a small mound is now a huge mountain.

During this process, another harrowing event occurs. One day, as I am carrying trash to the curb, a man informs me that his cadaver dog got a hit on the crawlspace under my parents' house. My mind races. I thought I had checked everywhere, but I never looked in the crawlspace. The man searches, but fortunately, he does not find anything. It must have been a false hit. He remarks that there is so much debris, it is confusing for the dog.

Ninth Fragment:

A month passes by quickly. The struggle continues, but on different levels. Volunteers bring water and food. One day a truck full of nurses goes through the neighborhood giving tetanus shots. They give me an injection because I do not remember when I last had one.

The official word is that the tornado killed at least 160 people and injured more than 900. This gigantic twister cut a six-mile swath, three-quarters of a mile wide, through the city. I realize with sadness that it destroyed a third of my hometown. An estimated 8,000 structures were damaged or demolished because of this monstrous force of nature. It has taken schools, businesses, firehouses, churches, homes, and one hospital. EF-5 tornados, it seems, do not discriminate when it comes to people or buildings. The damage is estimated to be in the billions of dollars.

Tenth Fragment:

I volunteer to help with the rebuilding efforts coordinated by Habitat for Humanity. The morning of my assigned work day, I hesitate to go. I am physically tired and mentally exhausted. I will have to walk to the site, and I'm not sure how useful I can be. I eventually decide it is the right thing to do.

I arrive at the site and meet some of my fellow volunteers. They are young, and some say they are from Saudi Arabia. God forgive me! I hesitate to walk two miles, and these people travel halfway around the world to help.

That day, I learn how to use a nail gun—a new skill for me. I successfully install several windows in a home. Creating something in the midst of destruction is therapeutic, and I am glad a family in need will have a new place to live.

As the rebuilding continues, volunteers and donations to aid Joplin's recovery come from across the nation and around the world. I am grateful for the outpouring of assistance. For the first time since the disaster, I have hope for the future. It occurs to me that weather disasters are a time when Mother Nature can be at her worst, but it is also a time when human beings can be at their best.

ELEVENTH FRAGMENT:

A year has gone by. Joplin continues to rebuild, and the building efforts for families often include putting in a safe room or twister safe. Beyond just homes, schools and churches are also adding these rooms to protect large numbers of people in the future.

We found a new home for my parents. Like other residents of Joplin who survived the tornado, I think they are on the mend, but sometimes it is hard to tell. My mother has no memory of the storm, but my stepfather recalls it all too vividly.

Violent storms are a part of life in the Midwest, but this particular tornado was different. The scope of its destruction has left permanent scars, and we realize life as we know it can be attacked and destroyed again—at any minute. Nothing can be taken for granted.

TWELFTH AND CONTINUING FRAGMENTS:

Almost eight years have passed since the 2011 tornado, and most of the city of Joplin has been restored. People literally came from all around the globe to help, and the efforts and compassion of both residents and volunteers have worked miracles.

The 2011 tornado devastated Joplin, but it also provided an opportunity for residents to rise from the destruction stronger and improved. The disaster gave us a chance to work together, side by side, not only to rebuild, but also to create an improved sense of community. Our town has experienced a renewal—a sort of rebirth of its citizens—and our sense of community is stronger because we have suffered together in loss, been supportive of each other during struggles, and built unifying bonds in our efforts to recover. The tornado caused great strife and sorrow, but it also led to positive changes. It gave us an opportunity to grow as a community and to grow as individuals.

For me, the disaster provided an opportunity to explore my own personal mettle and strength of character. I discovered that I am stronger and more resilient than I ever imagined. Today, I am more involved in my local community, more responsive to the needs of those affected by disasters, and more attentive to research directed at decreasing the negative impact of weather-related disasters. I have hope for the future, and I have learned to embrace challenges as opportunities for growth and improvement.

Like the mythical phoenix, Joplin has risen from the ashes and been reborn to a new life. Our new world is different, however, because we are different. We have been changed forever.

35

ORCHARD

BY MARGERY DORFMEISTER

Where is the sweetness now?
Petals look the same
pink-rimmed tufts of white
against a Wedgewood sky.
But where am I
the child intoxicated
by their scent
hugging herself
half-balanced in
a crooked Y?

Bees still buzz
and tanagers tip wings
in soft salute
but I have tasted bitter fruit
of many-a fallen flower
and lost the power
to sense the scent
of whiteness.

36

THE PATCH

BY JIM KROEPFL

Jeremiah and Dallin were flashing plastic behind the shelter before checking the fishing lines. That was everything on the Patch. Flashing and fishing. We'd staked out a nice chunk of plasti-swamp and were creating as much hard-float as we could before the ocean turned awful.

I know I might never go back. Never see the continent again. I'm okay with that. I've been lied to on the mainland. I've been hungry on the mainland. I've never been hungry with Jeremiah. And I knew he wasn't going to stay where we were. Jeremiah, my husband, was a man who would find providence.

His younger brother Dallin, on the other hand, is as impulsive as Mercury. But I think they both believe we're building a new place for everyone back on mainland. A place with maybe a bit more promise. A place that's maybe a bit more safe.

We'd come out on the *Exodus*. She's slow, but stable, and if you think you might encounter a rough Pacific, always take stable. I was starting to wonder if we'd gotten off course. But on the fourth day, we were all on deck and a screech from a curious seagull spun us around.

I don't know how, but a thousand miles from mainland, a seagull is still going to find trash.

The Patch comes on slow. Floating chunks of garbage here and there, tangles of netting and sludge, random lost buoys. You don't notice the plastic right away. It mostly floats below the surface in tiny bits.

Thick water, Jeremiah calls it. He's the smartest man I know.

It wasn't long before we were deep in it. A world of trash bound together in a plastic soup. You have to be careful not to explore where the water is too dense. You could get stuck in the sludge and wind up dying a slow, nasty death. Or you could run into raiders and die a quick death, if you're lucky.

We searched for days before finding the right place. A spot brimming with good material and protected by floating garbage islands. We set up solar and radar and fuel stills, and got to flashing plastic together with heat. We already built a fifty-by-fifty-foot platform along with a rough shelter and a berth for the *Exodus*.

We didn't need to worry about starving, though it's pretty much only fish, seagull, and seaweed. It's amazing how creative I've gotten with just those three ingredients. Salt is the key. We've been making dirt, collecting anything that might decompose. Anything. And the plastic particles make good sand to even out the muck. It stinks beyond belief, but it draws the gulls, and they're good bait.

We were starting to think we could actually survive. Electricity, salt, and the stars. Jeremiah has grand plans to grow things. Even wheat.

"When you can make bread," Jeremiah says. "God is with you."

A new start.

"Sarah, bring us two more flasher tanks," Jeremiah called out, his back to me as I came up behind him carrying the tanks. "We've still got an hour of daylight. Let's get another form done."

I tapped him on the shoulder, nodded at the tanks, not too sassily, and headed back to the refuse beds.

I understood his worry. Surface is life. We had food, water, and a bit of a shelter. But could we stay afloat when the ocean decided to throw us a storm? That would take a lot of surface. Probably more than we had.

When I married Jeremiah, I knew he wanted to pioneer the Patch. And I loved the idea of it. Just the three of us. Jeremiah, Dallin, and me. We wouldn't answer to anybody, and there wouldn't be problems between people, nor all the things in Jeremiah's memories about the mainland that disturb his sleep. I'm glad I'm younger and don't have as many memories of the time before.

Everything was going according to plan, except for the Babbits, who colonized a huge hunk of plastic about five miles to the south. There's smoke, thick and black, all day, every day. The Babbits are a big family, thirty or more. They run at least three tugs. Rusty and loud, but faster than you'd expect.

Jeremiah wouldn't let us spend time with them, even when we were working within sight of each other. "The best neighbors are never seen," he said. I think Jeremiah dreams about past neighbors.

We'd met some of the Babbits once when one of their smaller boats was lost. They eased up to our platform, and the crew was scruffy. Absolute flotsam. A man came to the bow. He was younger than the others, but he stood in a way that commanded attention.

"I'm Jeffrey Babbit from over there." He nodded to the south, to the towering black cloud. "Seen a small shuttle about?"

"Nope," Jeremiah called back. "Nothing at all."

"Sorry to disturb you," the young man said. Then he nodded to the man at the wheel and they headed back out. After that, we'd seen each other now and then; we'd wave, but the two families never spoke.

Once we'd stabilized the solar and gotten the fuel stills running and put together a decent enough surface, Jeremiah decided we should take the *Exodus* exploring and see what we could salvage. Fuel is precious, but so is having enough mass to live on when bad water comes. If we found something big enough to make a difference, it would be worth it. We made sure the battery was charged, the water was full, the fuel tanks were topped, and took off.

We pushed out in the *Exodus* through the sea of plastic, and it was amazingly still. Miles and miles of undecomposed trash, chunks of wood, and the endless soup of plastic particles. All the discarded materials from another time, waiting to be turned into a new continent. It wasn't beautiful, but it was hope.

We headed west for an hour before we saw the ship. A half-capsized, small freighter floating on a perfect list.

I felt the excitement in all of us. Even Jeremiah. But he held back.

"What's wrong?" Dallin asked.

"Shush," Jeremiah warned.

Nothing about the freighter appeared suspicious, but Jeremiah must have noticed something. He motioned to Dallin to put the *Exodus* in neutral. The boat slowed reluctantly, leaving a reverse wake of open water in the stew around us.

"Who's there?" a voice called out from the half-sunken ship. A masculine voice. Unwelcoming. Rough as sea wood. A few gulls flew up from the surface, annoyed by the disturbance of their floating buffet.

Of course, there are other people on the Patch beyond just the Babbits. Probably many. But this was the first time we'd encountered any of them.

Jeremiah looked back at me and our eyes held before he called out to the languishing ship, "We're just researchers."

"Come on over, *researchers*. We need help." There was nothing desperate or urgent in the voice. A chill seeped up my spine.

Jeremiah looked back at Dallin. "Ease back," he said, low and easy beneath the gulls' screeches. The lines in his forehead clued me in. We were two men and one woman in the middle of the ocean.

"Wait! Don't leave," the voice directed from the listing ship.

Jeremiah nodded to Dallin to keep moving backward. He touched the side of the dry box, the one with the shotgun. I couldn't tell if it was a signal or just a gesture to reassure himself. The hollows of his cheeks were tenser than I've ever seen them.

When we heard the start-up of an engine, Jeremiah yelled, "Go. Go. Go." He lurched to the wheel, grabbed it from Dallin, and spun it while gunning the throttle. We veered in a gut-wrenching one-eighty.

A boat jetted out from behind the capsized ship. Smaller than ours. Probably faster.

"Raiders!" Dallin shouted over the engine.

Jeremiah headed south, not toward our home. My heart began pounding so hard it hurt to breathe. Raiders kill you and take all you have.

The *Exodus* surged through the plastic, but she's only so fast. The raiders' boat began gaining on us.

"Take the wheel," Jeremiah yelled to Dallin. "Run her as fast as you can." He grabbed Dallin's shoulder and pointed south. "That way."

He whirled toward me. "Sarah, help him get through the plastic. Watch out for chunks!"

The raiders' boat was getting closer, and I saw three men. And I saw their guns. I tried to focus on the water, directing Dallin, hoping to avoid a collision. He swerved us around a sharp mass and Jeremiah lurched to the floor. He crawled over to the dry box and managed to get out the shotgun and some shells.

One shotgun wouldn't do us much good, unless we were right next to the raiders' boat. That's when I knew we couldn't outrun them.

Jeremiah was loading the shotgun as the boat moved beside us. Two of the men were aiming rifles just as Dallin swerved the boat to make a harder target. They shot off a few rounds and we heard a bullet slam through the bow. Then another.

"Get down, Sarah," Jeremiah yelled before blasting off a shot at the raiders.

They moved in front of us, well within range of their rifles. If they'd hit the fuel tank or the engine, we were done for.

That's when I heard the horn.

Dallin veered right, and I scanned the surface of garbage just as a rusty tug pulled out from a tall trash island.

"It's the Babbits," I yelled, pointing toward their tug.

They ran straight toward the raiders' boat, which made a hard right, circling away from the tug. The raiders cut back in front of us, way too close.

Jeremiah fired off another round, almost within range this time. The raiders turned away, which sent them back toward the tug.

Three Babbits aimed rifles at the raiders. There was no way their tug could chase down the raiders, but the Babbits landed a few good shots before the raiders' boat pulled out of range. One of the raiders slumped forward and I saw blood on his shirt.

The Babbits pursued the raiders for a few hundred yards before giving up the chase and trolling back. Jeremiah only loosened his grip on the shotgun when the tug pulled up next to us.

"Is everybody all right?" An older Babbit called out.

"We're all good," Jeremiah said. "Thanks to you." I heard a slight tremor in his voice, the smallest quiver that probably only I noticed.

"We've had trouble with them before. I'd avoid that area to the northwest if you're on your own."

Jeffrey Babbit eyed the bullet holes in the bow of the *Exodus*. "Your boat seaworthy? Can you make it back?"

"Think so," Jeremiah answered, and there's something different in his voice. Something accepting. "I owe you."

"Neighbors are neighbors."

For the next few weeks, we kept a watch but didn't see the raiders again. I'm sure it's due to our neighbors, the Babbits. We see them more often, and Jeremiah even invited them over once we get the settlement further along and can entertain properly. I'm starting to think about how to cook fish for thirty people.

For the neighbors.

37

MILKWEED

BY MEGAN E. FREEMAN

long after the monarchs
were only memories
and stuff of myth

our grandmothers
would place the fragile caskets
in our palms and whisper

see child?
they left their footprints
on the inner satin

I promise, child,
I promise.
they were real.

38

A REASON FOR TABLES AND CHAIRS

BY SANDRA MCGARRY

Magdalena says
blooms
on the hillside
near her home
so far away
as if she could
walk out the door
pick a vase's worth
for a table when asked
a thing she misses.

Her apron tied
bow in front
bright with stains
from hard work
down to the bone
she uses
to make soup
we hunger for.

With a broad smile
brown eyes dancing
perhaps to an invisible
flamenco guitar, she
says when it's served:

This recipe crossed the border
in a brown-skin body
that held little English and
a heart-full of left-behinds.

Ma-ma with words
to get the lizard
out of the soup.
Abuela laughing
hard into a long belch.
My chicken living
another day.
My family loves, too.
Eat.
It is a reason for tables and chairs.

39

FROM HOUSE TO HOME

BY R.C. SYDNEY

Kaylie fought to turn the key in the lock before she pushed once, then twice, barely managing to shove the mountain of stuff behind her apartment door enough to squeeze inside.

Her cell rang, muffled.

"Not right now," she sang to the cheery ringtone.

The door tried to fall shut on her halfway through her struggle.

"Come on you stupid—" With a final yank, she saved her foot from amputation. The door slammed shut. A precarious pile of boxes stacked behind it toppled with three dull thumps and a shatter that made Kaylie flinch.

Oops.

Well, it'd been six months or so since she'd moved: whatever that was, she probably didn't need it. She'd clean up later.

She sighed, glad to be home. She tied her hair—brown, *not* blonde, thank you—up in a bun. She chucked her keys in the general vicinity of the counter and tossed a handful of mail onto the table. Two letters, stamped in angry red, promptly slid off the massive pile already sitting there. No biggie; she mostly ate in the living room anyway. She slid her bag off her shoulder to the floor next to boxes of utensils and pot lids.

Kaylie hummed to herself as she glanced over the take-out menus on her fridge. Pulling out her phone, she skipped past the missed call from "Caller Unknown," found the restaurant's number, and dialed.

"Hey, Nate! Yeah, it's me again." She kicked her shoes off by the dishwasher, then picked her way around heaps of clothes to the living room. "Yeah, my usual please. No, I guess you don't need my card number anymore, do you?" She laughed. "Well, tell Jen to throw an extra ten on there for tip if she'll stop at a drive-thru and pick me up a coffee. Yes, Nate, I know it's not policy but come on! I've had *three* shifts in the last *two* days . . . What, you don't have bills? I'm drowning here."

She dropped onto the couch, punching the ever-present pillows and blankets into a comfortable arrangement. Then had to undo all her work to look for the remote.

"What if I have her grab you one, too?" She paused. "Thanks! I don't care what everyone else says, you're the best." She laughed again and hung up.

The remote was underneath the couch cushions. Between the blankets, pillows, and pile of laundry, she had no clue how it even got down there. Aggrieved, she flopped back down to flip through the channels. Something good *had* to be on.

Thirty minutes and a knock later, she gave Jen a hug goodbye then swept the stale containers off her coffee table onto the floor, making room for the fresh ones filled with steaming meat, rice, and—Jen was her best friend, oh my God—a double helping of dessert. Kaylie dug in, sipping at her triple mocha between forkfuls of saucy goodness.

Heaven. Pure heaven.

Just as she swiped up the chocolate syrup with a fingertip, and the sexy Heath knelt on one knee in the sunset, the phone rang again. Of course it did. She shot it the stink eye, then answered anyway.

"Hello?"

A smooth professional voice said, "Hello, I'm looking for a Kaylie MacCullagh?"

"That's me," she said, her tone customer-service bright. "What can I do for you?"

"My name is Trevor. I represent the Stageman and Clarke law firm. I'm calling because we've not heard from you, though our records show you signed for the packet we sent. Did you need any help deciphering the documents? Or did you need more time to look them over? We need a reply as soon as possible."

Kaylie glanced guiltily towards the kitchen's mountain of unopened mail. She didn't remember signing for anything, but that wasn't surprising.

This could take a day or two . . .

"If I needed more time, how much could you give me?"

Her Great-aunt Clara had passed away and left her the old manor, built nearly two hundred years ago when the family had come over from the old country. Kaylie remembered her aunt. A kind woman who let a young girl run around the house, play with the knockers, and jump on the antique furniture. Clara had shown her small magic tricks. A woman she hadn't talked to or thought of in years, and now she was inheriting her house.

The conditional clause for Kaylie receiving the house was that she had to live in it for a minimum of three months before she gained full rights to the estate. After those three months, Kaylie could choose to keep the house or sell it. However, those three months were nonnegotiable. So she pulled all her vacation time and put in a leave of absence for the rest of it. She would still have a job when she returned. Barely.

Now here she was, having driven nearly twelve hours upstate, into the mountains, staring in disbelief at the manor before her.

What? This was the house?

Kaylie stepped half out of the car, one foot on the ground and a hand still lingering on the steering wheel. Trevor had warned her of the house's neglected state since Clara had been moved to a home a few years before her death, but that didn't explain what Kaylie saw at all.

She remembered a sprawling estate, gleaming in the sun and looking like it came out of a fairy tale. She remembered green grounds, slightly wild but always beautiful. She remembered feeling like a princess with the long staircase, the shiny banister, and the many, many rooms she could roam about and explore.

Instead, the early summer light was almost swallowed by withered vines crawling over the crumbling brick of the manor. Plants that should've been blooming by now were dried and probably dead. She couldn't see through the windows for the dust and dirt, and she swore the house itself was smaller, almost shrunken compared to what she remembered.

There was neglected, and then there was *this*. If Kaylie didn't know any better, she would say the house looked bowed and depressed.

She left the car in the drive. She'd grab her bags later.

Her hair stood on end when she crossed the threshold. The harsh screech of the door hinges did nothing to deter the haunted house vibe. The whole thing smelled of dust and mildew. Sheets covered every available surface, and a thick layer of grime covered those.

No internet. No TV. A library she would probably be forced to take an interest in, but that was about it.

Three months in this? What exactly was she supposed to do?

———

Kaylie staked her claim in the lavender guest room upstairs. She tossed her suitcase and a handful of bags on the floor. The dustcover she balled up and threw in a corner, kicking large dust bunnies underneath the bed and dresser. She explored the much-diminished home, swearing all the while that there should have been a staircase here, or more rooms there. She couldn't even find the dining room, just a breakfast nook off the kitchen. At least the kitchen had pots and pans.

Sure, she'd been a kid, but her memory wasn't that bad, and no one had ever accused her of being imaginative.

Nothing happened that night.

She spent her second day bored and fighting a lonely pit in the center of her stomach. She needed to figure out how to get satellite; she couldn't take this quiet. At least the place had electricity.

Then the noises began.

Houses, especially old ones, settled in the night. They protested nocturnal temperatures with all the creaking groans of an old man.

Those noises weren't these.

The sound of heavy feet running up and down the hallway woke Kaylie from a deep sleep. She stifled a shriek and curled up against the headboard.

Thud. Thud. Thud.

Thud, thud, thud.

Thud-thud-thud.

Back and forth, in front of her door.

She cowered. She wished she wasn't here alone. She wished she was brave enough to get up and lock the door. Hell, she wished she was brave enough to grab the clock, or the lamp, or anything, and do something about it.

"Help me," she barely rasped.

The steps thudded louder.

She huddled there for adrenaline-lengthened minutes until the sounds stopped. Simply stopped. Just like that.

She wasn't getting out of bed, no sir. Her shoulders tensed; her eyes trained on the handle. Her legs were cramping and she was getting a headache, but she didn't care. She barely breathed until sunrise began to filter through the thin curtains on the windows.

Only then could she coax herself into unfolding from the bed and peeking outside her door.

Nothing. Not a hint that anyone had ever been there.

She crept downstairs, checked the foyer, peered out at her car. Everything was as she'd left it last night.

Was it a nightmare? Had she psyched herself out? It was so quiet up here. Maybe she was going crazy like Johnny in *The Shining*.

She tried to shove her unease to the back of her mind and set about boiling water for instant noodles. The nearest town was almost an hour away, and nobody delivered.

She slurped the noodles, drank half the broth, then abandoned the whole mess to wander around the grounds.

A chill shivered down to her bones even though the sun beamed through the leaves on this beautiful June day. Kaylie kept rubbing at the goose pimples on her arms. Bushes rattled and vines shuddered as she walked past.

"It's a squirrel," she told herself, "or a bird." It didn't matter that her surroundings were unusually quiet otherwise, because what else could it be? She needed to stop being stupid. She didn't know why Aunt Clara would do something weird like make her live in this old house for three months, but she'd been family. She had no reason to hurt Kaylie now.

Determined, Kaylie spent the rest of the day looking for an animal in the bushes. For all she chased the rustling, she found nothing.

———

The running sounds happened again that night. She almost made it to the door before she scared herself back under the covers, pulling a pillow over her head.

———

She startled awake to a deafening crack of thunder after dozing for only a couple of hours. When she dashed to the window, she saw no hint of a cloud.

"I hate this house."

Kaylie didn't try to leave her room that day. She dug out her laptop and watched the movies she'd loaded onto it. All four of them. She should have thought this trip through a little more.

For meals she subsisted off protein bars, tossing the wrappers to the floor. When the rumbling cracks thundered louder, she just put on her headphones and turned up the volume.

Two weeks. She put up with everything for two weeks. Two weeks of doors slamming shut on her and shutters that banged against the house on windless, sleepless nights. Two weeks of something following her around the house. Two weeks of her possessions vanishing one piece at a time. First her phone, then her laptop, and even her mp3 player.

She retreated to read in the library, and every book she touched gave her a papercut. The stove, even with how infrequently she used it, started burning her fingers. Pots fell. Mugs shattered.

She drove that hour to Greenwood, the old mountain town nearby, and talked to the locals.

"Clara's place? Yeah, she never invited a lot of people up, but when she did, it was gorgeous."

"Nope, never heard it was haunted."

"Well you know those old houses, always makin' noises, never what you think should be possible either."

"Here dear, have a slice of pie. You look absolutely peaked."

The consensus was the same. Old, not haunted, and oh wasn't it nice that Clara's niece was taking an interest in the place? At least Kaylie got a homemade pizza for her troubles. She studied the road leading out of Greenwood and pictured herself just driving away, right now, not looking back.

Only her things were at the house, and she really didn't have the money to replace them. Just as she reluctantly pulled the car back onto the grounds, the engine screeched and abruptly died.

That evening in the flickering lamplight, as Kaylie sucked on yet another papercut, she tossed the book she'd tried to read onto a table. Something yanked hard on her ponytail. She jumped to her feet.

"That's it! I don't know who you are, but I'm fucking done! I don't care if I have to *walk* home. You won't tell me what you want. You won't leave me alone. So guess what? You win! I'm gone."

She stomped up the stairs, kicked in the door to the lavender room before it could get stuck on her, and furiously began to pack. Clothes, blankets—not her electronics, of course, but most of the other things she'd brought with her. She stuffed her last remaining suitcase until it barely zipped, the others having walked off on her.

Moonlight spilled into the room, the only light she had since the electricity quit working upstairs days ago. Something on the bureau kept catching the light and throwing it in her face—an attempt to blind her, no doubt.

Kaylie didn't want to look—everything here brought her nothing but pain. This wouldn't be any different. With her bags, she tried to walk out of the room, but the door stuck fast. She pulled, she tugged, she kicked, she even set her bag down and got both her feet on the jamb to yank on the handle as if she were in a cartoon. But it wouldn't budge.

She loosed a scream as she flew to the bureau and snatched up the offending item with every intention of pitching it out the open window. It was a compass, a silver one. Kaylie stood with her arms poised for a long minute before she took a closer look at it instead.

Turning the compass over in her hands, she traced it with a fingertip. Part of her waited for something to happen, for it to bite her or snap shut on her burns. As she brushed the worst of the dust off, she felt an engraving etched into the metal. She wouldn't know where a rag was, but she took the hem of her shirt and buffed it in earnest.

There was no great revelation, no big reveal, but the compass itself was nifty. The etching was delicate and beautiful. Kaylie could tell a lot of work had gone into it, and when she managed to clear the inside, she saw a message engraved, "To Clara, with all my love, Thomas."

Aw, that was sweet! But who was Thomas? As far as Kaylie knew, Clara had never been married. She went to put the compass back, but it . . . looked wrong. For the first time she noticed—really noticed—the dust, dirt, and cobwebs. A beautiful token like that deserved better.

With a sigh, she headed down to the cramped kitchen. A dish rag or a towel had to be around somewhere.

The door opened without a problem.

Upon entering the kitchen, another light flashed out of the corner of her eye. She whirled around, fists up, ready for an attack. She waited a tense moment, then another, not trusting the haunted place.

Nothing came at her, but she didn't feel any better. Not until she noticed a door she could have sworn hadn't been there before. Sink, stove, and a closet of a pantry. That's what made up this kitchen.

Except, now she saw a second door next to the pantry. Trepidatious, she inched over, hands raised before her. When she got close, she tapped the door handle like it was a hot stove coil. In and out, barely grazing it. Nothing happened. She grabbed the handle, resting her hand on it. Still nothing. As carefully as a bomb disposal tech, she depressed the lever and pulled the door open.

Then she glanced around the side.

It was a linen cupboard. Shelves of tablecloths, napkins, and placemats lined the narrow space. Everything was dusty, but as she set aside her fear to look closer, she saw every piece was beautiful, elegant. Wow. She even recognized the brightly patterned flower tablecloth she and Aunt Clara had spread out in the garden for a fairy tea party.

"Now remember, the fair folk love cream, bread, and sweets. Always be polite, and be wary—or they'll take you away and leave a changeling in your place," Clara had said before tickling a tiny Kaylie, nearly spilling tea in the process.

Next to that cloth was a thick bolt of intricate lace. Kaylie thought it multiple cloths at first, but she unrolled it a bit and found one massive piece. What for? There wasn't a table that big in the whole house. Neat though.

She tossed it back on the shelf.

The door slammed shut.

"What? Hey!" She turned around and smacked at the door. "What the hell? Let me out."

Cut off from the light, she reached for the door handle. Only, when her fingers wrapped around the metal, it disappeared under her hands. There one second and gone the next.

What did this place *want* from her? First a door appears out of nowhere, then it locks her in. The house was trying to kill her. She knew it. She slid to the floor, burying her face in her hands. She should have left when she'd had the chance.

Kaylie sat there for a while. A long while. An hour, a day, a year, she didn't know, but eventually her butt fell asleep and her back hurt, so she tried to move.

When she leaned forward, she jammed her fingers against a crate resting on the floor. Ow. She pulled the box towards her and felt around inside. It felt like a bunch of small squares rougher than the napkins. Picking one up, she felt around the frayed edges. Rags?

A faint light, no brighter than a candle flame, filtered underneath the door. She immediately skimmed her hand over the wood, but the handle was still gone. She slapped the door again.

"What do you want from me?" she cried.

She was smart. She could do this. What'd she do different? She'd cleaned a thing, then came downstairs and found a new door. Went through the new door and got locked in for her efforts. Why conjure a new door only to trap her?

She looked over the tablecloths again and saw the bolt of beautiful lace in a crumpled pile, spilling over the rest of them.

No.

No way.

Kaylie lifted the bolt, meticulously smoothing it out as she began to rewrap it. She had to start over twice to get the lace to lay right, but it wasn't like she could go anywhere. At last it was folded, and she placed the lace tablecloth back on the shelf with the others, as if it hadn't been disturbed.

A muted click sounded behind her and the door swung open, practically bathing her in light. She was grateful, so grateful she almost ran out. But then she looked back at the crate of rags still sitting in the middle of the floor. She picked up the crate and took it upstairs with her.

She spent the night fighting her fatigue and set to cleaning the bureau around the compass. She wiped down the mirror, dusted every nook and cranny of each drawer, and even left to see if she could hunt down some polish. A closet appeared at the end of the hall, full of extra bedding, towels, and even some old cleaning supplies. She went back and polished the whole thing. It shined like she remembered. And when she placed the compass back, she—

Aunt Clara laid the compass down next to a letter that she ran a smooth, unwrinkled hand over.

"Thomas. Oh, my poor, Thomas."

An older woman, Great-Grandma Edith, walked through the door.

"I heard. I'm here, my darling girl."

Aunt Clara turned into her mother's shoulder and sobbed.

—Kaylie blinked. Whoa, what? That was freaky.

Kaylie stared at the compass before quickly picking it up and putting it back down. Nothing happened.

She'd seen it though, like she'd been there. She could still smell their old perfume and the flowers through the open window. She thought about carrying the compass around with her through the rest of the house but decided against it. The compass looked perfect, resting right where it belonged.

The exhaustion she'd been ignoring hit her behind the eyes. The burgeoning daylight indicated she'd spent the night up, again, and she suddenly didn't care about visions or haunted houses. She laid down, right on top of the covers, and went to sleep.

Kaylie awoke in the late afternoon on her own. No noises, no fake thunder. Cautious and waiting for the other shoe to drop, she went back downstairs. Other than the hall closet having vanished, nothing bad happened.

Running back upstairs, she touched the dresser and the compass. No visions either.

The kitchen door, the closet, the vision—it was just a dream, right?

But the polish and the dirty rags lay where she'd left them, and she sure as hell hadn't brought anything like that with her.

She had a theory. She went to the master bedroom and grabbed a jar of dried flowers off the dresser, upending it onto the floor.

Immediately the windows rattled and she felt a sharp yank on her hair.

"Ouch! Stop it with the hair. Jesus."

She knelt down to gingerly pick up the petals, making sure not to crumble any or grind them into the carpet.

"Message received. Clean the damn house. It's a good thing I'm here for two more months because that's how long it's going to freaking take!" she shouted to the unresponsive ceiling.

Frustrated, she sighed. Then she got to work.

Well, almost. She had to get lessons from the people of Greenwood on how to properly clean things in the manor, because the rattling windows and the growling floorboards told her she was *doing it wrong*. She also begged cooking lessons off the local café owner because her ramen kept disappearing, being replaced by raw ingredients in the fridge.

She switched between cleaning the kitchen and the upstairs. Cooking required a crap ton of dishes, even when she kept it simple. So . . . that became a thing.

"If you take care of your house, it will become a home and take care of you," Great-Grandma Edith lectured Kaylie's aunt and grandmother as little girls, herding them through the house.

The upstairs took way longer than expected because the rooms literally multiplied as she went. Her childhood memory wasn't as wrong as she'd thought. She would finish up one room, and another door would appear in the hall. Behind each one was a completely furnished room, ready for her steadily growing skills. The house eventually rewarded her by returning her things.

One morning she came downstairs to a greatly expanded kitchen. And another day, the library doubled in size. At the beginning of her last week, a ballroom appeared at the back of the house. A ballroom. Kaylie had never heard of this place having a *ballroom*.

The grounds took care of themselves, thank God for that. Every day they looked more orderly and a little more alive.

It wasn't completely terrible, though. As she cleaned, each room seemed to contain a . . . heart. Not a physical one, just an item that tied the room together—and to the rest of the house. Those always gave her glimpses of the past.

A toy soldier in the blue room gifted her a flash of an adolescent man throwing it to the ground, shouting he wasn't a child anymore and was ready to fight.

A porcelain doll in the rose room revealed a pair of sisters whispering secrets to each other and giggling until the small hours of the morning.

A tiny wooden cross and a white baby gown in the master bedroom conjured generations of births, all in a rush. Boys, girls, stillbirths, twins, she witnessed every joy and sorrow seen by those walls.

The ballroom held the biggest surprises. While Kaylie was on her hands and knees, scrubbing and polishing the floor, the world faded away.

A wizened, white-haired man clapped a hand on the shoulder of a younger one. "You will become the steward here, my son. The house needs a master and his family in order to keep its purpose, and its splendor. Be tied to it. Let its foundations become your roots here."

An imperious man with flame-like hair instructed the floor be carefully disassembled and packed to be shipped across the ocean.

An elaborate wedding with a younger version of the same man and a beautiful, dark-haired woman.

A dance.

Figures ghosted in front of brocade drapes, shining in brilliant candlelight. The elaborate gowns and tailored jackets shimmered in a way that wasn't entirely possible for cloth alone.

The people that waltzed over the ancient boards were strange. Their eyes were a little too wide, their ears a little too pointed, and their fingers a little too long. They danced with preternatural grace, and Kaylie swore a few of them were floating above the ground.

No. No way. The whole experience had been surreal from the start, but this?

When she came back to herself, she was surprised and relieved to see that she was completely done, three days early.

She had considered staying. She really had. After spending so much time with it, she fell in love with the manor's history. The stories, both beautiful and sad, made her feel connected in a way she'd barely felt for another person, let alone a place.

But with that connection came knowledge. Most of the memories showed children laughing, screeching, and playing. She'd seen more memories of Clara, who had chosen to stay but witnessed the slow decline of the house because she couldn't hold it on her own. She wasn't meant to.

Kaylie intuited the house had been rejuvenated by her, but without more people it would revert over time. And . . . well, she wasn't ready to be rooted.

So, she enjoyed the manor in its full glory for those few days, then made a call. Trevor helped her finalize the sale of the property to a family who also hailed from the Old Country, who *knew*. Kaylie could see it in how the father's eyes gazed in wonder and soft awe at the house. She felt it in how the air stirred around her, then them, saying good-bye and hello. She was distressed seeing it go, but she knew she couldn't give the house what it needed.

With her bags, her things, and her phone returned to her, she drove her once again working car back down the mountainside.

She'd been so consumed with the manor; she hadn't thought about her own apartment in weeks.

When she opened the door, she was immediately assaulted by the smells, and the mess, and—holy God, had she really lived like this? Kaylie saw her apartment with fresh eyes. Piles of boxes, piles of mail, piles of laundry, piles of rotten, moldy trash everywhere. She was surprised her landlord hadn't burnt the place down and started fresh.

She glanced at her phone for the time, ignoring the plethora of delayed notifications she'd been getting since she hit the base of the mountain.

At least her shift started late tomorrow.

"It's only a couple of rooms. It's not a mansion."

She adjourned to the closest bodega to grab basic cleaning supplies. As she wormed her way back into her apartment, her phone rang. The number made her smile.

"Hey, Nate! No, I'm not dead." She laughed. "Oh God, you did *not* send the cops over to my apartment! Well, I'm glad my landlord caught them or *you* might be under investigation for my murder."

Kaylie pulled out a box of trash bags and immediately started snapping bags open. "I was on a trip. Yes, a long one, but I'm back now."

She listened for a bit.

"Thanks, but I'm okay. No free coffee for you tonight. Give Jen a hug for me! You know, so long as it won't get you in trouble with HR." Kaylie started pulling the phone away from her ear. "Yes, I'm sure. *Bye,* Nate."

She began in the kitchen. The box that fell months ago turned out to be mugs abandoned by previous roommates. None of it was salvageable. She unpacked her kitchen, and stacked the unopened mail in an empty box to go through later. The sale should placate her creditors.

She used her new rubber gloves to pick up strewn-about take-out containers. Five trash bags later, she managed to vacuum before her neighbors went to bed. The vacuum she had unearthed from even more boxes in her closet.

Even scavenging, she couldn't find a single outfit for work tomorrow. Resigned, she threw everything else in baskets and boxes to haul to the laundromat. With the sale money, she might look into a washer and dryer, but for now Kaylie bemoaned the sleepless night. However, she couldn't go to work smelling like spoiled lattes and sentient takeout.

The bathroom, the bedroom, the kitchen, the living room—she straightened and washed and polished it all. She even cleaned her windows.

Maybe there was no magic to punish or reward her here, but her heart lightened all the same.

She finished in the wee hours of the morning, sweaty and dirty, but satisfied.

Great-Grandma Edith had been right.

"If you take care of your house, it will become a home and take care of you."

40

BIG HAMMER FORD

BY JIM BURRELL

Now! When I liberate my red machine,
a three-hundred-and-two cubic-inch steel
American fever-dream breaks quarantine,
stampeding the gate with a pagan squeal
and I'm smoke and lightning, heavy metal
thunder with the tachometer seeing red
and so—back on black down at the pedals—
shooting-star spirit shrieks ahead, now shred
hot meats, my V-8 reaches out and shouts
"Hey . . . baby, do you wanna dance this dance?"
A clear-channel romance, no doubt—kick out
those last few RPMs with just a glance
and then—road—hypnosis—will ease the pain.
Help me wander, yeah, 'cause I'm free again.

41

PORTRAIT: THE HOUSEKEEPER'S STORY

BY SUZANNE LEE

You wonder
why I do not lower my eyes
when your headlights
swing around the corner
and glare blindly at me.
You swerve a little.
I am unexpected.

You wonder
why I do not step out
of the street, why I do not defer
to the purr and bulk
of your prosperous car
as it surges past me
in the dusk.

You wonder
why my expression
does not change.

I will tell you.

Women like me
have walked this way
for a thousand years
head high, steadfast,
with weariness like death
in our bones, and, in our hearts,
the will to carry on
despite what you—
and all your kind—
may do.

I myself
have walked this way
two thousand miles,
two thousand miles
toward the pole star of hope,
through tropic heat and rain thick as soup,

Walking Woman

through wild pain and gripping cold, and terror
serrated like the rusting teeth of a trap.
I have walked invisible through borders
my feet silent as moonlight,
I moved like sunshine through leaves,
like water through a sieve.
Now
I am here.

You wonder
how I am content
to do the work I do. Why

I do not fear to walk
in the dusk to a distant bus.

I will tell you.

Your car's bright lights are nothing
to me. Walking two miles
to the bus stop
after cleaning your house,
and washing your clothes,
and cooking your meal,
and watching your soft, unruly children
all day, these are nothing
to me.

I have walked
a longer way than this,
and I am not
going back.

42

THE CINDERELLA WHO DROVE HER OWN COACH

BY MITZI DORTON

The trees stood with arms reaching, like a woman who had lost a child, weeping and wailing to the Lord. At least that was how Norita's life seemed in Beech Fork, bleak and without hope. There were fathers and brothers lost to the coal mines, children with no hope for a life without want, and women in bad marriages who had no choice. Her own father had recently been diagnosed with black lung. He had spells of coughing and wheezing off and on, while he held his ribs and moaned.

Norita could see a fingernail moon over the silhouette of a black mountain against the dark grey sky. She lay on a thin mattress in the stillness, with the occasional sounds of shifting coals in the potbellied stove, or a rollicking cough from her daddy's bedroom. If the dark part of the moon could point like a fingertip, would there be other worlds beyond Beech Fork, West Virginia under this same moon?

Norita slept, one of four sardines tucked into a bed, sideways, folding her knees up or sleeping at a slant to make it work. Her skinny younger sister, Teeny, snored like a kitten beside her, with a soft rattling purr. The other two girls were small too, with sweet and angelic faces, but she hoped one didn't wet the bed. It happened on occasion, and there was no place to turn from it.

The white sheets that Norita had smoothed and tucked under the thin mattress before bedtime were the work of all of the children in the family, walking miles, door-to-door, to sell candy. Norita remembered the luscious coconut bars with pink, brown and cream stripes, and the peanut-brittle squares. It was difficult to give them up on the rare occasion that someone bought them. Norita would imagine their children enjoying the sweet and buttery tastes that were denied to her and her siblings. All of the candy money went for linens: curtains, bedspreads, sheets, or tablecloths.

Norita recalled a conversation with a neighbor girl who asked, "Did you ever sneak a piece?"

"Girl, we knew better! We all wanted the candy, but we didn't touch it. We toted it in a wagon, and I put an old shawl over the boxes, so the little ones wouldn't hanker after it."

She had continued to explain to the girl, "Mama always bragged on us about earning the linens when company came. I had to sell thirty-one boxes of candy to get one bedspread. Why, I didn't think that old, ugly, orange and gold threaded thing to be especially pretty; I would have rather enjoyed the candies. When my cousin's mama heard about it, *her* daughter started selling candy, and she became our competitor, so they could have the sheets and pillowcases and bedspreads too."

"We never get any candy either, except at Christmas," her friend replied, assuring Norita wasn't by herself in the matter of being poor.

Norita didn't admit that she and her brothers and sisters had plucked pieces of tar from the road to chew, imagining the sweet taste to be something akin to the candies they sold. It was her brother's idea, tearing up fresh pieces that bubbled up from the street and encouraging them to try it. Oddly, it did have a sweet taste, but she was sure it was nothing at all like the denied candies.

The mining boss and his family had the most of what there was to grasp in Beech Fork, his empire perched on a hill above the miners' houses. Norita's life was as boxed in as the mountains that sprung up straight and tall in the distance, walling in her whole community.

Norita imagined for a moment, as she drifted off, what life would be like in the mining boss's family. She envisioned herself in a sparkly gown on the hilltop.

Then the reality of her daddy's husky cough smacked into the image she held and reminded her how scrunched she felt between three sisters.

Mama didn't seem to be feeling well either, so the garden fell to the children.

The following day, Norita marveled to Teeny, while they were digging potatoes as she gazed up at the hill, watching as the mining boss's wife directed some men who were planting bushes in her yard.

"I've watched their house. His wife sets a red book in the window on the days she wants Miss Elsie to come up and clean her house. I'm going to rise up and have a life like that woman's some day! Imagine owning the whole community of houses, the company store with all its fine merchandise, and being able to go in and pick out a new coat or any dress in there!"

Her younger brother, Bass, interrupted her thoughts, "I hate hoeing these old potatoes, don't y'all?"

"I don't know what we are going to do," Norita kept talking as she gazed up at the hill. "I've got plans bigger than Beech Fork."

The West Virginia sun hammered on her auburn crown and caused drips of sweat to drizzle down on her face, like rain on a windowpane. The sun was unforgiving, but they knew better than to quit. She wiped a dirty hand across a sweaty forehead and saw the postman bend down from the side of his familiar grey horse. He held out a letter.

Mama had seen him, too, and stopped on the second step. "Oh, it's from my aunt. They used to live down the road, before her boy took off preachin' down in Kingsport, Tennessee." She held her head and paused. "Oooh, mercy, I'm not feeling the way I used to," she floundered. "Plumb swimmy headed!"

"Better see the doctor, Mrs. McMullen!" the postman said. "You're not that old, you know."

She smiled at the compliment, and waved him on. "Mines dock too much out of the check to see anybody but the company doctor. He don't see nothin'," she added. "Can't afford to go to the city." She seated herself on the step, groaning loud enough for the little potato diggers to hear and wince. "It's a letter from Aunt Wannie!"

It was the grandest excuse to leave their post. Norita and Teeny went scampering down. "Wait a minute. You're not leaving me on this daggone hill," Bass cried out, as he followed.

"Read it, Mama. Read it!" Teeny exclaimed.

"Oh, my stars, she will almost beat the letter here!" Mama declared. "It says she's a comin' to Beech Fork today!"

The children moaned, because they knew they were in for a streak of quick housework. Their house sure wasn't in shape for company, more like someone had turned a billy goat loose in there. Norita, however, saw a crack of light for an opportunity to rise on that very day.

When Aunt Wannie and Radford arrived, Norita asked, "What brings y'all to Beech Fork, all the way from Tennessee?"

"We spent the night down the road in Ammonate with a preacher. We's on church business." Wannie explained. "Radford wanted to get Pastor Puckett to come down and speak for our revival in Kingsport. Your Uncle John had told us about your mama being sick, so 'course we wanted to stop by and check on her too."

"It's awful good to see you all." Mama said. Norita enjoyed seeing Mama smile.

Norita asked them questions about where they lived. She was excited to know, and it must have shown. They offered in passing to take Norita back to Kingsport with them for a visit. She surprised them and said yes.

She packed her few belongings in a suitcase, turned and exclaimed, "Thank you, Jesus!" when she and Teeny were in the bedroom, away from company.

Norita stood before the chifforobe mirror and straightened the damaged straw hat that belonged to her mama. Her brother, Bass, had pierced two holes in it to make a homemade mask. She remembered his blue eyes appearing through it, making her jump. She also remembered the thrashing from her father that Bass received for making it.

Norita had safety-pinned a wide piece of dark green satin scrap cloth from an old nightgown across the holes to mend it, but it looked nice, and Teeny said, "You wouldn't even know it!"

Norita looked back as she started to leave. She saw Teeny standing and watching on the front porch of the mining camp house. Teeny had always been part of her life. This would be her first trip away from home, and Norita felt a little homesick already, but she couldn't spend time dwelling on that. She moved toward the car.

A spray of sunlight broke from the clouds and seemed to shine down for a moment on the carriage that she imagined would whisk her away to her dreams. She blinked as though hope could disappear in an instant, as it often did in Beech Fork.

Norita placed her bag in the backseat next to her, while Radford sat in the front studying a paper map. Norita stared at the steering wheel and imagined her hands turning and guiding toward the routes of her own choosing. Aunt Wannie reached over and pointed to the map Radford held, mentioning the road they took yesterday, breaking Norita's thoughts.

Bass and Teeny ran and followed Norita's coach down the driveway and a little way down the road, waving at the windows and patting the sides of it. Mama and Daddy stood in the distance, waving with the little ones. Norita looked back at her family down the dirt road until they disappeared as the old car rattled over the hill.

Norita was in awe of the lights and the restaurants, the concrete sidewalks. The maple trees, with their branched-out, green leafy boughs, rising in arches over the two-way streets, like a welcoming arbor to a new beginning. Radford didn't talk much, but he did point out Maypole Street, a home lined with historic mansions and brick walkways. Norita had never seen anything as fine as Maypole Street in her life. "The richest people in Kingsport live here," Radford said almost reverently, shaking his head.

"Would you teach me to drive?" Norita spoke suddenly. Radford looked surprised. He hesitated, then offered, "I suppose somebody will need to drive your mama and daddy around when you get yourself a car." He pulled down a side street and let her take the wheel. He instructed her around the block. "You'll meet my wife, Verna Ruth, when we get back. She grew up here in Kingsport and knows all the roads. She won't mind to take you out a time or two and give you some practice, if you ask her. Be careful with my car, though."

"Oh, I will!" Norita promised. Norita felt very satisfied, and there would be no need to remind her to question Verna Ruth on this matter.

A few days later, Norita sat down with Aunt Wannie, trying to convince her to let her stay and look for a job. Norita insisted it wouldn't take long. She planned to go to every business within walking distance.

She landed a job within two days as a receptionist in a doctor's office, and her aunt let Norita stay rent-free and save the money to bring the family to Tennessee. The pay wasn't much, which is perhaps why it was not filled by someone else. Norita was proud to have the position though, especially since she had no formal work experience.

The telephone puzzled her. No one had one in Beech Fork. She heard the doctor speaking to someone on the phone about her, while she took a break in the back room. "I hired a new girl. She seems nervous, a mountain girl, but anyone can see she's not ignorant by any means, in spite of her cultural limits."

When Norita returned to her desk, she glowed, thinking 'not ignorant by any means.' He thinks I'm smart! She had encountered people in her job search who seemed to swallow a giggle when she said she was from Beech Fork, West Virginia.

The phone rang, startling her. She lifted the receiver, her first experience with one. She wanted to live up to what the doctor had said, and, trying to sound as sophisticated as she felt in her new job, said, "Dr. Sullivan's office, just a moment please!" She placed the receiver back on the hook and went to get the doctor.

He followed her back to the phone.

"Miss McMullen! You don't hang up the phone if someone wants to speak to me. You leave the receiver off the hook!"

She observed the doctor's furrowed brow and interpreted his tone of voice to mean he could possibly fire her. The thought of losing her job terrified her. To her surprise, though, he demonstrated the use of the phone. She could only imagine what he might say about her to someone now, but she would never make the same mistake again.

Norita went to the post office and purchased two stamps. She sent one along with the letter she wrote to her family, so they could write back.

July 6, 1938

I wish you all were here. Kingsport had a big parade with marching bands and baton twirlers. Aunt Wannie, her kids, and I went down to see it. Radford brought the fixin's for a picnic to celebrate the Fourth of July! We've been going down to hear him preach on Sundays.

How about this! I got a front desk job at a doctor's office! I've also been trying to get on at the Eastman. They have real good pay. I go every week at my lunch break to try and talk to the boss, but I haven't gotten on yet. When I do, I will try to bring you all here.

Love,

Norita

Norita felt terrible leaving all of the work in Beech Fork to Bass and Teeny. She didn't mention the watermelon she ate on the Fourth.

It reminded her of how much her own family loved the sweet, ripe, and rare treat. A travelling peddler had given Mama a couple of watermelon seeds when she bought some pie fillings a few years ago, but only one grew in the West Virginia soil. When they ate their watermelon harvest, Mama had hung the Sunbonnet Sue and crazy quilts all across their clothesline, so as not to make the neighbor children look in and feel hurt to see them burying their faces with glee into the rich garden prize.

Aunt Wannie's postman tossed a letter right through a slot in the door, and Norita happened to be walking by. She recognized the handwriting.

August 7, 1938

Dear Norita,

Daddy had to walk away from his work in the mines, and now we have no income other than what we can grow here. Uncle Johnny paid for Mama and Daddy to go down to the big hospital in Bluefield. He says Mama's eat up with cancer, and Daddy has heart dropsy, besides the black lung. Me and Bass do all the work for them and for the young 'uns too. We might expect the worst. The mine boss hasn't said anything about kicking us out. We can't believe this has happened to our sweet mama.

A pitiful old woman came to the door saying she had nothing at all to eat, and Bass went down in the cellar and got a can of beans and gave it to her. Daddy found out and whooped him for it. He talked about Bass going into the mines. Bass is only seventeen, though, and Mama sat out on the swing and cried.

Love your sister,

Teeny

P. S. On the bright side, Uncle John brought me some genuine cultured pearls, but Daddy put him out by the seat of his pants. Poor Uncle John!

Teeny's letter set off alarm bells; Norita had to find work with higher pay now. She had hoped to bring Mama down to Kingsport to see a good doctor, and they had a big hospital right here in town.

Now Daddy was in almost as bad shape and would need to see a doctor too. Teeny didn't mince words.

Norita did have to smile at the mention of Uncle John, though. He was a drinker, but he had a good heart, and he always brought gifts when he came to visit from over in Buchanan County, Virginia. The younger children would water down Uncle John's whiskey so he wouldn't get so drunk. Uncle John would exclaim, "Why, that's pure old rot gut!" He only came on rare occasions. And when he did, although the little ones loved him, Daddy would make a show for the children of lifting his brother by the back of his britches, and tossing him out the front door.

Norita applied at Eastman. A pamphlet she had taken from the woman at the front desk stated: "Eastman is Kingsport's largest employer, a modern plant which produces materials for making film, dyes, and fibers." She hoped for a position in the yarn plant. Though the CEOs migrated down from the north, many Eastman workers came from the surrounding farms and mountain regions. "I've got to get a job there!" Norita told Aunt Wannie. Her eyes stared off in the distance, envisioning life in the future.

Radford's wife Verna Ruth had taken Norita out for a spin in Radford's car on some of the main streets of Kingsport. So Norita was able to drive the borrowed car to her first interview at the Eastman Company, arriving thirty minutes early. She sat in the parking lot, waiting and very nervous. She hoped it would not show. Hopefully she didn't commence babbling in unknown tongues, like the women she'd heard at the brush arbor, where they held a Holiness summer church camp meeting back in Beech Fork. Norita spoke out loud in the car, practicing what she was going to say, until a woman wearing a smart hat with a little feather pulled up beside her, put on lipstick in the mirror and went inside. Looking down at her own outfit, Norita thought of the cardboard she'd stuck down in the soles of her old shoes, hiding the holes that had appeared in the bottoms.

The woman with the feathered hat sat in one of the waiting room seats when Norita entered. They called Norita first.

The man who interviewed her wore a suit and had a handlebar moustache. He smoked a cigar during the whole conversation. He did not seem to even see Norita as she told him what a hard worker she was. When she could see he was not even focused on her, even blowing a smoke ring at one point, she pleaded with him, "My father and mother are both quite sick, and no one is able to provide for my brothers and sisters I left behind in Beech Fork, West Virginia. I need a job with higher pay."

Mr. Holiday was a well-fed man who did not appear to concern himself too much with the problems of others, especially those in so remote a place as West Virginia. With a flick of his cigar in the big orange ashtray on his desk, he said in a singsong tone, "We will let you know if we are interested." "Next!"

His eyes glazed over, and he called to the waiting room. The woman with the feather hat whisked past her. Norita felt the cardboard slide in the sole of her shoe as she exited and headed for the parking lot.

Norita went back to Eastman and reapplied every chance she could. She'd heard this was how it was done at that particular company. Perhaps she could just show them her determination. The same man, Mr. Holiday, would interview her repeatedly, and she never got the job, but that didn't stop her from going back again. Once Norita thought she saw Mr. Holiday roll his eyes when she came in, but she couldn't be sure.

At dinner that night, Aunt Wannie slid a piece of paper around the big meal she'd prepared. "A letter came from your sister," she said, as Norita bit into a piece of cornbread.

August 30, 1938

Dear Norita,

*The mining boss has been knocking at our door. Mama gathered
me and the children and we hid at the side of the dresser. It was
frightful when he came around and knocked on the window right
beside us. The curtain was pulled, but we could see his shadow. Daddy
stayed in bed and held his cough. We are worried sick!*

Love,

Teeny

Norita took a deep breath and choked a little on the cornbread.
How long would the mine boss allow them to stay in the house
without her daddy working? They could already be set out, or it
could be any day now. The more she thought about Mr. Holiday, the
more the situation made her angry.

What did she have to lose? Time to try another tactic.

The Kingsport phonebook provided the address and the phone
number: Circle 5-5771.

Do I dare to dial it? she thought. "No," she told Aunt Wannie.
"I'll go there myself."

"Here," Aunt Wannie said, "wear Verna Ruth's high heels. Size
7? She won't care."

It was the perfect offer. Aunt Wannie talked Radford into letting
Norita borrow his car one last time, too.

The home was well built, unlike the shack where her family of
nine shared four rooms. Norita felt the soles of the empowering shiny
black patent heels step on Mr. Holiday's flagstone porch, raising her
to a new height. Her hand shook as she held to the white wrought
iron railing. She was a mixture of strength and doubts as she
approached the storm door, dressed in the best of what she owned,
starched, pressed, and spit spot polished.

She hesitated on the doorstep. No one else was going to lead her
family out. Bass was a year away from following in his father's footsteps. A lantern and a pickaxe awaited him. The image of poor Bass
with all his dreams squelched for a life of hard labor, or even an early

death in the middle of a dark mountain crevice, was all the encouragement she needed.

She knocked.

An attractive well-dressed woman with finger waves and fancy combs at her temples opened the door. Norita could not believe women walked about the home wearing earrings and heels, but this woman did. Her own mother wore a homemade cotton housedress, usually with an apron, and some flat brogain shoes.

Norita swallowed, and paused for a moment before saying anything.

When the woman said, "Yes?" Norita replied, "Mrs. Holiday?"

"Yes?" the woman repeated.

"I'm wondering if I might speak with you."

Mrs. Holiday looked worried. Norita bet that Mrs. Holiday was beginning to wonder if her husband was involved in some kind of love affair.

"Certainly, come in." The older woman motioned for her to follow. She ushered Norita into an unfamiliar world of gold-leaf-framed oil portraits and marble-topped tables. Norita had meant to sit up straight and brave, but the white, down-filled couch was soft like a fat marshmallow and seemed to swallow her as she sat.

"Now, what is this all about?" Mrs. Holiday spoke in a more demanding tone, probably expecting the worst.

Norita smiled timidly at the floor, stumbling on her words. "My m-mama-mother has just been diagnosed with cancer. I am the only one of my family who has come here to Kingsport. There are seven of us children. I am the oldest, and all of the others have not finished school. My father has heart dropsy and lung problems and can no longer work in the mines, even though he's forty-eight. I left this family behind, with only the end of our summer garden and what food they can get from the canning jars left in the cellar. Since my daddy can't work, the mine boss may put them out of the house any minute now."

Norita continued, surprised at her own bravery, "I'm a very hard worker, Mrs. Holiday."

A look of relief crossed Mrs. Holiday's face.

Norita continued, "As the oldest of seven, I'm used to taking care of all the young ones, plus cleaning and cooking. I am not a person who gives up. I need to bring my family out of that mining town, where there is no hope of a future for them. They might be homeless soon, and fall is coming. I want to find my mother a good doctor here, and get her some care. I work as a receptionist in a doctor's office, but the pay is not nearly enough. I have to be able to afford a place for my family to live here, and I need to be able to buy a car of my own. I've been to interview with Mr. Holiday ten times. Is there any way you can help me by speaking with him?"

The next day Norita received a call. She recognized Mr. Holiday's voice, muffled as though he had his handlebar mustache right up at the mouthpiece and was forced to say the words. She was hired!

Norita did her best to impress them. She ran from one section to another, always busy, always the worker bee, trying to impress. It was not long before they made her the supervisor of the yarn plant. She took her position very seriously. The women, all shapes and sizes, young and old, watched her as she moved from one area to the next, demonstrating to one the process of winding and assisting another with the bobbins.

In the meantime, Uncle John made a visit. He informed Norita that a notice had been tacked on to the front of the camp house. Her father had thirty days to get out of the Beech Fork mining camp house.

Norita bought a tar-paper-covered wooden house on stilts by Muddy Creek with a hundred dollar down payment, and she would make regular payments of twenty-five dollars a month. Teeny and Bass could pick up little jobs in town and help pay for it too. Now her mama and daddy could get help from the doctors in Kingsport, and Bass wouldn't have to go into the mines.

Norita made a payment for her own car, a used Buick, and drove it back on the weekend to Beech Fork. Tenny won't be able to recognize me, arriving in this coach, she thought, as she drove the twisting roads home. As she approached the curve that led to their camp house, she knew the boys would be out front. Automobiles didn't pass frequently.

Sure enough, at the sound of the engine they ran out to see. Norita pulled into the driveway as the boys inspected the car, stroked the exterior, and called for Daddy to check under the hood. Bass shook his head in disbelief. The younger sisters, Teeny among them, ran out to gawk.

Daddy hobbled out. "I expected it more of the boys. Shoot! I'm proud of you, girl." Praise didn't come easily from this stern man.

Norita broke down and cried.

Mama shook her head when she came out on the porch, walked over and wiped both her eyes, then dabbed Norita's with her cotton apron.

Everyone gathered their belongings in their arms. Norita watched Teeny fold the picture-day dress Mama had allowed her to order for seventy-five cents from the Sears catalog. Norita remembered the excitement of each of her younger brothers and sisters when her parents had let each child purchase one school photo during their elementary years. Norita was the first to have hers, a tiny postage-stamp-sized print, which she carried home as though it were a rare butterfly that might disappear into the winds without her careful guardianship.

Teeny, of course, made sure that she had Uncle Johnny's genuine pearls, too.

Bass had a rare all-day sucker he had saved from three months ago. He explained how he had exchanged the copper wire he scavenged around the coal camp and traded it in at the company store for three cents a pound. Norita insisted he pack his homemade shoeshine kit as well, because there were many more customers in Kingsport than in Beech Fork.

Norita's mama sat next to her in the front seat and held the youngest boy on her lap. Bass and Teeny sat in the back, with the other two little ones on their laps. Next to them, Daddy held a portrait of Franklin D. Roosevelt on his lap, with each of the children's one, tiny school picture glued around it. As Norita's car wound around the curves of the roads toward their new home, they left the coal camp in Beech Fork behind.

Catching the eye of Teeny in the backseat, Norita winked at her. Then she reached back and offered a small paper bag with enough sticks of horehound candy to go around. Squeals of delight echoed from the backseat. Norita saw Bass's eyes numbering the sweets, his mouth opening in wonder as each child tasted one. She observed his satisfied face in her rearview mirror as he sat back, laughed, and took a piece of his own. Bass offered another stick to his youngest brother, who was already reaching over the front seat for it.

As Norita turned her attention to the road before her, the happy little shrieks of excitement of her brothers and sisters lingered in her thoughts, and she made a note to herself.

Someday I will rise up and have a home like Mr. Holiday's on Maypole Street!

43

DANNY

BY JOCELYN AJAMI

Birthed on the steps of a church, buttressed
    by the love of an unripe mother,
he grows into Struggle,
    hobbling against the clench of poverty.
His toothless smile betrays the gnaw of hardship.
    In Chicago's frenzied Loop, he merges
into the urban din, a miscellaneous noise,
    an unheard beat
in the boisterous rhythm of the street.

Tall and slight, he blends into a parade
    of poles and posts, shrinking
towards a vanishing point. Unnoticed.
    Despite subzero temperatures,
he stands daily in the shadow
    of looming towers, extending
his hand with a generous grin:

    Streetwise, Streetwise

Stalwart and steady, he assumes the role
    of magazine vendor, sidestepping
the claw of homelessness and the flail of indignity.
    Many pass him by.
Those who stop are drawn by his fervent conviction.
    Their imagined benevolence shifts
to validation, welcoming his friendly nod
    and streetwise savvy:

> *Tickets-half price the day of the concert.*
> *Take a shortcut through the arcade.*
> *Thank you for your business.*

Danny is a man of authority, territory and purpose.
    He commands the corner, courting customers
into friendship. His presence humanizes
    the cold and neutral concrete.
On rare moments when he is absent, the street dims
    divested of essence.

44

BLACK-EYED SUSANS

BY JIM BURRELL

Here we are together again—
me, passing by on a prairie highway,
you, in your yellow dress, waving.
I know that part of you is gone,
as still as a summer memory,
yet your bold eyes remain
alongside me here these windmill miles.
It seems like I'm moving
though I see you out ahead,
restless as a blue-sky day.
Your open arms
make me open the windows—
hear that meadowlark?
He's more carefree than the both of us,
flying beyond the barbed wire.

45

WRITING LIKE A MULE

BY MARGARET MAGINNESS

I hate writing. Or it seems like I hate writing. I avoid it at every opportunity. And yet when I'm not doing it, I long for it: think about it constantly, imagine what I'm going to write, wonder why I don't write more and how to make myself write more. I puzzle over stories and characters and plot lines, imagining how I can piece them together and make them come alive, build an entire universe, and elucidate a corner of human experience.

When the time comes to actually write, I'd rather be anywhere else: cleaning the toilet, doing dishes, sleeping, watching movies, playing solitaire, listening to an audio book, petting my animals, clearing brush, building fences, pulling weeds, brush hogging (a particular favorite), ANYTHING but writing. Every molecule of my body says no, yearns for any other direction, and often gets away with it. And yet, in my heart, I know that I have something to say and that I desperately want to share it. Once I get started, I often enjoy it, and I sometimes write something that captures a corner of what I'm trying to show. Which is why I keep trying, despite the constant struggle.

The most common piece of advice a writer gets is simply to write.

A writer writes every day. Self-help authors, conference presenters, professors, bloggers—it seems everyone who knows anything about writing knows this. And while I want to bring my ideas to life, I continue to avoid writing. As I've been working to improve my writing habit, my best teacher was not another author or an expert, but my mule, Mikey.

I acquired my mule from a Craigslist ad in late 2015. He was shaggy, slightly underweight, friendly but wary, and cost $500. At eight years old and untrained to do anything other than be led around in a halter, he was meant to be a companion for the two horses I already had, and probably not much else. He has turned out to be so much more.

My two horses, Trip and Sully, were a key element in bringing Mikey and me together. Moving them from a large boarding facility where they were surrounded by other horses to the land where my husband and I were building a house proved very stressful for them, and in turn, stressful for me. My previously confident horses now became fraught when I separated them to ride one. The one left behind became so frantic he was at risk of injury, and the one I was riding wasn't much better. Horses aren't meant to be solo animals. It's one thing to expect them to leave the herd to go with you (a surrogate herd member), but it is another to leave them alone with nothing to occupy their minds except the instinct to reunite with their companion.

That's when I went in search of my mule. My criteria were that the mule must like people—an experienced mule enthusiast told me that was probably the most important quality—and that he or she must be a suitable companion for my horses.

If I believe in love at first sight, it's because of Mikey. He is irrepressibly handsome with a large head and Roman nose, expressive eyes with prominent boney brows, and most of all, glorious, long ears. Some people might think he looks common or maybe even too much like a donkey. His color is a plain red, called sorrel, with a lighter muzzle and belly, and a blond tail and mane. He has no fancy white socks or blaze on his face. But from the moment I met him, Mikey was friendly and loved to have his big ears scratched.

Aside from the love at first sight, our beginning wasn't terribly auspicious. He got in my horse trailer easily enough, but when I stopped a few minutes down the road, he was so nervous and scared that he was drenched in sweat. All I could do was pat him, tell him it would be ok, and hurry home, despite a flat tire on the way.

I soon discovered that he had a terrible case of thrush, a fungal infection in the soft part of the hoof. I could fix that. Within the first week he bit Trip's throat, ripping the skin open. Next he bit Sully's throat. I witnessed the next conflict, and the sight was terrifying and awful. Trip had reared up over Mikey, seeking to intimidate him. Mikey looked intimidated, but instead of fleeing, he stepped toward Trip, tipped his head up, opened his jaws, and clamped his teeth around Trip's neck just behind the jaw. With Trip's throat in his grip, Mikey held Trip's front end off the ground and forced him to walk backward on his hind feet. Mikey showed more strength and ferocity than I had ever seen in a horse, and I wondered what I had gotten myself into. My veterinarian promised that Trip's wound would heal quickly, and thankfully she was right. Eventually, Trip and Mikey reached some sort of understanding and their scuffles resemble the sort of horse play I'm used to seeing, but at the time I worried that one of them might get really hurt.

Over the next couple years, Mikey and I had quite a few mishaps. Once when I was trying to doctor his feet, he knocked me over and stepped on my arm, which by some miracle didn't break. I tried to teach Mikey to pull a cart, resulting in a few small successes punctuated with terrifying and life-threatening accidents and runaways. Mikey has now been permanently designated as a riding mule, NOT a driving mule.

You might be wondering why I kept Mikey, and if I am the sort of person to be so blinded by love that I refuse to see his true nature. Perhaps I am. But anyone who has spent much time with equines will have harrowing stories and quite a few mishaps. Most of Mikey's foibles can be chalked up to bad decisions on my part. But there was something special between me and Mikey.

What was different about Mikey was his ability and willingness to change—especially since mules are known for their stubbornness. We've made significant progress. He has turned into a stellar riding mule, notable for his willingness to go over or through anything I ask him to.

But Mikey's real gift to me is as a mirror. Through him, I am learning to treat myself with the same combination of patience, persistence, and forgiveness that I have in such abundance for him.

Last spring, I attended a three-day clinic with a mule-training specialist. Mikey thrived on my undivided attention as we camped at the facility for four days. I thought Mikey and I bonded more than ever and that he would be ready to do anything I asked of him in the future. When I got back home, I was excited and determined to keep working on the exercises we had learned. I saddled Mikey up, happy to revisit our recent successes.

Mikey had different ideas, which he made clear before we even got to the arena. As we neared the split in the driveway that would determine our destination—road or arena—he leaned right and drifted toward the road. I pressed my leg against his side, urging him left. He pushed back, letting me know that he wanted to go for a walk on the road, not to drill skills in the arena. I understood his sentiment, but for safety and convenience, I needed to be the leader and decider of this team.

My job as the leader is to make the wrong thing hard and the right thing easy. In the clinic, the trainer emphasized that you ask your mule nicely first. Offer them the good deal, use as little pressure as possible, and escalate the request from there. It was time to escalate.

I pulled Mikey's head around to the left, shifted my left leg back, and pressed it against his side. I wasn't using excessive force or kicking him. I didn't have spurs on or a harsh bit. But he knew what I was asking—we had done this before. He tried to continue right but quickly gave in and stepped his haunches to the right, away from my leg. Now his front end was facing the arena again. I released the rein and relaxed my leg.

And he started drifting right again. I repeated my response. Left rein, left leg. His haunches swung back to the right and we proceeded to the arena.

He started drifting again . . . and I repeated the process.

That right there sums up the next two hours. The exit was like a black hole pulling at him. I was like a tiny spaceship nudging at an asteroid, trying to change the trajectory. Every time I got the trajectory realigned and released my pressure, the black hole sucked him back in.

When I told this story to a writing friend and explained how I wanted to write about it, she instantly made a connection I hadn't seen. We'd been talking about how hard it can be to get ourselves to write. If I rewrote the description of getting Mikey to the arena and substituted my name for Mikey's and my desk for the arena, it was a good description of what it is like to try to get myself to write.

I can get myself to write, but the process is so draining that I don't do it often. Similarly, I could get Mikey to the arena, and I could keep him there, but I had to work at it, and that wasn't good enough. I don't want to have this argument every time we ride. It's exhausting. The biggest problem is that to have the success and adventures I want us to have, we have to conquer the boring basics first, whether it's getting into the arena or sitting down at the computer.

For me, it's not enough to just make it into the arena. Nor is it enough to write a paragraph that's technically correct but so boring no one would want to read it. I want my words to soar off the page, and Mikey and I to become a seamless team.

On that day last year, I'd planned to do a quick tune-up in the arena. Instead, two hours later, Mikey and I were dripping in sweat, grumpy, and tired. All we had done was walk and turn. The sun was setting. I wanted to quit. In my head, I begged Mikey to give in, to just stop leaning and drifting to the gate, so we could call it a night.

"Mules aren't stubborn, they're patient," the mule trainer had said during the clinic the previous week. "They are just trying to out-wait you."

If that was Mikey's strategy, it was working. I was frustrated and ready to quit, but I took another deep breath, probably my ten-thou-sandth, and stuck with the process. The methods we'd learned weren't new. It's an old art form that works—if the rider is consistent and skilled enough.

Fortunately, I'd had enough experience with this mule in partic-ular and training equines in general that I knew I had to have faith, be patient, and keep going. Finally, while there was still a little daylight left, I circled Mikey one more time, released my leg pressure and loosened the reins when we pointed away from the gate, relaxed my body, and thought *stop* with my every molecule—and Mikey stopped. I waited a moment, then asked him to flex his neck to the other side without moving his feet, a test of how comfortable and willing he was to just stay put. He stayed. I let out the last bit of breath that I hadn't known I was holding (he probably sighed, too) and patted him. I got off, loosened the girth, and left the arena by a different route than usual.

Success, sort of.

A week earlier, Mikey started the clinic with "lots of go and not enough whoa," he was excited and wanted to walk or trot faster than I was asking, and he either wasn't responsive when I asked him to slow down, or he started right back up again.

By the last day of the clinic, I had the opposite problem: too much whoa and not enough go. This worried me even more than the orig-inal problem. Had I done something wrong? Was he in pain? It was unlike him to be sluggish; he generally had the opposite problem. I asked the trainer about it.

"Your mule is like this one I'm on," he explained to me. "He just doesn't have a good work ethic."

The comment touched some sensitive part deep inside of me. I didn't like the sound of this verdict. A bad work ethic sounded a lot like lazy and no good. I quietly started to panic. I had trusted this man. He helped people with really bad mule problems, and I didn't even have a really bad mule problem—or I didn't think I had a bad mule problem until he said my mule didn't have a good work ethic.

Before I could process any of this, and definitely before I could verbalize it or form another question, the clinic was over.

As I drove home, and over the following week, the idea of work ethic continued to nag at me. I felt I could trust this trainer, who was the same man who'd said that mules aren't stubborn, just patient; a man who has dedicated his life to mule training. I had to be missing something.

In my world, inside my head, "no work ethic" is code for "lazy." And lazy is something I used to think I was, sometimes I still catch myself fearing that I am. Every time I hear someone say with disgust —and it's almost always with disgust—"Well, that's just lazy" or anything else with that word, I feel a tiny, poignant cut to my heart. No: to my soul, my self-worth, my self. To be lazy is to be worthless. Or even worse: a burden. And when I'm avoiding writing, I must be lazy. So there I was, a lazy writer with a lazy mule. More than anything, I worried that lazy was an incurable, innate flaw.

More than a decade ago, a therapist pointed out that maybe huddling in front of the TV with my siblings instead of doing our chores wasn't lazy. Maybe it was a coping mechanism. We were surviving the grief and loneliness of our parents' divorce, and in my case, coping with the depression and anxiety that have plagued me for much of my life.

Later, I wondered out loud to the same therapist if laziness even truly existed in the shameful way I'd always thought of it. Lazy is defined as averse or disinclined to work, activity, or exertion. Indolent.

Everyone gets tired and needs a break, but working for reward or a positive outcome is human nature. The things we're most proud of, our most joyous moments, almost always involve some sort of work and the resulting reward. The problems arise when we work without payoff.

Work can mean all sorts of things: talking through a rough patch in a relationship, doing a job, training a mule, washing the dishes. It doesn't always result in a positive outcome. Relationships fail despite the work we put into them. Some paychecks aren't enough to get by on. Your mule is hard-mouthed despite all your time. There are always more dirty dishes. But as long as we get some payoff, *some* of the time, it's usually enough to keep us striving.

Renowned horse trainer Ray Hunt said, "A horse [or mule] does one of two things. He does what he thinks he's supposed to do, or he does what he thinks he needs to do to survive."

Horses and mules aren't good or bad. They are trying to survive. Mikey was just trying to survive, to be safe and comfortable, and that included preferring a nice ride down the road to getting picked on in the arena. Could I blame him for that?

Does this reasoning apply to people, too? I think so.

I wasn't lazy and never had been. Anxious, yes. Depressed, yes. Fearful, indecisive, yes and yes. Surviving, coping; those were things I had done. No teacher or coach ever called me lazy. Quite the opposite, actually. With a clear task or goal, and someone to go to if problems or questions arose, I could go all day. I craved that sort of opportunity—still do. But school and sports have very clear indicators and measures of success. Life is rarely so simple.

The trainer from the clinic subscribed to the same school of thought as Ray Hunt. I don't think he meant my mule was lazy, and he'd already told me that he was impressed by my work ethic. So what did he mean? And what did it mean for my mule's future?

The next time I rode Mikey, it only took an hour and a half for him to start to relax and focus on me instead of the gate. Once he relaxed and listened to me, I got off, loosened his girth, and walked him back to the barn—his paycheck earned.

The next time, it took us forty-five minutes to reach that point.

Not many days later, he yielded his haunches perfectly and easily from the beginning of our groundwork session. I rode him around the arena and he turned with ease wherever I wanted. It felt as if his legs were becoming my legs. To reward him, I directed him out of the arena and turned toward the road. He was so excited by this that he started to take over, pulling me toward the road. I returned to our tiny circles and he quickly came back to me. Since then if he gets strong or pushy, we do our circles and begin again. It takes fewer and fewer circles.

Mikey is like my mind wanting to escape the hard work. I have to be ready to be the responsible one, bringing myself back over and over again. But it is that discipline that allows us to advance, to go down the road and on larger adventures, fording rivers and climbing mountains.

On the first day of the mule clinic, the trainer said, "A lot of these mules don't know what it means to get a paycheck." He explained that mules and horses learn from the release. You ask them with leg pressure or the reins to do something. When they respond, you release the pressure. The release is how they know they did something right. That's how they learn what you want.

The release is the paycheck. It may sound strange or harsh, but for equines, it's natural. It makes sense. Herds have rules, and the reward for following them is membership in the herd and freedom from pressure. If a horse wants another horse to move out of the way, she applies pressure, from an ugly look to a kick or bite. When the horse moves, she releases the pressure.

When riders and handlers pull and kick without a prompt release or a clear intention—when there isn't a paycheck—the animals respond by actively resisting or learning to tune us out.

As I puzzled this out, I realized that the trainer wasn't saying that Mikey was lazy, but rather that he didn't understand the paycheck system yet, and maybe that Mikey's forgiving nature lends itself more toward tuning out than to volatility and acting out.

My own work ethic, I started to understand, had been damaged or underdeveloped. My depression and anxiety got in the way of my paychecks so I'd rarely felt the satisfaction of a job well done, and I didn't reward myself for working hard. I had no "good boy" or release of pressure, no pat or scratch on the withers. I was always kicking and pulling myself along, like a donkey sitting in the road, refusing to pull the cart a single step farther.

All Mikey needed was more time and patience, rewards and releases. The more times I ask him to do something, and then reward him for doing it, the more work ethic I deposit in his bank account. Even a year later, he will still occasionally drift or lean toward something he'd rather be doing, but it's easier and easier to bring him back to a place of focus.

I could clearly see myself in Mikey, but how could I translate the cure to my dilemma? What is the equivalent of leg pressure and reins on a wily, mulish human?

It has taken me almost a year to figure this out and put it into the words you're reading now. What I needed is what I gave Mikey, and what Mikey needed was not so much the right rein or leg pressure, but persistence, patience, and forgiveness. I don't get mad at him when he leans toward the road. Getting mad at a mule is like putting another stone in your pack. Criticizing myself gets the same results.

Mikey Mule weighs at least 1,200 pounds. I cannot make him go into the arena or stay there. I can only continue asking him until he begins to understand that it's easier to just go. Eventually he will feel or know that it's best to go with me, that I am a good and benevolent leader to be trusted and followed even into circumstances he wouldn't choose. Likewise, I cannot beat myself into writing. I can only keep leading myself there every day and, most importantly, keep forgiving myself for the struggle.

Even now, months after I first drafted this essay, I have to bring myself back, slowly, patiently picking the computer up after a long absence for one more edit, one more rewrite. Sometimes my return to the keyboard is brief, but I don't give up. I keep coming back. I write more and the change is reflected in my writing.

Training Mikey has taught me to have hope for myself and not to be discouraged or deterred by setbacks. When I started this essay last year, the frustration at not being able to fully articulate these ideas was so palpable and painful that I quit several times. But I came back, again and again. As I learn to trust myself and have faith in the process, writing gets easier; I need less and less internal circling and my repertoire of movements and skills is growing. I am becoming for myself the leader that I am for Mikey. Just as I look forward to future adventures with Mikey, the mountains to climb and rivers to cross, I can see myself doing the same with my writing.

46

MY HUSBAND'S HANDS

BY LUANN ATKIN KOESTER

Damn, there they are again,
sitting on top of my dryer,
stiff, arthritic-like fingers, contorted
and stained
with blood, and oil,
with sweat and dirt.

Once they were soft, supple,
the fingers smooth and pliable.
Once tanned to a subtle russet,
the suede palms may have caressed my cheek.

Cattle dander and wheat dust
settle in the crevices,
stick to the stains,
make my dryer dirty and my nose itch.

They smell like the pickup,
the dog,
the diesel overran this morning.

An old, frayed band of black and red
circles each wrist.
The small silver buckles undone
for the night.

Ugly,
but when cinched tight around his wrists,
a white calf gripped snug between his knees
as he tags it his,

they are
strength,
beautiful and sexy.

To Mary –
Enjoy!
John Chistenson

47

A TREE GROWS IN THE MAN CAVE

BY JOHN CHISTENSON

At the risk of becoming the media's *cause célèbre* once again, I'm going to pen an article entitled, "Five Warning Signs Your Husband Might Turn into a Tree." We may be the first couple this has happened to, but I doubt we'll be the last.

These are the signs I ignored at my own peril:

1. My husband was born in Long Branch, New Jersey.
2. He drove a Toyota Sequoia, the only vehicle named after a tree (when he could still drive, that is, before he took root).
3. When he was a stockbroker, before getting laid off a year ago, he told his clients, "You won't get rich overnight, but your money will grow slowly over the years, like an acorn into a mighty oak." Yes, he really said that.
4. His drink of choice was single malt whiskey aged in oak casks, and
5. This one should have been obvious: His name was Forrest.

Let me amend that: His name *is* Forrest.

But did I heed any of those signs that my husband of thirty-five years would get all leafy on me? I did not. Did I notice when bark and branches replaced bald head and beer belly? How could I, when I didn't see Forrest at all in those days? You might say I couldn't see the Forrest for the trees, if the trees were the demands of being a geriatric nurse working a 12-on 12-off schedule at the hospital, too exhausted when I came home to do anything except call out goodnight in the general direction of the den before collapsing into bed.

In my defense, Forrest's beloved Tar Heels were in the Final Four, and whenever one of his teams made the postseason he retreated to his man cave for the duration, glued to his 72-inch, ultra-HD smart TV. I was accustomed to never hearing a peep out of him during those marathons, since he watched them from the most tricked-out Barcalounger on the planet, where he also ate and slept.

How long before I realized what had happened to Forrest? Not as long as you might think. As for the authorities and Forrest's mother, that was a different matter.

The day I walked into the den and discovered the melding of bark and Barcalounger had started out as one of the best days of my life, a day I'd been looking forward to for a long time. When my 4:00 a.m. to 4:00 p.m. shift had ended, I'd walked into the personnel office and signed my separation papers. No fanfare, no farewell party, no fare-thee-well from anyone except Margaret, an elderly patient ravaged by cancer and dementia whom I'd grown attached to. She'd grabbed my arm with a force I didn't think she had left in her and whispered, "Alma, I know what a burden life has become for you. You've shriveled up until you're nothing but a dry husk."

I'd smiled and patted her cheek, and thought nothing of her words until I merged onto the freeway for my last, hellish commute. Margaret was right—life had become burdensome. I felt like I no longer mattered, no longer made a difference to anyone. Nursing, which had once been my calling, had become a reverse IV drip, draining me of hope, contentment, a sense of purpose. I had indeed become an empty husk. I'd only vaguely been aware this was happening, but now the truth of Margaret's words hit me with such force I almost drove into the guardrail.

"Oh, Forrest," I whispered, "we never . . . we couldn't have kids, we only had each other, and I let you down. But that's going to change, I promise."

I thought of our youthful passions of long ago, mine for travelling the world, Forrest's for painting. Perhaps we could combine them—plein air painting of the Grand Canal, followed by *aperitivos* and romantic dinners on the Piazza San Marco. We could bask in the Italian sun, no longer merely marking time as we'd done for years.

I made it home without an accident and marched to the den, Final Four be damned, to raise the curtain on our new life.

"Forrest," I called. "Forrest, honey, we have to talk."

No answer. And no sign of Forrest. That was the first time I beheld the tree. A sturdy-looking specimen perhaps a dozen feet high, it stood under the skylight in the cathedral ceiling exactly where the Barcalounger had been. Its brown bark, roughly the color of the knotty-pine paneling covering the walls of the den, swirled like the whorls in fingerprints. This was odd enough, but the blue, silver, and white streaks running through the leaves disturbed me even more. At first I didn't understand why, but then I had it—they were the Tar Heels' team colors.

The tree wasn't in a pot like the ficus and the lemon tree, one on either side of the television, but appeared to be rooted in the floor. I gingerly touched the bark, then quickly recoiled. It was . . . pliable, almost like skin. Extremely wrinkled skin. And it may have been my imagination, but it felt slightly warm to the touch. Then I noticed the most disturbing thing of all.

The Barcalounger was still there.

Well, parts of it, anyway. The flip-up footrest protruded from the base of the tree's trunk, covered with that cheesy Naugahyde Forrest loved. And armrests seemed to be growing out of the trunk, like mutated branches. It looked like the tree had settled in to watch sports and munch nachos (speaking of cheesy), just like Forrest would if he were here.

"Forrest!" I called. "Where the hell are you? This isn't funny!" I circumnavigated the den, checking to see if Forrest was crouching behind the furniture or hiding behind the drapes. No Forrest, and, except for a thick coating of dust, no changes since I'd last darkened the door of his den. When was that, exactly? I couldn't remember.

"Forrest!" I repeated as I widened my search, examining the rooms of the house, then the yard, even peeking into the garden shed, and finally the garage. Forrest's Toyota Sequoia was still there, and since he didn't have any friends left, at least none that I knew of, he couldn't have gone far.

Ah. I had it—the basement. "Okay, we have to talk," I said in a no-nonsense voice as I clomped down the narrow stairs. It was full of a lifetime of uncollated junk we kept out of sight and out of mind. I turned on a light and began my exploration. Nothing unusual in the main part of the basement or the furnace room. One last place to check—a storage room directly under the den. I entered the room cautiously, steeling myself for, I didn't know what, maybe the lifeless eyes of my husband staring up at me after dying of a myocardial infarction like his father had when Forrest was a boy.

I could only stand and stare at the sight that greeted me. My heart hammered like I was the one having an MI. A pair of gigantic, twisted roots filled the room. I peered upward and saw that they were coming through the room's ceiling. They must belong to the tree in the den.

I didn't know what to do now. Forrest had vanished, and all I had was a tree that couldn't possibly be here, but it was. I looked around for any clue that could help me. Something about the ends of the roots seemed odd. I knelt down to get a better look and let loose a scream.

Each root had a boot attached to the end of it. There could be no mistaking Forrest's blue-and-white boots, silver Tar Heels logos embossed on the toes. He always wore them for good luck when his team made the playoffs, even while sitting in the Barcalounger.

I started to run out of this root cellar and get as far away from here as possible, but decided instead to confront this horror and get to the bottom of it. I knelt and tugged on one of the boots, harder and harder, until it suddenly came free, causing me to fall backward and land on my butt. I reached into the boot and pulled out the tattered remains of an argyle sock that looked like Forrest's, then examined the now-exposed end of the root. Instead of tapering to a tip, the root ended in a foot complete with five toes, glistening with a ghastly white sheen like something that had never seen the light of day.

I must have fainted dead away at that point because I awoke lying on the basement floor, my cheek pressed against the cold concrete. After retreating upstairs, I located a bottle of Forrest's precious whiskey in the den and went to the kitchen to fortify myself with several shots.

A myriad of possibilities spun in my head, ranging from a scenario where Forrest had met his demise at the hands, as it were, of a man-eating tree, to one where he'd masterminded an elaborate practical joke, even though his sense of humor was nil. I shelved those ideas for the time being and called Jeanette Williams, a social worker who lived across the street. She was the closest thing I had to a friend.

"Jeanette, it's Alma. Have you seen Forrest lately?"

"No, I haven't seen him in . . . I can't even remember when I last saw him. Why do you ask?"

"Because, um . . . he's missing. Forrest is gone, but his feet are still here."

"Slow down, Alma. Tell me what you know."

"Forrest is gone, and there's a tree where he used to be, and the basement is full of roots, and the roots have boots, and . . ." I stopped, horrified at the gibberish spewing from my mouth.

"Alma, are you all right?"

"No, Jeanette, I'm not. I retired so I could spend time with my husband, and what did I find when I came home? A damn tree!"

"It sounds like he's left you, Alma. I'm so sorry. It happens all the time. Maybe it's only temporary. Do you want to talk? Do you want me to come over?"

I was too upset and exhausted to be sociable, so I said, "No, that's okay." Then I added, "I'm sure he'll show up in a day or two," even though I wasn't certain of that at all.

"Sure he will. Feel free to call anytime."

I called a few more people on our block and asked about Forrest in the most nonchalant tone I could muster, since the last thing I needed was panicky neighbors. No one had seen him. Then, not wanting to alert the police at this point but wanting to do something, I called the local university and asked to speak to an arborist. They connected me to the forestry department, and a male voice said, "This is Jacob Matheson."

"Mr. Matheson my name is Alma Ritter, and I have, ah . . . I have an anomalous tree to report."

There was a pause. "I'm sorry, did you say anomalous?"

I took a deep breath. "Yes sir. It's growing in my husband's den, where his easy chair used to be, and it has roots that are . . ." I caught myself before I said, "roots that are feet." Instead, I told him, "It has a digital root structure."

"Digital root structure?"

"Yes, and soft, pliable bark. You see why I say it's anomalous?"

There was a longer pause. "Ma'am, perhaps I can help if you email me pictures of the tree. My address is on the university website."

Suddenly, frustration and fear hit me and I blurted out, "The roots appear to be my husband's feet! They're white and slimy and horrible, but they *smell* like my husband's feet. That sounds crazy, but trust me, I'd know that odor anywhere. And the tree resembles my husband in a woody sort of way. I think the tree has eaten him or subsumed him or whatever it is trees do. I need help, so please don't hang up! I—"

At that point there was only a dial tone. I snapped pictures of the tree, the roots, and that horrible foot and sent them to the arborist for all the good they would do.

Imagine my surprise when I received a call shortly after that from Jacob Matheson, saying he'd like to examine the tree. The university was close by, and he arrived in a few minutes. First, I showed him the tree in the den, then took him down to the basement. He flinched when he saw the root-foot, from the sight or the smell, or both, I couldn't tell.

He asked if he could pull the other boot off, and I said, "Be my guest." At first I couldn't look, but when I finally forced myself, I saw another foot, glistening with the same deathly whiteness as the first one, like something you'd find under a rock.

After a long silence, the arborist said, "I've got a sample bag in my truck. With your permission, I'd like to take scrapings from the bark and roots and have them analyzed."

"Then you believe the tree ate my husband?"

He shook his head. "I don't believe anything at this point, but if you'd be willing to give me a toothbrush that belonged to your husband, I can test this bizarre theory of yours."

"Toothbrush?"

"To cross-match the DNA." After he'd collected samples from the tree and left, I wandered back to the den and slumped onto the vintage lime-green shag carpet, next to the tree.

I put my head in my hands. "Oh Forrest, please tell me what this all means. I need to talk to you, to open my heart to you the way I haven't done in forever. I still love you, but that love has shriveled into a dry husk, just like Margaret said. If you were here, you'd say my love was an acorn in winter, waiting for spring so it could take root and grow."

Was I crazy? I was talking to it, baring my heart and soul like I used to do with Forrest long ago. I caressed the soft bark, which shivered almost imperceptibly at my touch. The idea that Forrest had turned into a tree verged on insanity, but a visceral feeling filled me with utter certainty that he was here, and that we were still inextricably entwined together.

"Forrest," I said in a hoarse whisper. "The tree didn't devour you after all. You *are* the tree."

I gently touched the tree's leaves and realized they were heart-shaped, like those of the Bodhi tree under which Buddha had attained enlightenment. And so, in that spirit, I meditated under the leafy canopy and found my way to a difficult but wondrous truth—that Forrest, and more importantly his spirit, had withered and died during a long, hard winter. But, in a way I didn't yet fully understand, he'd been reborn from the earth and was reaching upward, toward the sun and the sky.

The next day, Forrest's mother, thin as a stick and sporting a cane, showed up for one of her unannounced visits. In a moment of irrational idiocy, I thought this woman—who thoroughly despised me because she held me responsible for everything from the loss of Forrest's job to his chronic foot odor—should know the truth about her son. So, I showed her the tree, taking care to point out the bits of Barcalounger protruding from it.

Her face twisted into a rictus of pure loathing. "What are you trying to pull here, Alma? Just tell me where my son is."

"I will," I said. "But first we have to go down to the basement."

The old woman brandished her cane at me. "I'm not going near the basement. You've killed Forrest and hid his body down there, haven't you? And now you want to do the same to me!"

"Your son is here," I said, "right in front of you. I know how crazy this sounds, but he's transformed into a tree."

"Of all the . . ." She swung the cane at me, showing surprising agility for her age, and almost connected with my skull. "You've never cared about anyone but yourself, and now you've disposed of my son like you were taking out the trash." She swung the cane again, and I blocked it with my forearm.

"Please, Mrs. Ritter," I said as I massaged my arm, "you have to listen to me. Forrest is here!"

Mrs. Ritter hurled more invectives at me before calling the police.

That, of course, was when my private nightmare became a public spectacle, ending with my story plastered across every tabloid, news outlet, and social media site. I won't bore you with the details, but suffice it to say that the authorities decided from the get-go that I was behind Forrest's disappearance. The *National Enquirer* paid me more for this story than I'd made in a year of nursing, and I acquired a fanatical following who believed in my innocence. But that didn't sway the District Attorney.

The most damning piece of evidence was from Jacob Matheson—he'd determined that DNA from the root-feet matched the sample from Forrest's toothbrush. I'd been in favor of the DNA profiling in order to find out the truth about the tree, but it had backfired horribly. When the case went to trial, the prosecuting attorney told the jury this constituted prima facie evidence that I had cut up my husband's corpse in some satanic ritual à la Jeffrey Dahmer and attached his feet to the tree. The case against me seemed open-and-shut.

But then, miracle of miracles, the estimable Mr. Matheson provided a ray of hope. He'd given his samples to a research biologist at the university, who had analyzed them and now believed what I'd known ever since my tête-à-tête, or tête-à-tree, as it were: Forrest was still alive, even if he wasn't kicking. The biologist concluded that my husband had been transformed into a tree; that Forrest and the tree growing in the den were one and the same. When asked to elaborate, he said he'd discovered a combination of arboreal and human genetic material in the tree, creating an entirely new genome. His term for this process was spontaneous arborogenesis—the creation of a new type of tree-like organism.

I could tell by their expressions that this testimony convinced neither the judge nor the jury. Things went from bad to worse when Forrest's mother took the stand to testify for the prosecution as a character witness. She said I'd always hated her son (a total lie) and wasn't surprised I'd done away with him. The attorney seemed nonplussed by this statement and asked if she had any evidence. Had I ever hit her son or verbally abused him? Had I talked openly about killing him? Mrs. Ritter admitted she had observed no such behavior.

"Then what do you base this assertion on?" the attorney asked her.

"Alma always criticized him. She didn't like what he wore, especially his boots, didn't like what he ate, didn't like what he watched on television, never listened to him at all."

This, I had to admit, was partially correct. Okay, it was mostly correct.

"And she didn't want anything to do with him after he lost his job," she continued. "I think she was ashamed of him."

"That's not—" I started to blurt out, then shushed myself. I was going to say that wasn't true, but in fact it had a seed of truth. I had grown tired of explaining that Forrest was whiling away his days watching TV. Finally, I'd stopped talking about him, out of a sense of despair, hopelessness, and yes, shame. And lately I'd used my job as an excuse to avoid Forrest completely. Damn that woman, she was right.

But she was telling only half the story. What about Forrest? Didn't he deserve some of the blame? Hadn't he made a decision, conscious or otherwise, to check out of this marriage? True, he hadn't physically walked out on me, but he'd found a way to turn himself into another species, as the biologist had said. One that didn't have to defend a sedentary lifestyle.

"She wanted him out of the way when she retired," Mrs. Ritter said, "so she could enjoy herself."

Because of the seriousness of the charge against me, my lawyer petitioned the court for a temporary change of venue. He wanted to move the trial to my house so that the tree could be examined first-hand. The prosecution hesitantly agreed, but the judge wasn't going to allow it until my lawyer cited precedents, mostly in situations where the defendant was too ill to appear in a courtroom. That wasn't quite the same as this case, but after mulling it over, the judge finally assented.

The next day we reconvened in Forrest's den. It was a tight fit, which meant the public and the media were banned. The judge and jury examined the tree, then went down to the basement to see the roots. Some of the jurors were whiter than Forrest's root-feet when they returned to the den.

Forrest's mother almost got herself ejected from this makeshift courtroom when she waved at the tree and shouted, "Hi, sonny, how's my boy? I hear your bark is worse than your bite." When the bailiff attempted to quiet her, she said, "What's the problem, am I making an ash of myself?" and dissolved into hysterical laughter.

When she finally quieted down, the prosecutor called me to the stand (one of Forrest's barstools). After I was sworn in, he asked how I could be certain the tree was my husband, since the biologist's tests could only confirm taxonomy, not identity.

I shook my head. "I don't understand. He found Forrest's DNA in the tree."

"Yes," the attorney agreed, "but I still don't find the idea that the tree and your husband are one and the same to be credible. Isn't it far more likely that you somehow incorporated your husband's DNA into the tree as a diversion to keep us from discovering how you disposed of his remains?"

Instead of answering, I stared at the dappled sunlight coming through Forrest's leaves, creating lovely patterns on the worn carpet. Peace and contentment once again flowed through me. My breathing calmed, my heart slowed, and the anger engendered by Forrest's mother drained out of me.

"It's true that I resented my husband because he didn't listen to me," I said. "But now he hears and understands everything. Not just my words; he hears *me*."

"Surely," the attorney said, "you can't believe you're in communication with this tree?"

"Forrest is now more than just my husband," I said. "He's

husband, father, mother, whatever I need him to be."

Mrs. Ritter stood up. "Oh for the love of God. Do we have to listen to any more of this?"

A sudden impulse made me grab her hand and force it to touch the tree. She opened her mouth as if to scream, but then a look of melancholy came over her and tears filled her eyes. She kept her hand on the bark even after I let it go.

"It was his favorite tree," she said after a long silence.

"I'm sorry," the judge said. "Do you wish to make a statement?"

Her voice grew louder. "A gigantic cottonwood in our backyard, been there since the land was homesteaded a century earlier. Forrest went there to play, to read, to think, to hide from his older brother who beat him up all the time." She paused and took a deep breath.

"Mrs. Ritter," the judge said, "are you all right?"

She nodded. "It happened so suddenly, on Halloween night when Forrest was eleven. He'd just gotten home with a bagful of candy and found an ambulance and firetruck at the house. He had to watch his father being wheeled out on a stretcher, beyond the help of the EMTs. He threw the bag of candy down and ran off. I didn't find him until the next morning, almost frozen to death, huddled in a tree-house his father had built for him in that old cottonwood. He insisted on sleeping in the tree for months after that, no matter how cold it got. There were times when I caught him talking to the tree, like he was talking to his father. I tried to comfort him, but I never could."

She bowed her head, and the court was silent.

Mrs. Ritter's testimony hit me so hard I could hardly breathe. Forrest had never told me the details of his father's death. I walked around the tree, gazing up at the branches. "You felt hopeless when your father died," I said to Forrest, "like there was no way forward. And that's how you've felt this last year, like your life had no purpose." A sob burst out of me. "It was the cottonwood that saved you. Maybe it contained your father's spirit, I don't know. And now . . . you've saved yourself the only way you knew how."

Forrest's mother gently took my hand. We looked at each other in silence. And even though there were no words, we were truly speaking to each other for the first time.

That was the end of the session. When we reconvened back at the courthouse the next day, the jury returned a verdict of not guilty. Not because they believed the tree was my husband, but because of the lack of sufficient evidence that I had murdered him.

That was a year ago, and the media coverage has finally abated. I'm obviously not able to sell the house and move, so I've used the money from the *Enquirer* to build a high security wall around the property. I've also expanded the den into a glass-enclosed atrium so that Forrest has room to grow, and I've provided a continuous water supply in the basement to nourish his roots. The boots now rest atop the remains of the Barcalounger's footrest. A 98-inch TV has replaced the 72-incher, with the hope that Forrest can still enjoy sports after a fashion—especially, of course, his Tar Heels.

I've been to the Piazza San Marco, and even though Forrest wasn't able to travel with me, I could still see him and talk to him via a Tree Cam. His mother accompanied me, and it turned out she was an accomplished painter in her own right. She said her paintings, which now hang in the atrium where Forrest can see them, or at least sense them, express Forrest's deepest feelings, feelings that bind him to the earth.

Oh, and she's moved into the house. We still face hurdles in overcoming more than a quarter-century of animosity, and so far we've only achieved an amiable détente, not a true level of understanding. But no matter what is happening in our lives, we always find time to sit together under Forrest's protective canopy.

I often sit alone under Forrest and talk the way we hadn't done since the early years of our marriage. He's been reborn in all his arboreal splendor, and in turn he's helping me achieve my own rebirth. The more we converse, sharing thoughts and feelings beyond the reach of words, the more our roots grow deeper and stronger, breaking through years of isolation and loneliness as the earth rolls on around the sun and winter finally gives way to spring.

48

COTTONWOOD

BY JOHN BLAIR

copse surrounds
a two-top giant ypsilon
framed by November's
lenticular cirrus
azure edges.
Should there be more leaves?

It sends sugars through roots
nourishes companions
together surviving in
an east sloping arroyo
where meagre implies
perishable.

It would do me good
Jim,
to see you,
broad shoulders, shy smile,

calm, self-effacing, loyal
you nurtured us,
me
a cottonwood among cottonwoods.

49

A LOVE STORY FOR ALL SEASONS

BY SALLY JO

Spring and Summer fell in love
Much to the surprise of the stars above
He filled the air with blossoms for her
Her heated kiss made his lifeblood stir
But her warmth and exuberance became too much
He withered away under her firm touch
Then an older Summer fell in love with Fall
They thought each other best of all
Their feminine curves soon blended together
They flirted with heat and with cooler weather
But Fall was needy and smothered her lover
Her cool embrace caused the death of Summer
Then love between Fall and Winter came
She donned her bright colors, he whispered her name
He threaded his fingers of frost in her hair
She shivered for him as he stripped her bare
But he was too cold to hold onto her heart
Soon his freezing touch caused her soul to depart
Then slowly Winter fell in love with Spring

Spring's warming body made Winter's blood sing
Their masculine energy played across the land
They worshipped each other, didn't understand
Spring's heat was melting Winter's frozen soul
He disappeared slowly as Spring became whole
Then again to the shock of the stars up above
Spring and Summer fell in love

50

AIR SUPPLY

BY KRISTIN OWENS

After five mind-numbing hours at Sierra Trading Post and REI, my husband acquired all the necessary gear scribbled on his list. I had no idea the cost of roughing-it equated to purchasing a small Mazda. Three different water filters, assorted weightless pots and pans, flashlights of every shape and size . . . the pile of equipment was astonishing. We owned tools for any plausible emergency. No, it wasn't for an expedition to Nepal, but for a brief stint in the Colorado woods. Surprisingly, as the cashier totaled our wares and tried to locate larger shopping bags, I was calm.

Some background. For an East Coast girl, the outdoors usually spells trouble. Hiking and camping inherently have the potential of doing without. Without what? Anything that equates to comfort or convenience. I like clean, sanitary water that magically dispenses from a faucet. A flushing toilet. And a comfortable mattress. But after relocating to Colorado, my dreams of vacationing in luxurious five-star Fifth Avenue accommodations soared out the window. New nightmares starred hungry bears, torrential rain, and forgetting coffee filters.

My husband knew this and *still* married me. Not one to duck a new experience, I said *I'd try*. I'd try to camp outdoors. I'd try to go hiking. As long as we didn't forget a corkscrew.

Our outdoor adventures started small: an overnight in a state park. Not completely roughing it, but I required baby steps. In the time spent unloading our newly purchased gear and pitching our tent, I had opportunities to ponder random thoughts. First, no iPhone or TV to distract me. Disconcerting! I struggled with the tranquility.

Given this new occasion for thoughts to wander, existential questions found their way in and nagged. Such as, *why* do we camp? To feel more connected to nature? In my modern, tech-centric life, I did everything in my power to protect myself *from* nature. Normally I spent hours planning for her not-so-funny surprises. Thus, letting nature *in* was counterintuitive, an internal conflict providing hours of stress. I wondered: in the end, who would win?

Later that night, securely zipped into a rain-resistant tent, with my headlamp within arm's reach, I dreamt strange dreams. I floated on a raft down the Amazon with hungry alligators nipping at my feet. My toes were being munched on like free appetizers at happy hour. I struggled, trying to get away, but my uncooperative raft kept spinning around and around. It slowly collapsed from a hole made by a gigantic alligator tooth. The raft grew smaller as I clawed to remain afloat. Suddenly, my husband shook me awake. He was less than an inch from my face, as both of us had rolled and sunk into the middle of the deflated air mattress. The dog had taken all the covers, and my frozen feet poked out of the sleeping bag. I whimpered, "This is not fun."

In spite of the crappy air mattress, we had a good time. Camping made things simple. Grilled hotdogs and a bag of potato chips provided an uncomplicated supper. The campfire kept us toasty warm. We burrowed into sleeping bags, giggled, and peeked out at the moon's reflection on the lake. Small nagging distractions disappeared. No internet meant no inconsequential pinging. The doorbell didn't ring. Glancing over my shoulder, there were only trees looking back. I spent an hour thinking without interruption. Peaceful. Calm. I could breathe.

Nonetheless, I got dirty and smelly. But when marshmallows got stuck in my hair, I didn't mind. I felt like a kid. And that brought back memories of easier, stress-free times. The ever-present knot in my chest loosened and untied itself. Maybe the outdoors wasn't so bad. Surrounded by plenty of food, my ever-resourceful husband, and a sweet pup, I really lacked for nothing. I felt safe. In the morning, the crisp and clean air invigorated me. A new day. I concluded I could do this again.

Newly inspired, I was game for a longer jaunt. I figured the more the merrier, so we asked our adventurous next-door neighbors along for a weekend getaway. These folks have seen the world—the intimidating, non-European parts like Nepal, Antarctica, and Bhutan. Also, we had previously day-hiked together, resulting in epic picnic lunches. I knew they had their priorities in order. Plus, they had nicer gear. And they could cook.

An empty campground awaited us, and we claimed it all to ourselves. All sixty-two spaces. We laughed loudly, let the dog run free, and spread ourselves out. How glorious to sit with a glass of wine, squint in the sun, and watch the trees sway on the mountainsides. I contentedly relaxed, balanced on my camp chair while approving the vistas. The guys spent the afternoon drinking seasonal beers and shooting slingshots at a target in the trees. The gals read six months' worth of magazines and chatted. No agenda.

Again, with the fresh air and space to breathe, my mind opened up. I contemplated, why do modern humans feel the need to rough it? To prove we still can? Primal needs certainly must be met: food, clothing, and shelter. But as a society we've become horrifically soft. Drive-throughs, Amazon, Alexa. We want everything fast and cheap. It's a wonder we survive. On that note, did Maslow ever camp?

I'm not certain if the four of us actually roughed it that weekend. We may have slept in tents, but our meals were Michelin-star quality. For dinner, we made hobo pies; sliced potatoes, exotic spices, and grilled steak steamed in aluminum foil over the fire. I brought an Austrian wine—Grüner Veltliner—and although not an ideal pairing on paper, we all declared it fantastic. Dessert was a tower of designer cookies from a local bakery. Next morning at breakfast, we ate pancakes with real maple syrup and fresh blueberries. Certainly no one starved.

Just when we finished a meal, the cleanup dance began. We boiled water, washed dishes, dried with the still wet dishrag, re-puzzled mess kits, disassembled stoves, and stowed it all in the car. Only to start the next meal minutes later. Though we were stuffed, the sandwich maker made an appearance at night around the camp-fire. White Wonder bread with the cheapest no-name pie filling, squirt butter, and voilà—a pie!

We burned our lips, tongues, and fingers on scorching hot pies as childhood memories came racing back. Each of us had camped in varying degrees as children and we compared long-forgotten memories. Whose father told the scariest ghost stories? Which state parks did we camp at? How many stickers collected on the station wagon? More sidesplitting stories and laughter. Our commonalities or differences didn't matter. So much to talk about, and we liked each other well enough to listen.

Later that night in teeth-chattering 25 degrees, elk partied and bugled at the next campsite over. Scared to die a trampled death, I froze in my sleeping bag and clutched my lip balm, thinking of new names for my husband. This was *not* the way I wanted to go. My entire body, petrified in fear, refused to move the slightest inch . . . Elk don't smell fear, do they? Do they eat meat? Why is the dog still snoring? Doesn't he hear them? Why did we even bring the dog? The next morning, my husband dismissed my concerns and grumbled that I hogged the air mattress. When I refuted, he showed me the zipper mark embedded across his forehead from the tent window. Apparently, our sleeping arrangement still needed work.

Like the previous adventure, the air mattress was my chief complaint, in addition to experiencing night terror while listening to wild animals fornicating. As the four of us packed up on Sunday afternoon, and with our bellies full of eggs benedict, we vowed to make camping an annual event. Once home, it took hours to unpack and clean everything . . . The smell of campfire smoke had permeated throughout the gear. I had no postcards or souvenirs, only great new memories.

I reflected while unzipping sleeping bags and hanging them off the patio to air out. Solitude can be unnerving, yet I was learning to welcome the quiet and peace with nothing between me and the outside but a thin tent canvas. With each trip into the unknown (and all the ambiguities) I was learning flexibility. I was bending and not breaking.

The next year, I wanted to try something a little more comfortable and less exposed to marauding wildlife. I did some research and learned a fun fact: Mongolia is approximately 6,189 miles away from Colorado. However, it turns out both have yurts. Yurts are basically treehouses for grown-ups. Round in shape, they have a floor, a roof, and proper walls, which provide a nice layer of protection from outside animals, unless they know how to knock. Colorado yurts are popular and tend to rent fast, so by the time the four of us got ourselves organized, a walk-in option with a parking lot approximately ten minutes away was the last choice for the season. We booked it for a weekend in September.

We found a wheelbarrow in the parking lot. After three trips rolling over uneven ground, we finally schlepped all our gear to the yurt. Obviously, we brought too much. Each couple, thinking about the luxury of extra space, packed two of everything. This resulted in four lanterns, four frying pans and lots of alcohol. I didn't complain.

It turns out that *yurt* in Mongolian means *home*, and ours was just that. The yurt came equipped with all the essentials. Locked bear box for food on the outside porch. Table and chairs for both outside and in. Brooms, dishtowels, everything needed to keep the yurt clean and tidy. Two charcoal grills, a woodburning stove with two cords of firewood, and a gas cooktop with a large propane tank underneath for plenty of hot eats. It also had an outhouse. It was yurtastic!

We oohed and ahhed at this latest upgrade. Then abruptly stopped and sucked in our collective breath. Bunk beds. The website touted sleeping for four, but bunk beds never crossed my mind as a conceivable option. I hadn't slept in one since Girl Scout camp in 1976. Quickly, terror filled my heart as I envisioned the whole thing collapsing, and my husband's obituary reading, "Cause of death, chunky wife." Still . . . it was better than an air mattress.

Our earlier conceived cooking plan went into effect; each couple prepared one dinner and one breakfast. I brought chili and corn-bread, which was easy to heat on the stove. Dessert followed with the sandwich makers. Boxed wine and beer bombers made for lively games of dominoes the rest of the evening. Silly stories, teasing, and new jokes to laugh at. Clutching our sides, we howled into the wee hours of the night. This kind of fun usually happened to other people.

Unfortunately, the next morning I woke up with laryngitis. The small cold I brought with me turned into a rampaging plague. Having had so much fun the night before, I hated to leave. But I also didn't want to infect everyone else in such a tight space. Reluctantly, my husband and I loaded the wheelbarrow with our gear and headed back to the car. I gazed longingly at our sweet yurt off in the distance as we drove away. Our neighbors stayed, enjoyed the beautiful scenery and lovely views from the porch. The fabulous Colorado fall colors were just beginning to pop. They said it was dull without us and not the same. Apparently, more *is* merrier.

Change is good. After four years in Colorado, my hiking boots are nicely scuffed. Our garage is filled with outdoor gear. But most importantly, we have lifelong friends. Ones we have seen in the same set of clothes for three days. I am still ambivalent about camping, but my anxiety level has certainly decreased. If I forget to pack some-thing, I am now 99.9% positive our neighbors packed theirs, and definitely a spare. Also, my reference points for camping include a lot of laughing.

And as a bonus: it's pretty outside. Blooming wildflowers. Rippling brooks. The changing leaves on the hillsides. The wilderness provides an opportunity to reset expectations. Camping and all its inconveniences remind me of the value of living more simply. An air mattress is a good tradeoff for the experience. The trees, water, mountains . . . an unlimited air supply. I just needed a reminder to breathe it.

51

ARS POETICA

BY BELLE SCHMIDT

(*After William Carlos Williams*)

If I when my spouse is sleeping
and the dogs Butch and Maxine
are sleeping
and the sun is a yellow-orange ball
in vaporous veils
above waking earth,
if I in my studio loft
twist slowly, impossibly
on my floor
inhaling breath deep into my lungs
and meditating,
"I am relaxed, relaxed.
I was born to inhale, exhale
I am in the now."

If I admire my tree pose,
my downward dog, rooster, cobra
against the blue yoga mat—

Who can say I am not
in the moment?

52

AUBADE FOR THE MAD KING

BY FRANK COONS

goldfinch & oriole
　　　　cowbird & jackdaw
harbingers of his dawn & his ten minutes
of clarity
he awakes
from another murderous night aggrieved
askew
and thinks again　　　any king
who sleeps well
　　　　is already dead
　　　　　　not a sunrise
but a fire encroaching
birds already turning to winged demons
the short chains of long-
dead
would-be usurpers　　rattling
rattling beneath the bricks
he'll
eat

no
    honeyed
       porridge
just unpeeled fruit   a pot of tea
he makes himself

then
to the sudatorium where he bites
the head
off a red-wattled cock   asks
      his fool
    to read
   the entrails
what's foretold:
more gold eggs from the goose
the ass still shitting persimmons
the split-tongued asp guarding the jewels
all good news
      sire
       all good news

53

PREAMBLE

BY JOHN BLAIR

Before their wedding, before his telephone marriage proposal, before 71 love letters, he attempts to rationalize the gnawing in his gut, Friday, April 19th, 1974.

I think that at last I will leave you and end our relationship . . . but can't. I miss you, your allure, your innocence. Struggling with the meaning of friends versus lovers, I feel abandoned. You study night after night except Thursday when Mark asks you to walk. And you join him! Already the green contagion has hold of my entrails. I wait for your knock, I wait for your step across my threshold, I wait for long blonde hair to sigh across silk. Like teaching an aria to a hog, tone-deafness echoes in my bungling sentences, my misplaced words. Where are you? Who are you with? I need you . . . the sound of you, the smell of you, the taste . . .

54

CLIMBING DOWN THE MOUNTAIN

BY KATHERINE VALDEZ

(Names have been changed to protect privacy.)

Coming down from the mountain, I have seen the lofty glory
I will go again someday, but for now I'm coming down.
— The Meat Puppets

I'm not ready to die today. Ice axes in hand and crampons strapped to our boots, we descend the snowy ridge of Mt. Richthofen in the Never Summer range near Walden, Colorado.

"It's just five steps!" my husband Johnny yells, encouraging me to start down-climbing and front-pointing the short wall of packed snow he finished a few seconds ago. This is the crux: the place where I could fall and die.

Sunny blue sky, crisp morning air, mountains surrounding us.

I hate it.

And I hate my husband for forcing me to climb another peak, another unroped route that could get us killed. I picture tripping and tumbling to my death. *If I live, I will never climb this fucking moun-*

tain again, I scream inside my head. *I won't climb any mountain, ever again.*

"You need to jam that ice ax in, solid!" he yells. "Be very sure of it!"

"Okay," I say, faking confidence. He'll get mad if I show fear. And I can't handle him yelling at me right now. Do it. Deep breath. The metal spikes scrape against a patch of exposed rock as I walk to the edge and turn around to face the peak. Driving the ax into the snow on my right side, I lower my right leg and kick the front points into the wall. Stick my left fingers into the hole made by Johnny's ax, lower my left leg, and jam those points in. Solid. I grip the ax so hard, my right hand will cramp later.

Reposition the ax. Repeat the process.

Relief. Deep breath. I'm on less steep terrain now, and I allow myself to smile. My eyes sweep across the snow-covered mountains in front of us. Looking down at the frozen blue expanse of Lake Agnes, I imagine walking along its shore, my boots crunching across the pristine snow, through the trees and back to the car.

I must figure out how to avoid climbing that damn mountain—any mountain—again. I'm forty-one, we've been together seventeen years, and I don't want the rest of my life to be like this: not allowed to skip these trips, not allowed to make friends, not allowed to pursue my own interests. Yelled at almost every day for being "weak-minded," "stupid," "fat," and "lazy."

I'll never return to this place.

My underwear was full of holes. Faded Fruit-of-the-Looms in sickly pale pink, yellow, green, blue. They were high-cut, not granny-panty full briefs, but still. Boring. Tattered. Depressing. Johnny didn't want me spending money on new ones, so I used thread and needle to mend them every few weeks. Same with my socks, their see-through heels embarrassing me at work, where the interns wore better clothes than I did.

Our spartan lifestyle was the reason we could pay cash for our house, so who was I to question him? He was the smart one, the one who kept our life in order. He was also the one who led us up mountains.

I started rebelling in small ways. I met business acquaintances for coffee or lunch. I bought a package of underwear and didn't mention it.

"I noticed you bought some new underwear and didn't tell me," Johnny said quietly. The cold voice betrayed his calm face.

I stared at him. "It's *underwear*! It was, like, $5. You do the laundry. It wasn't a secret."

"That's not the point. I tell you about every penny I spend. It's about respect."

Arguing would make it worse. "I'm sorry," I said. "You're right. I should've told you."

I don't remember when he stopped calling me by my name. I became "Hey!" Abrupt, loud, annoyed. Annoyed because I was careless and drove over a pothole, or left a strand of hair on the bathroom floor, or forgot to put away the dumbbells.

He had plenty of other names for me: bitch, cunt, imbecile, retard, crazy.

"Freak," he said, when my insomnia came up. I assumed my trouble staying asleep was due to a lack of peace inside myself. I couldn't figure out who I was; never had a strong sense of self. I tried on other people's personalities like they were clothes: is this who I am?

It didn't occur to me that Johnny was the real reason I woke in the middle of the night, haunting the kitchen, reading, and sipping herbal tea until I felt sleepy again. It's laughable now to think how stubborn I was in denying the truth. He told me many times I wasn't living life fully. That I was dead inside. A corpse.

Suicide was one way out. "Do it," he said, spitting the words at me. "The world would be a better place without you."

"Maybe I will," I retorted.

I imagined cleaning out my desk at work and giving away treasured possessions. I could pretend to leave in the morning, then stay in the garage with the engine running and the windows rolled down: fall asleep and never wake up. Easy.

But I didn't want to hurt my family. And I didn't really want to die. I wanted a way out of this marriage, a way in which I wouldn't have to face the shame and embarrassment of being divorced. *She couldn't make her husband happy.* He had convinced me I wouldn't be able to survive on my own.

I tried to forget the indignities he'd inflicted: he spit in my face on two different occasions, shoved me forward to get me to jog up a hill I would've rather hiked, and forced me to eat all the dinner he cooked, even though I was already uncomfortably full. "I'll eat the rest of it tomorrow," I'd plead, and he'd say, "No! Finish it." So I'd stand up, walk around, and attempt to will my body to digest the food faster.

I longed to drive to the library, or to the store—anywhere—on weekend mornings when he would sleep until 11:00 a.m. But I knew he'd hear the garage door open and yell at me for going somewhere. So I stayed inside reading or slipped out the door to walk around the neighborhood. I was supposed to sleep in as late as he did, after a Friday or Saturday night staying up until 1:00 a.m. He didn't consider that I had been up since 6:00 a.m. to prepare for my full-time job. He wouldn't accept that I was too tired to stay up late.

Coming home from our weekend backpacking trips, he'd force me to drive while drowsy. I was "weak-minded" if I couldn't stay awake. He wouldn't let me pull over and take a quick nap, and would pinch me or pour capfuls of water on my head to wake me up. I was terrified that we'd end up in the river while driving the narrow, winding road down Poudre Canyon.

One Sunday, I could barely keep my eyes open. I pulled into a turnout and parked, saying I needed to close my eyes for ten minutes, and he immediately started yelling. "It's your responsibility to drive! You agreed! That's our arrangement!" I had no energy to argue and pulled back onto the road.

On another weekend, when we backpacked twenty-six miles over two days on the Barr Trail to Pikes Peak, I drove us back home from Colorado Springs, north on I-25, and fell asleep for a second, drifting left into another lane. I woke up, heart pounding. Johnny merely raised his eyebrows.

Later, my therapist pointed out we could have killed someone.

It wasn't always like this. We met in California during my first job as a newspaper reporter after college. He was a photojournalist, and I was impressed by his intelligence, talent, and strong work ethic. No one worked harder.

We became friends, dated briefly, then kept in touch when I took another reporting job on the central coast. Over the next year and a half, I realized I was in the wrong profession but became paralyzed with the knowledge that I had failed.

We grew close. Johnny could tell I was unhappy, and when he proposed that I quit my job and move in with him, I saw him as my savior, the older and wiser independent thinker who would help me get my life together.

Looking back, I gave him too much power. I ignored early warning signs.

When people asked me what brought us to Colorado, I told them we didn't want to wait until retirement to enjoy life, so we saved as much money as we could for a year, quit our careers and moved to Fort Collins, without jobs or housing lined up. I had never seen this city but embraced the idea. We would build a new life together.

We settled into a routine. I worked as an office manager and brought home a paycheck, and Johnny—who was now "retired"—did everything else: cooking; cleaning; maintaining the car, house, lawns, and garden; planning all our trips; and even packing my backpack so we could leave as soon as I finished work on Fridays. He was responsible for our quality of life.

From the outside, it was an equal partnership, and we appreciated each other's roles. But he felt that he did more than his fair share because he did the majority of the big thinking. He was the miserly financial planner, and I handled the books. He was the visionary, and I was his disciple.

"If you would grow up, we could be happy," he said. "Please. Let's just be in love."

"If you love someone, you don't call them names and yell at them," I said more than once, my voice thick from crying. "You don't treat them like that."

He'd dismiss my complaints by blaming me: "If you would pay attention and think more about what you're doing, I wouldn't have to." Our life was all about improving ourselves, being better than everyone else.

Whenever I brought up the idea of going to see a counselor, he immediately criticized it. "You think talking to a stranger is going to solve your problems? They'll make me out to be the bad guy."

We spent most weekends from May to September backpacking and "tagging peaks," racking up thirty-five fourteeners, thirty thirteeners, and hundreds of other peaks over nine years. I kept a small journal in which I wrote the details of every mountain trip, proof that I could be tough, that I could accomplish *something*.

Johnny believed we served a higher purpose by spending most of our time in the wilderness and shunning society. Mundane activities like going to the movies, or out to dinner, or to museums had no place in our lives.

We steadily improved our minds and bodies. I read *Moby Dick*, *The Brothers Karamazov*, and Dante's *The Inferno* at his insistence, and we became voracious readers of mountaineering classics such as

Annapurna by Maurice Herzog, *Annapurna: A Woman's Place* by Arlene Blum, *Starlight and Storm* by Gaston Rébuffat, and *The Mountains of My Life* by Walter Bonatti.

We hiked or ran or lifted weights and did various strengthening exercises almost every day after I came home from work. We regularly hiked up and down the Foothills Trail with dumbbells, or rocks, or plastic jugs of water in our backpacks. Once, at Greyrock, I even hiked the Meadows Trail back down to the car to get an extra gallon of water (eight pounds) and up again while Johnny set up camp, adding an hour and a half of exercise to my day.

Our life was perfect, basically. That's what we portrayed to the world. That's what I convinced myself was true.

The reality: I was utterly alone.

I never talked with anyone about his behavior. I was the one forcing him to be cruel. It was my fault.

Mutual acquaintances wondered aloud if I really shared Johnny's passion. "I once had a boyfriend who was really into the mountains," my colleague Helen said, alluding to the possibility that I was simply along for the ride, that I didn't really love these outdoor adventures as much as he did.

I was offended and instantly defensive as I tried to squash their doubts. *They don't think I'm tough enough to handle this.* A united front was crucial. Us against the world.

Small moments of happiness and normalcy scattered throughout our days weren't enough anymore. Yes, I felt peace on some of those mountaintops, and was glad to see Johnny happier there than anywhere else. But my world was shrinking. He increasingly isolated me from family and acquaintances. Making my own friends was not allowed, and his behavior became more cruel and extreme.

In 2010, I mentioned to Johnny several months in advance that I wanted to fly to California and surprise my mom for her seventieth birthday. He didn't say "no," so I thought I had his grudging approval. As September approached, I bought the plane ticket, then mentioned it to him in passing.

He exploded. "If you go, our relationship is over!"

"You had said it would be okay!" I was shocked. "It's her seventieth birthday!"

He was adamant: if I went, it would be one less weekend to climb mountains before winter weather hit. I was crushed. But I cancelled the flight.

Many months later, I called the employee assistance program and spoke to a counselor. This conversation gave me the courage soon after to pack a few things—including my mountain journal—and take a taxi to a motel. We had only one vehicle, his fifteen-year-old Tercel.

The next day, I walked three miles to get a rental car, then drove to my office to call apartment complexes. I made one mistake. I checked my voicemail. "Please come home," Johnny said. "Please call me."

I called and stayed another night at the motel before going home. But things didn't change and he didn't change. So I did a radical thing: I visited a counselor.

Amy was a licensed clinical social worker who specialized in domestic abuse. During the first session, I told her how Johnny treated me, and she said, "It's called 'the crazymaking.' The abuser convinces you that you're the crazy one, that you're the one with all the problems."

"He's never going to change," she said. "You need to leave." Her face crumpled with sympathy as I began sobbing. "I'm so sorry."

With Amy's help, I planned my escape. He'd be out of town for a few days during a solo backpacking trip at Rocky Mountain National Park.

I almost blew it when I forwarded the mail to my apartment too soon, just before he left for his trip. He'd been waiting for the backpacking permit to arrive, and when several days went by with absolutely no mail, he got suspicious. I feigned ignorance. But then he called the post office.

"They told me your name is on the request," he said in a voice-mail message at my office, his voice steely.

I panicked, and called a Crossroads Safehouse counselor I had been meeting with regularly. She calmly asked me if his birthday was coming up. It was. "Tell him you bought a birthday gift and wanted to surprise him."

I happened to walk by a rack of used books for sale in downtown that day, and couldn't believe it when I saw a battered old paperback of *Annapurna*. This was my alibi.

He believed me.

When the day came to drive him up to the park, I kept thinking, *This is the last time I'll see him.* I was on my best behavior so he wouldn't suspect anything, and I also wanted to make our last hours together blemish-free. We hugged goodbye, he smiled at me, then I watched him disappear up the trail into the forest.

A strange mix of sadness and relief filled my head on the way home from Estes Park. The morning sunlight on the trees was beautiful. I was alone. And finally free.

I packed all my possessions into several boxes, made one trip to my new apartment, then met a co-worker at the house to help me transport everything else in a second, final trip.

The next day, I called Johnny's one friend and asked if he would please pick up Johnny at the national park on Thursday. "Sure," Andy said.

Andy's younger brother, Evan, was there when I arrived. I handed them a six-pack of a local microbrew as a thank you, along with the house key and map.

As I waved goodbye, Evan said, "Read *Harry Potter*. Read *Twilight*." And I knew instantly he understood who my husband was. He was saying in code, "Read what you want. Do what makes you happy. Because Johnny's not around to criticize your choice of reading material or anything else."

"I will," I said, smiling as I walked away. *Thank you, God. Someone understands.*

Later, after I bought two novels in a favorite series and Taylor Swift's CD *Speak Now*, I settled in at my new apartment and conjured up images of Johnny's reaction to reading the note I had left on the kitchen table. I thought of lyrics from the song "Comin' Down" by the Meat Puppets, which we had listened to on many trips.

Sadness tinged the following weeks—especially as I fielded voice-mails, phone calls, and one surprise delivery to my office. A friend who'd been through worse (her husband was physically abusive), predicted he'd do anything to win me back.

"I guarantee you'll get flowers," she said, and I nodded, although I didn't believe her. *He wouldn't do that because he knows I'm allergic to flowers.*

She was right.

The flowers came to my office in a small vase, pale orange lilies and baby's breath. I was not happy, but smiled at the flower delivery person so she wouldn't be disappointed with my reaction. I didn't want to be rude. My co-worker looked at me as I read the card. "Is it from him?" she asked. I gave the flowers away.

I didn't waste time creating my new life. I took yoga, Zumba, and Nia classes. I started hanging out at a local yarn store for the weekly knitting circle, and joined two writing organizations. I attended the symphony, theater, and other cultural events, by myself and with new acquaintances.

I analyzed why I stayed with Johnny so long because the question came up over and over again as I made new friends. Out of dozens of reasons for keeping the marriage together (we had invested so many years into our relationship, we had joint bank accounts, we owned a house together, we kept hoping it would get better), a couple stood out. One, I had believed in the life we'd created, the life designed to help us become as strong as possible and fulfill our potential.

And two: "We're women and we have womanly feelings," my friend Lily told me long-distance from California. "You love someone and you want them to be happy."

She was right: my fatal flaw had been wanting Johnny to be happy, not wanting to hurt him. I made it worse by staying many years longer than I should have.

My sister visited a month later and we played tourist around Northern Colorado. Before visiting Rocky Mountain National Park, we stopped by a big box store for snacks. I was thinking only of granola bars. Anna had other ideas.

"You gotta try boy shorts," she said, pushing the shopping cart toward women's lingerie. "They're so comfortable!" We stood in front of the underwear racks, where cheery packages shouted out bright colors: neon pink, blue, orange, green, yellow. Solids, stripes, and polka dots. Teeny bikinis. No-seams microfiber.

These were the panties of liberated women.

I had spent nine years wearing cotton briefs that frayed after a few washings. They were boring, but comfortable.

"Uh . . ." I said, hesitating. I was skeptical. They'd probably be uncomfortable and ride up.

"I'm buying them for you," she said, smiling. She'd always been the bold one.

I didn't want to seem ungrateful, so I allowed myself to relax. Time to adjust my attitude.

I settled into my new life and felt the joy of freedom, of simply being alive, of feeling good about everyone and everything. I smiled at strangers. Friends told me I look great. At the market I'd think, *Wow, I can buy this basket of raspberries and enjoy it with my oatmeal in the morning. I can buy new clothes for work. I can read and watch a movie and write a letter to my family and hike all in one weekend.*

I can do anything I want!

Even buy new underwear. Or find a new mountain to summit.

55

TRANSFORMATION

BY SUZANNE LEE

I felt a burden
in the service for eight,
in the accompaniments
and ramifications of butter knives
and grapefruit spoons,
of bread plates, dessert plates,
demitasse and tea cup,
table cloths, runners, the array
of napkin rings, centerpieces,
and candles for every season,
occasion, or mood.

I'm lighter now
with my array of odds and ends,
my decorations inspired
by the moment and created
by the happenstance that catches
my eye. My life, no longer perfect,
glows kaleidoscopic.

56

WHAT WE KEEP

BY MELANIE KALLAI

Three summers ago, I decided to get my eyes done. I was tired of hearing people say to me, "You look tired," or "Rough night?" or "Do you have allergies?" A simple outpatient procedure and I'd finally look rested, refreshed, and maybe even a few years younger. My best friend Rachel was a proponent for Botox injections, so even though I felt a little vain going under the knife for the sake of my looks, I was okay with it. We'd fight this aging thing together. We'd been a team since the age of four—middle age wasn't going to get us down.

I had my procedure on September 15th. The day after, I was a swollen, red-eyed, just-had-a-reaction-to-the-topical-antibiotic mess. Rach would find this hilarious since it had become an inside joke that I react to just about everything except Tylenol. I couldn't cry about it, though—not a good idea when stitches and glue are precariously holding your eye skin together.

When Rachel called me that day, assumedly to check on my progress, but instead told me that her cancer had become terminal— my life turned upside down. "Maybe you have a year," her doctor had said. *What the fuck? Don't cry. Can't cry.*

Don't cry.

Rach had been fighting cancer on and off for a couple of years—cervical, caused by HPV. She'd been through two rounds of chemo and radiation, had a hysterectomy, and was getting back to life as usual. She was running again and working on her dream of developing a program to get healthier food into public schools. She'd even married her middle-school crush—who she had pined for all through high school and most of her adult life (except for that time she got married to someone else and gave birth to one of the most beautiful creatures on this earth).

Her doctor must have misspoken. Rach was an invulnerable beast when it came to her health; she'd never even had a cavity. Mighty Viking blood flowed through her veins, and a little cancer was not going to take her down. *Was it?* I mean, yes, we'd read the statistics, but Rach was the exception. She was going to be in that 30 percent who lived longer than five years after the initial diagnosis. She would beat it. Rachel was too strong to become a number.

Rachel was determined to prove her doctor wrong, and I hopped on the "Team Rach" train, cheering her on at every stop. She started applying to immunotherapy drug trials. It was a complicated process because her type of cervical cancer was extremely rare. It was microscopic, and therefore undetectable until there were tumors—which grew to debilitating size in a matter of months.

While waiting to be accepted into a trial, three tumors wreaked havoc in her abdominal cavity. She could no longer eat; anything she tried came back up in violent bouts of vomiting. By Thanksgiving, she was starving and hospitalized. A tumor was blocking her intestine, and since she had undergone so much radiation, her intestinal tissue was not healthy enough for a resection (or a re-route). This meant that the only way to keep her alive was to give her an ileostomy —a forever-open hole in her stomach, higher up in the digestive tract than a colostomy, where her food could come out into a bag worn on her stomach. It nearly broke her spirit. Over the next year and a half, she'd add two more bags to the routine, one for each failing kidney.

Rachel was born two days before me, but we were twin souls, having both been conceived on Valentine's Day. We met in a tap class at the age of four. Rach was a rosy-cheeked bundle of energy with purple yarn holding her reddish-brown pigtails in place, and I was a shy skinny-minny with knobby knees in a homemade purple dance skirt. We danced to "Yellow Submarine" at our first recital, and we continued dancing the number well into our thirties. I think it's a rare thing when you meet someone and instantly feel gravity pulling you together. Maybe it happens all the time, but I've only felt it a few times in my life. I definitely felt it with Rach. She provided me refuge when I needed it most.

I was fifteen and falling in love for the first time with a boy from my church youth group. Rachel had gotten in trouble and had been sent to the youth group by her mother, in the hope that the teens there would be a better influence than her school circle. Now, I don't know if this is true for all church youths, but the teens at my church were far more deviant than anyone I knew from school or elsewhere. It wasn't uncommon to see my church friends smoking pot or taking pregnancy tests in the fifteen minutes between Sunday school and church. It was a noble effort on her mom's part, but I'm pretty sure it didn't change Rach in the long run. It did, however, provide the opportunity for Rach and me to become closer.

We were about to turn sixteen, and I'd planned a big party at my house, when the unimaginable happened. The phone rang on my birthday. I was hoping it was my boyfriend, J.D., but it wasn't. It was our church friend Kyle. He told me J.D. had picked up his dad's gun and shot himself in the head.

Believe me when I tell you that I suffered some long-term psychological damage from that one. It's been twenty-seven years, and I still struggle with questions—and loss.

As horrible as it was, J.D.'s death signified a turning point in my friendship with Rach. That was when we became inseparable—as in walking together with our arms linked and being physically attached at the hip. We became so close that rumors started about us at school. We didn't care. Those kids who talked about us didn't get it. I was grieving, and Rachel kept me from losing myself. She was my light, and I loved her.

We were insane together back then. Laughing our asses off at jokes that only we got. Others in our circle sometimes wanted what we had, but, unfortunately, they didn't get the joke.

Since we came into this world at the same time, birthday cards were our thing. The perfect card would not only make the other laugh but also inspire a plethora of new jokes that would keep us laughing at least through the week—or even years (I'm looking at you, monkey card). The older we got, the more our cards portrayed spunky old women breaking the law, being hilariously senile, or not giving a fuck about what came out of their mouths. That kind of sass was something to aspire to, and we truly believed that one day we'd be those awesome old women, sitting on a pier, drinking margaritas at noon on a Monday, and deciding which men on the beach were too old for their Speedos.

Shortly after Rachel learned about her end-of-life-countdown, my husband got a job in Colorado and my family made the move. It was hard to be away from Rach, and my family, but I was lucky enough to be able to travel to Florida frequently. I'd leave my toddler with my parents while Rach and I would go out for pedicures and lunch. Or we'd make all day trips to the cancer center where she'd get her blood drawn, vitals taken, chat with the nurse practitioner about any side effects the trial drugs were causing, and wait around to see if her blood was healthy enough to receive more drugs. Then, if she was eligible, she'd get the infusion, and I'd get french fries for us to share. Usually by 5:00 p.m. we were on our way home, exhausted, but hopeful.

Rachel was an optimist. I'm a realist, and each trip to Florida, my heart broke a little more as I could see the noticeable differences in her appearance. She never believed she was going to die from cancer —at least not until she was near the end. She told me more than once, while reclined in a fake leather chair at the cancer center being pumped full of a concoction of trial drugs, "I'm not glad this happened, but if it was going to happen to one of us, I'm glad it's not you. You'd never be able to handle all these drugs. You'd be a goner." Then she'd smile, confident the magic potion dripping into her chest port would provide her the cure and this would all be over soon.

Two years passed after the terminal diagnosis, and because Rachel had lived far beyond her doctor's timeline, she had real hope. Unfortunately, when death has your number, you can't outrun it for long. Viking or not, Rachel's condition began to rapidly decline.

She was kicked off her immunotherapy trial—it just wasn't working. Rachel's tumors were growing, limiting her food intake, and penetrating everything in her pelvic region. I traveled as often as was financially possible, even racked up credit card debt to be with her. Rachel desperately looked for other treatment options, and finally, in June of 2018, her doctors put her on Keytruda as a "compassionate care" option. What this really meant was, "There's nothing more we can do for you, but we'll give you drugs so you can maintain an ounce of hope." And because of Rachel's eternal optimism, she clung to that hope and expected to get better.

That September, on a Saturday, another trial came my way. I almost lost my husband. The day started as ordinary as any other, maybe even better. We took our four-year-old son to the park and cheered as he climbed to the top of the rock wall for the first time. We went for a hike and met a horsewoman who let our son take a ride. We played in the garden and had lunch outside. Then my husband said, "I'm going for a mountain bike ride. I'll be back in an hour."

An hour and a half later, I was standing in the trauma ward of our nearest hospital, watching at least twenty doctors, nurses, surgeons, and other various hospital staff scramble frantically around my broken husband. They cut off his clothes, transfused blood, yelled at each other to "get out of the way" and "get a chest tube now!" The hospital chaplain held me as my husband bled on the floor, blood pressure tanking with each shallow breath.

When the chest tube was in, only partially relieving the internal bleeding caused by his fall, the trauma surgeon took my arm and said, "You need to tell him goodbye now." I nodded, walked over to him, and placed my trembling hand on his forehead, not able to process the depth of what I was about to do. He looked up at me with drugged, bewildered eyes, which asked the only question that mattered in that moment, "Is this it?"

The chaos of the trauma ward kept its pace in the background while I kissed him on the forehead and said, "I love you. Keep breathing."

He did.

Somehow, by the grace of God, my husband pulled through. I canceled my latest trip to Florida and became a full-time caretaker to my husband during his recovery. He not only needed me to feed, bathe, and clothe him, but also to lift him out of bed, connect him to his bedside oxygen machine, change his wound dressings, and wake up in the middle of the night to administer injections of blood thinners right into his belly. I was happy to do it, but exhausted. Thankfully, help arrived. My mom, aunt, and close friend Kim stayed with me through the most challenging time.

Then, in November, Rachel and her family came to Colorado to see me. It was a nearly impossible trip because her pain was so intense she could barely walk.

How did she make it? I don't know, but I was in crisis and, without me asking her, she showed up. It was our 43rd birthdays.

It was heart-wrenchingly obvious that Rach was living on borrowed time, and our usual old lady birthday cards were no longer appropriate. So, I did what any friend would do. I bought her a shitload of pot and some Mentos. She spent most of the weekend sleeping in my recliner, but I was happy to have her. By that time, her daily pain medication regimen would have the average person over-dosing in the ER, and it was barely easing her agony. Goddamn, she was strong—even then.

By January, my husband had sold his mountain bike and was actively practicing his golf swing—quite a long way from fifteen broken bones, a punctured lung, internal bleeding, and pulmonary embolisms. He has two titanium ribs now and diminished lung capac-ity, but he is here, healing, and I am grateful.

Since my husband could be safely left alone, I booked a flight to see Rach. We got pedicures, had lunch, and spent a day at the cancer center. Business as usual, except it wasn't. Something in Rachel had changed. We sat together on her couch one afternoon, and she turned to look at me, not lifting her head from the back of the couch. "I don't want to die," she said and began to cry. I held her hand, knowing there were no words of hope left to offer, and cried with her.

Two days after I returned home, I woke up to find a missed call from Rachel's husband on my phone. My heart sank, and with shaky fingers, I called him. "She's alive, but I don't think she has much time. How fast can you get here?"

Frantically, I opened my computer and found a flight at 2:00 p.m. *That's not soon enough.* It was the earliest available, so I booked it, grabbed a suitcase, and threw in a bunch of mismatched clothes for my son and me. During a second call with Rachel's husband, I learned that one of her tumors had severed her right iliac artery, and she had begun bleeding out. She lost consciousness during the ambu-lance ride and had lost all blood flow to her right leg. The doctors weighed the option of amputation to try to save her life, but the window to do that passed too quickly, and she was placed on "but-terfly watch."

On the way to the airport, I explained to my perplexed son that his Aunt Rach was going to die, and we were going to be with her family. The plane ride was brutal, being out of touch for three and a half hours. I prayed that I'd make it in time to say goodbye. I remember looking out of the plane window at the clear, bright blue sky and thinking, "Rachel, you picked a beautiful day to die."

Finally, we landed. I called our dear friend Kim, who was already at the hospital.

"She's still alive, but get here as fast as you can."

My father picked us up from the airport and raced me to the hospital. Kim and Rachel's sister met me by the elevators, shaken with sadness. I found Rachel's daughter and pulled her into a hug. Then, I went into her room. She'd never regained consciousness, and her breathing was quick and shallow. I took her hand, kissed her forehead, told her I loved her, and thanked her for being my best friend. A tear rolled out of her eye, and she tried to squeeze my hand. I know in my heart that she heard me. Half an hour later, her heart slowed, and then stopped. She'd waited for me. Rachel left the world surrounded by the people she loved the most, and I think that's not a bad way to go.

If Rachel's life taught me anything, it is that the human spirit is more powerful than circumstance. I've also learned that grief is forever. It doesn't fade, and we don't get over it—it becomes a part of who we are. Pain reminds us of the beautiful people we've lost and lets us keep them alive in our memories, our hearts, and our actions. Sometimes, if we're lucky, we become the parts of them that we valued most, allowing them to live on while we grow into more complex humans.

Because of J.D., I take chances, and I always tell people how I feel about them. Because of Rachel, I am bold, I make friends without judgments, and I know how to laugh at myself. Sometimes the hurt takes center stage, and sometimes it waits in the wings, but it's always there. I know that I will never get over Rachel's death as long as I live. I miss her laugh already, but I know she'd want me to keep laughing, even if I am the only one now who gets the jokes.

57

THINGS WE FORGOT TO REMEMBER

BY KARI REDMOND

I just today remembered
the dragonfly on the middle of your back,
like it was yesterday, like it was
every day.
And I'm sorry.
I didn't mean to forget.

It took a photograph to remind me.
A printed one, we used to call them snapshots.
Kept them in shoeboxes.
Piles and piles,
faded and sticky.

You are running away from the camera.
Your straw colored hair flying behind you
and that dragonfly.

It fell out of a book,
marking the place of another thing
I never finished.

You know the picture I'm talking about.
You are topless.
In those days, you were always topless.

There was a time the very thought
would make you blush.
The crimson of shame
rushing up.

I don't think that's you anymore.

It makes me wonder
what else
I've forgotten.

BIOGRAPHIES

SHORT FICTION

AUTHORS

Jonathan Arena was born with a pen and cried for paper. Now he's older and you should be worried. Fiction is his lover and he struggles to go a day without her. It's why he has a past with novels, novellas, short stories, flash fiction, poems, film screenplays, television screenplays, comics, video games, and so on. It's also why he has a past with action, adventure, drama, thriller, suspense, mystery, historical fiction, alternate history, science fiction, fantasy, satire, literary, horror, and so on. He will never conform to a style or genre even if it hurts his marketability. He just loves words and stories too much and wishes to explore it all. Find out more about this strange man on www.cavewritingonthewall.com.

John Christenson writes fiction for children and adults. He lives in Boulder, Colorado with his wife, who paints watercolors, and a cat who is fond of penguins. His short stories have appeared in the *New Mexico Review* and the Rocky Mountain Fiction Writers anthology *False Faces*.

Mike Kanner is a relatively new fiction writer, having previously focused on history, political analysis, and decision theory. A few years ago, he tried his hand at historical fiction with "Home," the story of a German immigrant returning to his hometown as an American soldier during World War II. Since then, Mike has branched out into literary and genre fiction, and has been published in several anthologies as well as on Spillwords (https://spillwords.com/author/mikekanner/). He has two novels in progress, both of which regularly yell at him to complete. Mike lives in Longmont and is a lecturer in security and international politics at the University of Colorado, Boulder.

Jim Kroepfl writes short stories of mystery and adventure, and YA science fiction novels with his wife, Stephanie, from a rustic cabin in the Colorado Rockies. Their debut novel, *Merged*, was published by Month9Books in 2019. His short stories and articles have been published in literary journals in the United States and England. Jim and Stephanie often speak at universities, festivals, and conferences. When not writing, Jim is a musician. He and Stephanie are mythology buffs and world travelers who seek out crop circles, obscure historical sites, and mysterious ruins.

Katie Lewis lives in the shadow of the Rocky Mountains with her husband, their furry son, and a vast collection of geekdom sundries. When not at her computer, she can be found taking long walks through the nearby cemetery or rolling multi-sided dice to save the world. Like any good writer, her search history has likely placed her on several government watch lists, especially concerning that one thing. Inspired by everything from Arthur Douglas to Stephen King to Tolkien, she strives to always push boundaries and explore the more frequently overlooked aspects of society. Katie wishes to thank the Misfits, the Ehlers clan, and her online family for their tireless encouragement and support.

Sarah Reichert (S.E. Reichert) is a writer, novelist, poet, and blogger. She is the author of the Southtown Harbor Series (*Fixing Destiny, Finding Destiny,* and *Fighting Destiny*) and is a member of Northern Colorado Writers. Her work has been featured in the *Fort Collins Coloradoan, Haunted Waters Press, Tuliptree Publishing's* 100-*Word Dash* and *Sunrise Summits: A Poetry Anthology.* She is the site owner and operator of The Beautiful Stuff (https://thebeautifulstuff.blog), a blog about writing and fostering a creative and balanced life. Reichert lives in Fort Collins, Colorado with her family, two ridiculous cats, and one finely-aged basset.

Jennifer Robinson is a Colorado native born and raised in the northeastern plains and is a Colorado State University graduate. By day she works in insurance, but by night she is busy writing her first novel. When not writing fiction you can find her cooking, baking, reading, and traveling. She currently resides in Fort Collins, Colorado with her cat and her soul sister. Follow her journey and find news of her upcoming works at jenniferrobinsonbooks.com.

David E. Sharp is a noisy librarian. While he insists his middle initial stands for intrEpid, this remains unproven. He never pronounces the t in often. He has written and produced three plays, and published various other works. His novel *Lost on a Page* is available on Amazon and chronicles the plight of fictional characters from various genres who intend to murder their authors. Were this a biographical work, he might not be with us today.

Cindra Spencer has an affinity for dark mysteries, so she is often on the road inspecting health facilities. Occasionally, she dusts off her keyboard and pretends to be a writer. Her small works of fiction can be found in *Paws and Claws, Terror at 5280, Coffin Bell,* and *The Blue Pages*. She is (yes, STILL) working on a mystery novel set in Colorado. Twitter: @Cindra_Spencer

---

From Great-Grandpa telling tales on a Nebraskan porch to Dad expounding upon M.A.S.H.-like military anecdotes, ***R.C. Sydney*** grew up around storytellers. The crazy stories led to a voracious love of books; which then spurred the desire to connect with people through the written word. As a student of life and a lover of things, Sydney can be found haunting local coffee shops or slowly creeping up on a keyboard so as not to startle the plot bunnies.

NCW member ***Shelley Widhalm*** is a freelance writer and editor by day who writes fiction during the other hours, occasionally dabbling in oil painting and drawing. She's written six novels, a collection of short stories, and hundreds of poems, plus she blogs about the writing life. Her current projects are literary adult, *The Fire Painter*, and young adult, *In the Grace of Beautiful Stars*. She is the founder of Shell's Ink Services, a writing, editing, ghostwriting, and consultation service based in Loveland, Colorado. Her work has been published in anthologies, and she's won a few contests. She holds a Master of Arts degree in English from Colorado State University and worked in journalism for 20 years, bringing that background to her storytelling ventures. She can be reached at shellsinkservices.com or swidhalm@shellsinkservices.com.

NARRATIVE NONFICTION / MEMOIR

AUTHORS

When **Mitzi Dorton** received the P. T. A. Literary Arts Award in high school, her parents feared her destiny was to become a starving artist if she pursued writing as a vocation. Their dream for their daughter was to study education. She became a starving teacher instead. She worked in the field of special education, her choice, with the purest of hearts and enjoyed serving as a learning specialist for a community college disabilities center in the southeast. She was twice a VEA/NEA grantee. Old loves die hard when "it's my time now," and she revived writing. Her work has been featured in *Good Old Days, Annie's Publishing*, and in the literary journals *Bloodroot* and *Cleaning up Glitter*. While her roots and tendrils are from the mountains and foothills of southern Appalachia, they are now mingled with her love of the Berkshires region, where she resides.

Jaclyn Maria Fowler is an adventurer, a lover of culture and language, a traveler, and a writer. She is an American woman of Irish descent who is married to a Palestinian man; she works as the English

Faculty Director and Associate Professor at American Public University System and as a writing coach for Northcentral University. Fowler earned a doctorate in education from Penn State and an MFA in creative writing from Wilkes University. She is the author of the novel, *It is Myself that I Remake*.

Kate Hansen is an Idaho girl living the dream in Colorado with her husband and two children. She graduated summa cum laude from BYU-Idaho in 2013 with a bachelor's degree in English. Kate worked as a content writer and user experience designer, but now primarily takes care of her children and writes essays about them. She has been published in *Segullah, the Ensign,* and *Connotation Press*.

Millicent Porter Henry discovered at age seven she was a terrible artist. She was crushed. But a tender second-grade teacher showed her the gift of writing, that words have the power to paint stupendous pictures, and so her stories began. She lives and writes in Columbia, Missouri on a YA novel about baseball . . . with the able assistance of her sports-alcoholic husband and a multitude of baseball-loving boys. Her work appears in a variety of publications.

Becky Jensen is a freelance writer and podcast contributor living in Northern Colorado. Her work has appeared in *Misadventures, Mind + Body* and *Fort Collins* magazines, and on the *Out There* podcast—an award-winning show that explores big questions through intimate stories in the outdoors. An avid hiker and road tripper, Becky is also the proud mama of Jake and Dane—two loving, funny, and kind human beings who recently fledged the nest. "Follow the Hula Girl" is adapted from the memoir Becky is writing about running away from home and into the Colorado wilderness for five weeks when she was forty-five. Clips, recordings, portfolio pieces, and more at becky-jensenwrites.com.

Melanie Kallai is an active member of the Society for Children's Book Writers and Illustrators, Rocky Mountain Fiction Writers, and Northern Colorado Writers. Her publishing credits include a science fiction novel, *Eternity Rising*, and two etiquette-focused picture books, *Afternoon Tea* and *Ballet Class*. Melanie has enjoyed a twenty-year career as a dance teacher to children, tweens and teens. She also holds a BA in Evolutionary Biology and Ecology. Melanie lives with her husband and son in beautiful Colorado but is a Floridian at heart.

Margaret Maginness (pronounced like MuhGuinness) spent most of her life in Steamboat Springs, Colorado, then moved to Missouri to study journalism. Ten years later, she found herself married to a Missourian and still living in Missouri, a place that most Coloradans can neither remember, nor identify on an unlabeled map. Her professional endeavors have included ranch hand, ski patroller, high school biology teacher, goat milker, and community organizer. She has earned two master's degrees: an MS in environmental education, and an MA in journalism. Her labors of love (and sometimes despair) include writing, caring for and learning from her horses and Mikey the mule, observing nature, asking lots of questions, and drawing her own conclusions.

Kristin Owens earned a Ph.D. in Higher Education Administration at Penn State, and held academic positions at University of Maryland, University of Alaska Anchorage, and Mat-Su College. She also taught a variety of subjects (from ballroom dancing to graduate counseling) and was awarded 2016-17 Teacher of the Year, chosen by students at Aims Community College. Now a full-time writer in Colorado, Kristin has published over seventy articles for *NOCO Style, 5280, The Coloradoan, Thirst,* and *The Pint.* Her personal essays have appeared in *Writer's Digest, Women Writers-Women's Books,* and *Outpost.* Her first manuscript, *Elizabeth Sails,* was selected as a Judges' Favorite in the 2017 Ink & Insights contest. Her essay, "War Bride," won Honorable Mention for the 2018 New Millennium Writing Awards and was a finalist for the 2019 New Letters' Conger Beasley Jr. Award for Nonfiction.

Billie Holladay Skelley received her bachelor's and master's degrees from the University of Wisconsin-Madison. Now retired from working as a cardiovascular and thoracic surgery clinical nurse specialist and nursing educator, she enjoys focusing on her writing. Crossing several different genres, her writing has appeared in various journals, magazines, and anthologies in print and online—ranging from the *American Journal of Nursing* to *Chicken Soup for the Soul.* An award-winning author, she also has written seven books for children and teens. A mother of four and grandmother of two, she lives in Missouri with her husband and two cats. Billie spends her non-writing time reading, gardening, and traveling. Connect with her at www.bhskelley.com.

Katherine Valdez is an award-winning author of essays, flash fiction, and microfiction that have appeared in *Havok Magazine,*

Pooled Ink: Celebrating the 2014 Northern Colorado Writers Contest Winners, Baby Shoes: 100 Stories by 100 Authors, Open Doors: Fractured Fairy Tales, WritersDigest.com, The Coloradoan, and *Zathom.* A former journalist and communications director, she promotes diversity and inclusion as publisher of DiverseFortCollins.com and has attended national conferences on racial equity in Chicago, Detroit, and Albuquerque. Valdez is from California and has called Colorado home since 2002. She counts among her greatest achievements summiting 65 Colorado fourteeners and thirteeners, and dozens of other peaks around the West. Read about author events and literary festivals at "Secrets of Best-Selling Authors" KatherineValdez.com, and reviews at NoSpoilersMovieReviews.com and NoSpoilersBookReviews.com. Follow her on Amazon, Facebook (Author Katherine Valdez and Diverse Fort Collins), Goodreads, Zathom, Instagram, and Twitter @KatValdezWriter and @DiverseFortCollins.

Wren Wright is retired from a global telecommunications corporation, where she managed one of the company's technical libraries and got to buy lots of cool books. She holds a BA in Communications, with an emphasis in Literary Journalism and a minor in Women's Studies, from the University of Denver. Her work has appeared in several anthologies (most recently *Us Against Alzheimer's*), literary magazines, and local publications. She also wrote a column for *Senior News* about her life as a caregiver when she briefly lived on the North Coast of California. Her first book, *The Grapes of Dementia,* is a memoir of her and her husband's passionate midlife romance and marriage cut short by early onset dementia. She and her muses are working on her second book. Wren lives in Loveland with the new man in her life.

POETRY

AUTHORS

Jocelyn Ajami is an award-winning painter, filmmaker, writer, and founder of Gypsy Heart Productions. Jocelyn started writing poetry in 2014 as a way of connecting more intimately with issues of cultural awareness and social justice. She has been published in the *Journal of Modern Poetry, The Ekphrastic Review, bottle rockets,* and *the Kusamakura International Anthology for Prizewinning Haiku* (2018), among others. She has won additional awards from New Millennium Writings (finalist, Flash Fiction, 2017) and Poets and Patrons (first prize for "Chicago Burning," 2016). In 2017 she was a semi-finalist in the 24th Annual Gwendolyn Brooks Open Mic Awards for "Still Until." In 2018 she won First Prize in the National Federation of Poetry Societies award competition. She lives and works in Chicago, Illinois.

John Blair grew up in Denver and graduated from Colorado State University. He pursued a career in trust banking management, now retired. He served in leadership roles for many educational, arts, and social service non-profit agencies along the Front Range. John and his spouse Anne enjoy a passion for performing arts, often attending concerts, theatre, dance, and opera. He began writing poetry 20 years ago to fulfill a childhood dream.

Jim Burrell was raised in flatland Illinois, where cornfields, woodlands, and demanding English teachers encouraged his love of reading and writing. Since then, he has worked and travelled widely in the American West, often jotting down observations or snippets of interesting word combinations. He is fascinated by the world of rhythm and sound available in English. Jim's work often tends toward the lyric, but he prefers to read and write plain, modern language. His major writing challenges are finding the right words, a deepening exploration of themes, and typing. He lives with his family in Fort Collins, Colorado.

Frank H. Coons is a veterinarian and poet living in Colorado. His work has appeared in *The Eleventh Muse, The Santa Fe Literary Review, Pilgrimage, Pacific Review, Pinyon Review, El Malpais, Fruita Pulp, Caesura,* and elsewhere. His first collection of poems, a chapbook titled *Finding Cassiopeia,* was a finalist for the Colorado Book Award in 2013. His second book of poems, *Counting in Dog Years,* was released in 2016. Both books were published by Lithic Press.

Margery Dorfmeister is the longest living member of the Chaffee County Writers Exchange. She was trained as a journalist at the University of Wisconsin, Madison and published two books and numerous articles in midwest and eastern U.S. newspapers and magazines. She moved to Buena Vista, Colorado, in 1978 where she founded a local theater group for which she wrote a series of musical plays based on local history and folklore. She also taught Creative Writing at Colorado Mountain College, served as a book editor for About Books Publishing Company, and acted as a radio news reporter and hosted her own talk show for KVRH Radio, Salida. While continuing to freelance to local publications, she fortunately discovered Shavano Poets Society, based in Salida, which is now her favorite bounce-off place for self-expression. She realized then that her penchant for songwriting had qualified her as a poet all along.

Megan E. Freeman writes poetry and fiction, and her debut poetry collection, *Lessons on Sleeping Alone*, was published by Liquid Light Press. Her poetry has been selected as texts for musical compositions commissioned by the Los Angeles Master Chorale and Ars Nova Singers, and she has been published in many poetry anthologies, as well as literary and educational journals. Megan has over twenty-five years of experience teaching in the arts and humanities, and is nationally recognized for her work leading professional development programs for educators. Megan is represented by Deborah Warren at East West Literary Agency.

Sally Jo lived the first seven years of her life in Illinois then grew up in Colorado, where she now lives with her fiancé, two cats, and a puppy. She's been writing since she could hold a pencil and, despite a brief lapse into madness when she wanted to be an engineer, has always wanted to be a writer. Now a technical writer by trade, she also publishes poetry on Instagram as @sallyjopoetry. The words she finds within herself often embrace nature, enchantment, and relationships. Her first collection of poetry, *Droplets: Of Four Sisters,* celebrates her younger sisters and their relationships.

Luann Atkin Koester graduated Cum Laude from Colorado State University with a Bachelor of Arts degree in English in 1994. She received a Masters of Arts in Teaching from Colorado College in 2009, and a Post Graduate Certificate of Expertise in Creative Writing from the University of Denver in 2013. In 2003 she was recognized by the Boettcher Foundation as a Boettcher Educator, MIT in 2009 as an Influential Educator, and in 2015 by the Colorado Family, Career and Community Leaders of America as a Friend of FCCLA. She has taught High School Language Arts classes at Merino High School since 1994. Mrs. Koester enjoys teaching, traveling, spending time with her immediate and extended family, writing, and playing golf.

Ellen Kramer is an Ohio native currently living in northern Colorado. Frequently hospitalized and homebound throughout her lifelong struggle with the genetic disease Cystic Fibrosis, Ellen has long explored the world of books for freedom from places of confinement. After graduating from The Ohio State University in 2012, Ellen worked as a dietitian for children with eating disorders and in a bakery until her declining health forced her to put her career on hold in 2016. No longer able to work in the "real world," she was inspired to write about her own world, which had come crashing down. Through both poetry and prose, Ellen navigates the grounds of debilitating illness and loss in the ultimate pursuit of meaning and beauty, even in the most barren landscapes. Ellen is a member of Northern Colorado Writers. She resides with her fiancé, a hospital chaplain, in Arvada, Colorado.

· · ·

Suzanne Lee is a historian and writer. She grew up in small towns in Arizona and New Mexico where she developed a love of the landscapes, spirit, and people of the southwest. Her poetry has appeared in journals including *Snowy Egret, Sow's Ear,* and *Snowline,* and in *Weaving the Terrain* (Dos Gatos Press). As a professional writer of nonfiction, she has published investigative reports, monographs in military history, and articles on varied topics for organizational, professional, and denominational publications.

Sandra McGarry lives in Fort Collins, Colorado. She has been writing for years and has been published. She is a former elementary school teacher who moved from the east to the west to be challenged by the mountains and their beauty.

Marilyn K. Moody is a poet and writer who lives near Denver. She grew up on the Illinois prairie and still prefers wide open spaces and distant horizons. In addition to Northern Colorado Writers, she is a member of the Poetry Society of Colorado and Rocky Mountain Fiction Writers.

Kari Redmond is an English as a Second Language teacher living in Fort Collins, Colorado. She has recently completed her first novel, *This Story Takes Place in a Bar,* which required extensive research in various bars throughout the world. She is currently working on her second novel, *What We Let Go.* She also writes short stories, flash fiction, and poetry. Her work has been published in *The Tulip Tree*

Review, Brilliant Flash Fiction, Flash! 100 Stories by 100 Authors, and *Sunrise Summits- A Poetry Anthology.* Aside from writing, her passions include music and festivals, SCUBA diving, reading, and especially traveling. She has a goal of visiting every country in the world. She has just returned from Georgia and Armenia—her 61st and 62nd countries.

A Canadian native, **Belle Schmidt's** first published work appeared in *The Quill,* her high school yearbook. During her career, she worked in advertising and public relations for a statewide bank in Seattle. Currently, she is a regular contributor to Colorado's *Prairie Times* publication. She studied journalism at the University of Washington and was graduated from its Certificate Program in Poetry. Her work has appeared online and in numerous anthologies, newspapers, and international magazines. The latest of her five books is *In Our Bones.* Schmidt is a member of the Northern Colorado Writers and the Longmont Writers Club.

Sherry Skye Stuart is an author, writer, artist, and a certified yoga teacher. Under her previous name (Sherry Johns) she authored four books on local history, and edited and published five memoirs for older women. She wrote numerous newspaper columns, a local history blog, and produced over a dozen programs on local history. Currently she is finishing *The Early History of Penrose.* Sherry loves to delve into the lives of marginalized women in history, teasing out their stories and bringing them to light. Ladies of the evening, female felons, and old cemeteries particularly intrigue her. She also writes poetry, prose, short stories, flash fiction, and has numerous book ideas. Writing historical fiction and silver romance are in Sherry's future. Sherry holds two Associate Degrees in Library Science and Fine Arts from Pueblo Community College. Teaching and practicing yoga keep her centered and balanced.

Greta Tucker is a senior at Fossil Ridge High School in Fort Collins, Colorado and has been president of the school's writing club since her sophomore year. Ever since she read her first novel, Greta has been obsessed with writing something of her own. She is inspired by science fiction and fantasy and loves creating anything from poetry to a full-length novel. She dreams of writing something that inspires others to become writers, just as past writers have inspired her.

EDITORS

Holly Collingwood is a freelance writer and editor in Fort Collins, Colorado. She was raised on wild blueberries and basketball in cold, snowy states: Alaska, Montana, and Oregon. Her work has appeared in *Mamalode, Sierra Trading Post, Flash Fiction Online, Molotov Cocktail, Glimmer Train,* and local publications. When she's not reading or writing, she loves hiking, skiing, kayaking, gardening, and meeting with her critique group.

Laura Mahal splits her time between writing, copyediting, and hiking. Her work appears in various literary magazines and anthologies, to include *Fish, DoveTales, Still Coming Home, Sunrise Summits,* and *Veterans Voices.* Laura is a two-time winner of the Hecla Award for Speculative Fiction and was the recipient of the Gladys Feld Helzberg Memorial Award for Best Poem in 2019. She offers free editing for veterans and serves on the board for PFLAG of Northern Colorado. Her home base is Fort Collins, Colorado, but she is happy to travel wherever the spirit moves her . . .

Bonnie McKnight is the owner of Lady Knight Editing, LLC and the Membership Coordinator for NCW. She has been a freelance editor since 2015—but she's been correcting people's grammar since she was two (ask about the legendary fog vs. mist debate of '92). She earned her MA in the History of Books and is more than happy to gush about ancient Mesopotamian literacy or Victorian fiction magazines. Born and raised in Fort Collins, Colorado, Bonnie sees the mountains as home. She enjoys playing games and doing cryptic crosswords with her family, reading, collecting first editions, and not hiking.

Dean K. Miller has edited two anthologies, one of which was a 2018 Colorado Book Award Finalist. He has published four books of poetry, one children's coloring book, and one book of personal essays. Currently he is on the road in the mountains of Colorado looking for a place to live, hike, bike, fly fish, and resume his writing.

Sarah Kohls Roberts is a member of Northern Colorado Writers and SCBWI, and has published several technical papers and articles. She 'retired' from chemistry to spend time with her three kids, and now experiments with words. Sarah writes picture books and is a strong believer in the power of reading with children. She volunteers in many capacities, most notably as a Girl Scout troop leader. She enjoys hiking, but can more often found baking, reading, or spending time with family and friends.

Ronda Simmons is a former field geologist who used to get paid to go camping and look at rocks. After years of technical writing and editing, she was lured by the siren-song of make-believe and is now writing fiction. She serves as Program Coordinator for the Northern Colorado Writers and is one of the award-winning bloggers on The Writing Bug. She is committed to volunteering with several organizations that combat hunger and homelessness in her community. In her spare time, Ronda can be found hiking in the foothills of the Rocky Mountains with her family and dogs.

Lorrie Wolfe is a technical writer and editor living in Windsor, Colorado. She is passionate about volunteers, creating community, and about the power of words to unite and move people. Her poetry has appeared in *Earth's Daughters, Progenitor Journal, Tulip Tree Review, Pilgrimage, Pooled Ink,* and others. Her chapbook, *Holding: from Shtetl to Santa,* was published by Green Fuse Press in 2013. She edited and contributed to the 2017 anthologies *Mountains, Myths & Memories* and *Going Deeper.* Lorrie was named Poet of the Year at Denver's Ziggie's Poetry Festival for 2014-15.

Amy Rivers is the director of Northern Colorado Writers. She is the author of three novels—her most recent an award-winning psychological suspense novel, *All The Broken People.* Her short works have been published in several anthologies including *We Got This: Solo Mom Stories of Grit, Heart, and Humor, Flash!,* and *Chicken Soup for the Soul.* She has degrees in psychology, political science, and forensic criminology; a few of her favorite topics to write about. She lives in Boulder, Colorado.